BALANCE OF POWER

TOOTH & CLAW
BOOK 3

AMELIA FAULKNER

Ravensword
Press

First electronic publication: December 2014.
First paperback publication: March 2025.
https://ravenswordpress.com

Balance of Power is set in the UK, and as such uses British English throughout.

CONTENTS

GLOSSARY

Areet: All right. E.g. *Y'areet there, petal?* or *It's areet, in't it?*

Aye: Yes. *Aye, it was me.*

Barmpot: Fool. This tends to be used as a term of mild frustration or exasperation. It isn't too derogatory, but it's not all that fond either. *The fella's a total barmpot!*

Cadge: Borrow. *Can I cadge a tenner? I'll pay it back…*

Daft apeth: Fool. This is a term of fondness or endearment while still expressing how silly you think someone's being. *You don't have to pay me back ten quid, you daft apeth.*

Earwig: Eavesdrop. This can either be in, on, or as-is: *I was earwigging in on Albert t'other day* or *Oi, stop earwigging, it's rude!*

Gradely: Good. Excellent, even, especially combined with reet: *Aye, it were reet gradely!*

Happen: Reckon. *I'll 'appen as it'll take a few days.*

In't: In the or isn't. *I'll be over in't morning* or *It in't time for dinner yet!*

Owt: Anything. *I didn't bring owt with me. Were I s'posed to?*

Reet: Right. Very. *I'll 'appen as it were reet gradely!*

Petal: Term of endearment. *Y'areet there petal?*

Tosser: Wanker. From 'tossing off', i.e. wanking. *Aye, 'e's a reet tosser, he is.*

Wazzock: Idiot. Mildly derogatory. *Then the wazzock dropped 'is trousers an' we all had a good laugh!*

ONE

"WHAT DO YOU WANT FOR CHRISTMAS?"

Ellis laughed and leaned away from his desk at Randall's question. "I don't know. A year's supply of dog food?"

Randall let out so much air that it sounded as if he'd been punctured. "I can't afford that!"

"A month?" was Ellis' counteroffer. "A week? Anything to save me shopping. I don't know. Ask Christy. Christy, what do I want for Christmas?"

Ellis heard her pulse quicken as she took a sharp breath, and he hid a smile behind his hand while he pretended to rub his stubble.

"Jay has advised me," she said with all the neutrality she could muster, "never to involve myself in a domestic."

Randall barked a laugh. "He's far too smart."

"Aye." Ellis' smile faded. He dropped his hand to find and fuss Tiberius' head. "That he is."

Randall's question had brought about that uncomfortable truth: Christmas was only a week or so away and Ellis hadn't yet picked up any gifts. He didn't like shopping, and he liked

Christmas shopping even less. There were far too many opportunities to be caught — or more specifically *not* caught — on camera for his liking. The trouble was that the longer he left it the worse it got.

Usually Jay would help him. They would sit in his office together until late at night while Jay scoured websites and described items to him, and then Ellis would decide what to buy and for whom while Jay ordered them. He'd hired Christy to take some of the pressure from Jay and that was all well and good, but she wasn't quite there yet on the level of personal connection required to let her do his shopping.

Plus, Christy had no idea that her employer was a vampire. Or that his boyfriend was a werewolf.

She was a fast learner, though, and Jay was able to spend more time with Han as a result. Ellis missed having Jay around so much, but he'd felt so guilty that his best friends weren't able to spend their married lives together that he'd relented and hired someone to share Jay's job.

It didn't seem to make Jay any happier. Whether there was trouble at home or he felt guilty for not being around so much Ellis couldn't tell.

"Well, if you won't tell me, you'll just have to put up with whatever tat I get you." Randall's voice was filled with warmth even as he teased, and Ellis heard the werewolf's clothes rustle as he leaned over to take Ellis' hand.

Ellis squeezed those warm, living fingers and smiled in the direction of Randall's words. "I can live with that, petal."

To say that their relationship had progressed swiftly was an understatement. Ellis had never been one to ignore his own feelings, true, but they'd gone through more together in a few months than most people endured in a lifetime. A killer on Ellis' heels, a new pack on Randall's territory, and far too many close calls to mention had pushed them together fast.

Now they lived together. Randall's flat was a ruin and his previous pack's Alpha was probably keeping one eye on it waiting to exact revenge for his wife's death. That seemed a good reason to offer the werewolf space in Ellis' own home, but he would be lying if he said he didn't worry that Randall might think it all a little bit too much, too soon. Now that Randall was an Alpha himself his confidence seemed to be growing, but he was still a far more reserved creature than Ellis was. He took time to adjust to his feelings; time which Ellis hadn't given him.

He'd been selfish.

He loved Randall so deeply that any thought of harm to the shorter man fetched up an anger from so deep within him that it felt almost animalistic. He had no doubt at all that this was the man he wished to spend his life... his undeath... whatever it was, with. Randall was kind and gentle, compassionate and thoughtful. He was a delight in bed, all whimpers and pleas, his muscles and strength for naught as they writhed in surrender. He gave everything of himself without hesitation or fear.

Even his blood.

That wasn't normal, was it? Was it right? Randall's blood was potent stuff. When Ellis had first fed from him it was overwhelming. Shifter blood was enough to regrow his arm within minutes. It enabled him to go out in the sun. He felt vibrant and alive without drinking anywhere near the amount he used to need from humans, and he only had to feed every few weeks. It was pleasurable for them both, and it kept Ellis alive without the need to seek sustenance elsewhere. It made clear logical sense, and Randall was good with logic.

Christy cut through his thoughts. "If you two are getting kissy, I'm going home for the day."

"Are we?" Ellis lifted his chin.

3

"Oh yeah." She chuckled. Her chair rubbed across the carpet and her shoes squished the pile as she stood. Her computer fan cut out and left a sudden void in the sounds of the office. Ellis heard her footsteps, then the lining of her coat swish as she pulled it on. "That and it's gone six. Have a great evening. See you tomorrow. G'night, Randall," she added on her way out the door.

"Night, Christy," Randall chuckled.

Ellis turned toward Randall again and gave him a sly grin. "What were you doing?"

"I dunno what you mean."

"No? Why'd she think we're about to leap on each other, then?"

Randall laughed and took Ellis' jaw in his palm. His skin was soft and warm. His breath came closer, and Ellis parted his lips in anticipation moments before Randall's met them with a faint groan.

Ellis felt for Randall's thigh and ran his hands up toward the werewolf's hips, which he gripped and pulled closer until Randall landed in his lap.

"I know," he whispered against Randall's inviting mouth, "what you could get me."

"Name it."

Ellis grinned and nipped lightly at Randall's lower lip. "You. Naked. Maybe with—"

The office phone trilled loudly, and Randall jolted in surprise, then laughed. "Jesus, that scared the life out of me. Shall I get it?"

Ellis huffed and leaned back. "Would you mind?"

"It's fine." Randall levered out of Ellis' lap and headed for Christy's desk. "Hello, O'Neill Gallery, Randall speaking. How can I help you?"

"How about now?" Edison bellowed out of the little

speaker. "Is he there now? No? Don't bother to lie, whoever the hell you are! Tell him dad's had enough!"

Ellis heard his older brother's yelling from across the office. Edison shouted so loudly that Ellis was willing to bet he could have heard it even without his undead-sharpened senses.

"Er—" Randall began. The line clicked, then Randall lightly set the receiver back down. "Er," he said again.

"Randall, Edison. Edison, Randall." Ellis shook his head. "Sorry, petal. You okay?"

He listened as Randall's pulse levelled out. "Yeah. God, I thought Jay was being mean when he said your brother was an arsehole."

"It's all true." Ellis slid fingers up his wrist and felt across his watch for the ball bearings. Almost half-past six. "When's that thing out in Ilford?"

Randall sucked in air. "Shit. Is it... Bugger. I'm supposed to be there at seven. You going to be okay?"

"No," Ellis deadpanned. "I am going to be terrorised by customers any moment now, and all of them will suddenly want to buy out all our stock."

"Ha." Randall came over to kiss him again. "You're horrible."

"I love you too." Ellis squeezed Randall's arm. "Go roll around in the grass, or whatever it is you and your pack get up to."

"Sniffing each other's bums mostly. Love you."

"I'll see you later."

Ellis listened until Randall's heartbeat left the building, then turned to his display and tried to find some enthusiasm for Google. He would have to find somewhere that could deliver his purchases within the next few days and not be stymied by the volume of post that clogged up the postal service this time of year. He should have done this all by now. It would be in the bag if Jay had been around.

Ellis pursed his lips and pushed the display away. That was unfair of him and he knew it. He'd grown far too dependent on Jay, and for a man who prided himself on maintaining as much of his independence as he could, that realisation was a grim one.

"All right, Tiberius. Let's go. I've about had enough of today." He tidied his desk and reached for Tiberius' harness. He steered the German Shepherd to the coat hooks and grabbed his jacket, then once he had it on he took up the harness and turned the lights out. It made no difference to him, but it would make a difference to the electricity bill.

He barely took two steps out of his office before the gallery door downstairs opened. Its hinges made the faintest of squeals, and the draught excluder rasped over the doormat. Ellis turned an ear toward it and waited for any sound which could identify the newcomer. There was a heartbeat, which was almost always better than the alternative, and the faint click of an analogue watch. Footfalls were soft and faintly squeaky, so the newcomer wore trainers rather than shoes or boots. The human walked straight into the gallery without dithering at the door or drifting like a stranger toward the paintings.

"Jay?" Ellis called down the stairs.

"Hey! Sneaking off early?"

Ellis grinned at the familiar sound of Jay's voice, and he stepped toward the top of the stairs. His hand found the rail and rested over it. "Guilty as charged. I didn't think you were working this evening."

"I'm not." Jay's trainers slapped against the steps as he bounded up them. He reached Ellis in only seven footfalls, so he'd taken them two at a time. "No Randall?" he puffed once he was at Ellis' side.

"He's got a thing with his pack." Ellis took his hand from the rail and turned toward Jay, who placed his arm where Ellis would find it.

"Butt-sniffing." Jay's chuckle was brief. Tense. "I don't see the point unless there's tongue too."

Ellis slipped his fingers around Jay's elbow and frowned faintly. "What's wrong?"

"Nothing," Jay said, far too quickly. "We, uh. We haven't got your Christmas presents sorted yet. Have you done that? What are you getting for Randall? I think he'd love some new boots you know, his ones look so ratty. Or maybe that's okay. Does he shred his clothes when he goes all rawr? Wouldn't want to destroy a nice new pair of Timberlands—"

"Jay." Ellis squeezed his elbow. "I can hear it. Your heart is going ten to the dozen and you're too fit for it to be a few stairs. Your vocal chords are shaking and it's affecting the pitch of your voice. I mean, really? You're going to make me list the ways in which I can tell how upset you are? Tell me what's wrong."

Jay's breath rasped in his chest, and Ellis felt the position of his arm drop slightly. "We need to talk."

"Areet. You know where the office is." Ellis nodded.

It took seven pumps of his heart for Jay to respond. "It's about Han."

Ellis turned toward him with a frown, and Tiberius' claws clattered lightly against the mezzanine floor as he moved to remain at Ellis' left. "What about him?" Ellis blinked, and added, "He hasn't cheated on you, has he? He wouldn't! Whatever's going on, I know Han. He's a good man, Jay, he—"

"No," Jay said. He even laughed. A weak, angry laugh. "Oh

god if he were cheating I'd be over the moon compared to this."

Ellis straightened his shoulders. "Then... what?"

"He—" Jay's voice shook and his throat closed around his words. Ellis heard him swallow and take another breath. "He's dying." Jay's voice wavered as he spoke, and he sobbed softly. "Oh god, Ellis, Han's dying!"

TWO

RANDALL RAN ALL the way to Bond Street tube station and had a less than comfortable time on the Central Line to Liverpool Street. While the overground to Ilford was only about ten minutes it didn't run anywhere near as often as the tube, and he didn't get to Mr. and Mrs. Uddin's house until quarter past seven.

Zev's mum and dad were amazing. Their own pack was just themselves and three other shifters well into their fifties, but all of those families' children were part of Zev's — and now Randall's — pack. Despite Zev's death only a couple of months ago, his parents had welcomed Randall like a lost son and fussed over him when Ameera told them he had been raised by and among humans.

Arriving late was deeply embarrassing. He ran the last mile from the train station along suburban streets which had grown familiar to him, but he couldn't run fast enough to turn back time, and he took a breath on the doorstep before he knocked.

The door opened almost straight away, and Ameera pulled him inside. "You're late!"

"I'm sorry. Ellis—"

"Is irresistible, yeah." She smirked and fussed with his shirt. "You're sweaty. Nice one, oh great leader."

Randall smiled softly. "It'll be fine. Are we in the garden?"

"We're everywhere." Ameera beckoned and led him through the cramped hallway and into the cramped living room.

It was *heaving*. The house was a little three-bed terrace on a row of identical three-bed terraces, and it seemed plenty of space for two adults living together, but the living room was a riot of bodies and colour. Randall was too short to see over everyone's heads and count them, but there had to be at least fifteen people in here, and the place smelled of the uniquely woodsy scent of shifters.

Well, that and the drool-summoning scents of Mrs. Uddin's cooking. The woman was, Randall had discovered, a master of Bangladeshi cuisine. For a gathering as huge as this she had probably spent at least two, maybe three days preparing dishes and sweetmeats.

He felt another pang of guilt at showing up late when his hostess had worked so hard to prepare for it.

"Randall!" Mrs. Uddin waved to him as the crowd parted a moment.

"Ha. In you go!" Ameera gently pushed his shoulder, then hurried after him. "Mum!" she called.

Randall eased through the pack, all of whom smiled and nodded as he passed them. Around half of these people were his pack. The other half were unfamiliar to him, but he greeted them nonetheless, until he reached Mrs. Uddin. "I'm sorry I'm late."

Mrs. Uddin was even shorter than he was. Her brown skin creased as she smiled, and emphasised her flawless white teeth. Her hair was parted neatly down the centre and tied in a bun at the base of her skull, and there was barely a grey hair to be seen. She assured him once that werewolves aged graciously, their health as excellent in advanced years as it was in their youth, and for a woman over fifty she certainly only looked to be in her early forties. "Quarter of an hour, Randall," she laughed as she hugged him. "It's hardly the end of the world. Hasan isn't even here yet."

Randall couldn't help but smile at her. "You're far too good to me, Mrs. Uddin."

She squeezed his arm. "Wasn't your fault, Randall. Not even Sadia thinks that it was."

Randall's smile fell away at the mention of Zev's widow. "Is she here this evening?" He hadn't seen her since the night of Zev's death.

"Oh, no." Mrs. Uddin shook her head. "Four months and ten days of mourning. Only after then is she able to come into contact with men who are not mahram." At his questioning expression she added, "Mahram are relations one is forbidden to marry. During her period of mourning those are the only men who may be in her company."

"Right." Randall gave a slight nod.

He'd been immersed in two alien cultures at the same time. While he himself was born to a human mother, and his brother was human, Randall had changed when he was fifteen and only the good fortune of running into Preeti at a party saved him from a potentially terrible future. But Preeti and Briar were lost cubs themselves. The entire pack had formed from stragglers, from shifters born to human parents who had been forced to work out who and what they were without much help from the outside world. Zev, Ameera, and Hasan were born to shifter parents with a long and strong oral tradition and decades of experience.

Then there was also the fact that as well as shifters, the

Uddin family were Muslims too. Randall hadn't had such in-depth contact with Islam before, so sometimes he had to stop and work out which of Mr. and Mrs. Uddin's advice came from their experience as werewolves and which came from their faith, and mahram sounded much more Islam than shifter.

"She would like revenge," Mrs. Uddin added more gently. "Once she is able to return to the pack."

Randall chewed the inside of his cheek. He understood, he really did. If he lost Ellis he'd be baying for blood. But he was Alpha. He had to keep a level head, for the good of the pack.

Could he agree to set his entire pack to the task of hunting down and slaughtering Briar?

"Ah, you are a wise young man." She smiled fondly up at him. "The head must rein in the heart sometimes. You must wait and see Sadia after her iddah. If her love remains, she may wish to leave your pack to prevent conflict within it. If she has moved on she may remain and need your gift."

The gift of an Alpha came from their love. All these years Briar's pack believed it was something you were born with, and it turned out it was available to all, but a pack could only bear one Alpha pair. If Sadia's love for Zev persisted enough for her to retain the gift it would be best for the pack to decide who wished to follow which Alpha and for them to part amicably.

"But he will be a problem, I think," she added as she took him by the arm and steered him toward a table. It was piled high with nibbles, samosas, bowls of fruits and nuts, and other things Randall didn't know the name of but had prior experience of their deliciousness. Mrs. Uddin released him to pick up a paper plate and napkin, and she used the napkin to load two hand-sized samosas onto the plate. "Here! You should eat! Perhaps it will make you taller!"

He laughed as he accepted the plate with both hands. "Might be a bit too late for that."

"Never lose hope!"

"With the greatest of respect," he mumbled, "you're shorter than I am. They don't seem to have worked for you."

"That's the point of hope." She laughed and took his arm again. "It's there to protect you from reality."

Randall winced. "Ouch."

"Eat. Eat!"

Randall did as he was told, and Mrs. Uddin dragged him back into the throng to introduce him to werewolves he couldn't have even hoped existed three months ago.

———

RANDALL EVENTUALLY WORKED out that nobody batted an eyelid at what he considered lateness because it took well over two hours for the rest of the party to arrive. They came in twos and threes until, by ten o'clock, the party had spilled out into the back garden and there was a serious dent in the buffet. Many, Ameera told him, would wait until the last prayers of the day were completed, while others paused in their partying to participate in them.

Randall hadn't been raised among any religion. His mother was an atheist — although it said Church of England on her birth certificate — and he had no idea who his father was, let alone whether he was a religious man. His first real encounter with faith was when he was old enough to notice that some children were exempt from school assemblies, and when he asked them why they would tell him that they didn't partake in Christian prayer because they were Jehovah's Witnesses or Muslims.

He had no real comprehension as a child that the stuff they all had to recite in assembly was a prayer, or who it was aimed at. It all seemed silly once a teacher explained it to him. Even sillier was her shock at his question.

Still, by and large, faith was an understated thing throughout his childhood. Everyone kept theirs to themselves if they had any. Neither Randall nor his brother Kieran believed in any sort of higher power, so to be suddenly immersed in a deeply religious community was a surreal experience. He tried to keep his observations subtle whenever the evening turned to prayer.

"It's okay," Ameera whispered at his side once the last prayers of the evening were done.

Randall blinked. "What is?"

She gestured to the party. "Nobody's going to be offended if you ask questions, Randall. And nobody's going to be offended that you don't take part in prayer."

He wiped his fingers on a paper napkin and adjusted his stance sheepishly. "I'm that obvious, yeah?"

"Islam is very forgiving." She chuckled at him. "This life is just a preparation for the next, and in the next life pretty much almost everything can be forgiven or atoned for. Being a nice guy who takes care of people and animals isn't going to get you punished by Allah."

"What about being gay?"

"That depends on who you ask." Ameera turned and grabbed a small pastry shaped like a Danish from the buffet table. "As with all things centuries old which are translated and retranslated throughout the years, it is open to interpretation. Most will tell you that homosexual thoughts are a challenge to overcome, and that the only sin is in acting upon them. Whether there is punishment pretty much depends on where in the world you are."

Randall's mood soured. He scrunched up his napkin and tossed it into a bin, then let his gaze roam across the party. There were over thirty people here now, every last one of them a werewolf. The music was subdued out of respect for the neighbours. Nobody wore a burka or niqab, but he could see a few hijab headscarves among the women, both young and older. Most of the men wore neat shirts and trousers, although Hasan had rolled up in jeans and a t-shirt, and Mrs. Uddin had given him a light cuff around the ear for it.

Was it possible that each and every one of the people he had enjoyed a wonderful evening with thought of him as some sort of pervert or sinner? Did his own pack think such things of him?

Ameera gently nudged his elbow, and Randall blinked.

"You're fine," she said gently. "Everyone's own sins are between them and Allah."

"My *sins*?" he hissed. "Is that what you think love is? A sin?"

"No." She poked his bicep with a slender finger. "I'm answering your question. If you want to know what people in this room think personally, you are going to have to ask them."

Randall glowered at her.

"Hey you're the armchair anthropologist here, perving on prayers from the garden like a creeper." She grinned at him. "If you want to get to know people, though, you've got to talk to them. Come on, let's go do a poll!" She grabbed his arm and began to drag him toward the crowd.

"Ameera!"

"Nope! No assumptions!" She grinned at him. "If you've got questions, you come on in and you ask them! Mum? Hey, mum!"

"Ameera!" Mrs. Uddin turned with a warm smile.

"Randall wants to know what you think about homosexuality!"

Randall groaned.

THREE

"THIS ISN'T FUNNY." Ellis's grip on Jay's elbow tightened. "Jay, don't lie to me about this. Han's fine!"

"I'm not lying!" Jay yelled, and his voice tore through him in a way no human could fake. His heart pounded and his body grew tense as it shook with the vehemence of his words. "What am I going to do? I can't lose him, Ellis! It isn't fair! What, are we supposed to just have a few years and then that's it? He's gone? He's the best man I've ever met! I love him!" Jay broke into sobs which shook him so hard that Ellis had to cling to his elbow to hold him still. "I love him!"

"Office, Tiberius," Ellis said quietly. As Tiberius began to lead him that way, he tugged on Jay's arm. "Jay, come away from the stairs, aye? Tell me what's going on."

He heard Jay's trainers drag over the carpet as his assistant let Ellis pull him, and once they were through he released Tiberius and turned on the lights. He yanked his glasses off and stuffed them into the pocket of his jacket and steered Jay toward the centre of the room where the light would be strongest. It wouldn't be enough to see by, but he could at least be sure he was doing his damndest to look in Jay's actual direction, not three inches left of his ear.

The pale blob that was Jay's face finally swam into view. Ellis drew the taller man into a tight hug and could feel his body tremble with fatigue below the shudders of his crying.

Jay gripped Ellis' lapels and sobbed into his shoulder. Ellis could hear the soft pat of each tear as it broke free and landed against his shoulder. There was a light fragrance of something clinical about Jay's body up close, lying beneath the scents of grooming products and London transit. Disinfectant, perhaps, or some other industrial chemical. The sort of odour it took days to be rid of.

"Jay," he prompted softly.

"Oh god." Jay sniffled. "Oh god, I'm sorry." He pulled back and wiped at Ellis' shoulder. "I've got snot all over you."

Ellis did his best to keep his expression steady. "Not sure that matters right now, eh? Do you want a cuppa?"

"Okay. Yeah. I'll get it."

"Rubbish. Sit down. I can make tea." He propelled Jay toward a chair and moved toward the kettle, hands out to feel for the worksurface and along it until he found what he was looking for. He lifted it from its cradle and used his hip against the worktop to guide him to the sink.

The chair flexed with Jay's weight as the other man sat. His breath struggled to slow down. His heart still pumped in anger.

Ellis rested a fingertip over the edge of the kettle's filter compartment and ran the tap until his finger was wet. Once it was filled he closed the lid, returned it to the cradle, and felt his way through the cupboards for a cup, the teabags, and sweetener. His surroundings became a rhythmic collection of different regular sounds: Tiberius' heart; Jay's pulse; the drip of water through the kettle's filter; the high-pitched electrical hum of the light; the lower buzz of the refrigerator; the faint and indistinct sounds of the hotel next door. When the drips halted he felt for the kettle's On switch and flicked it.

He turned and rested his backside against the worksurface, with his hands on either side of his hips. "Jay," he prompted softly.

Jay's chair shifted. "It's called dilated cardiomyopathy," he groaned. "It's genetic. Half of his heart has got really weak and it doesn't work properly." Jay huffed and Ellis heard him fidget in his seat. "He was getting tired, like, all the time. We thought it was just stress with his company, you know? But then he was getting out of breath like all the time and they did all these tests, and..." He tailed off and took deep breaths.

The kettle clicked. Ellis turned and used his finger as a guide to pour the boiling water into Jay's mug.

Being a vampire was weird in more than the obvious way. Ellis's remaining senses were sharpened beyond any human capacity, and yet pain which would have left him in tears while alive was little more than a simple sensation. It only hurt if he were in serious danger from it. Barnes' knife had hurt like nothing he ever wanted to experience again, but a couple of seconds of boiling water was a mild irritation which healed quickly.

He finished the tea and took it to his desk. Placing it on the surface with care, he turned the handle towards Jay, then perched beside it and rested his hands on his own thigh. "Can't they treat it?" he eventually murmured.

Jay took the tea and blew on the surface. "He's going to need this defibrillator in him. It's like a pacemaker but whenever he has a heart attack—" his throat closed around the words.

Ellis leaned forward and felt for Jay's shoulder to squeeze.

Jay took another deep breath. "It'll shock his heart back

into a proper rhythm. But his heart's only going to get weaker. He needs a transplant."

Ellis grimaced and sat back. "That's horrible." He frowned. "He has to wait for someone to die? How's he taking that?"

Jay gulped down some tea and hissed at the heat of it. "The odds we'll ever get a compatible heart are pretty much nil. There's thousands of people on the waiting list and only a couple of hundred transplants a year, and Han's ethnically Chinese. Pretty much every donor is unsuitable. And then he could die from the transplant itself even if it ever happens—"

Ellis leaned in to squeeze his shoulder again before Jay could work himself into another panic. "Why didn't you tell me?"

"I just did!"

"I mean—" Ellis sighed and shook his head. "Sorry. That were a reet stupid question." He ran a hand through his hair and scratched his scalp. "How's Han taking it?"

"Philosophically." Jay sniffed. "You know what he's like."

Ellis nodded. He leaned back and crossed his arms loosely. "If there's anything you need, Jay, you know you can ask. Time off, support, a shoulder to wipe your snot on, you name it."

Jay laughed, but his laugh cut out. "There is something you could do."

Ellis leaned in at the sharp stab of hope in Jay's voice. "Name it."

Jay's heart quickened. So did his breath. "You could save him."

"I... what?"

"Ellis! Oh my god, why didn't I think of this sooner?" The cup clanked against Ellis' desk, and the shadow of Jay's body loomed over him as he stood. "You can save him! Make him a vampire!"

The rush of enthusiasm, of relief, in Jay's tone was painful to hear. Ellis stood himself and squinted up at Jay, but the light was behind him now, and all he could make out was a shape.

"I can't," he whispered.

"Don't give me that!" Jay grabbed his shoulders and shook him. "Don't you *dare* give me that! When Jonas did this to you, *who* came to your rescue?"

Ellis grit his teeth and shook his head. "That isn't fair."

"All this time!" Jay screamed the words. "All this time I've stayed late, I've come out in the middle of the night to find you, I've worried myself sick about you, and all this time I could have spent that time with my *husband* and now he's *dying* and you won't do this for us?"

"Jay!" Ellis planted his palms against Jay's chest to steady himself. "It isn't that simple!"

"Yes it is!"

"No it bloody isn't!" Ellis shoved at him, but Jay wouldn't release his shoulders. "Jesus, Jay, if I turn him and the Council ever find out they'll destroy us both!"

"You keep saying they'll destroy me if they find out I know what you are. Well, guess what? They haven't found out, and they won't find out about Han!"

"It's not the same thing!" Ellis sagged slowly. "He could die either way, whether I do this or not."

"Then it doesn't matter, does it?" Jay sighed as the fight left him. "Please. God, I've never asked anything of you, have I? I left a job at Han's side to come here and help you when your sight started to go and I've been by your side ever since. I've pulled twelve hour shifts. I've left Han in bed alone to get in a taxi and track you down. I've never even billed you for the cab fare. I did all of it because I believe in you. I believe in your business. You're a decent guy. You're Han's best friend, and you're mine too. He namedrops your gallery every time he has clients visiting, you know."

Ellis ran his tongue along the inside of his teeth. "I know," he relented.

Jay let go of his shoulders. The darkness looming over Ellis disappeared and his chair groaned again. "I'm sorry. I'm sorry, I don't… It isn't fair. And I don't want you to ever think I was, like, banking hours in exchange for a future favour or something. God, I'm an arsehole."

Ellis returned to his desk and sat on it. His feet swung slightly and he placed his hands on his knees while he listened to Jay finish the tea.

He'd have to be a total bastard not to empathise with Jay's position. It had to seem to him as though Ellis held some magic panacea for an otherwise incurable, fatal disease and he withheld it out of nothing more than choice. Were it Randall in Han's position Ellis knew damn well he'd fight for the cure no matter how dangerous it was. Perhaps even no matter how much it might change the man he loved.

He rubbed his stubble, then drew air to sigh with. "I would need Han's permission," he said quietly.

Jay launched to his feet. "You'll do it?"

"Hey, that isn't what I said, is it?" Ellis scowled. "I'll need Han's permission, which means I need to offer Han a choice."

"He'll say yes. He has to say yes." Jay's footsteps hurried to the door.

Ellis slid from his desk, landed lightly, and fished his glasses from his pocket. He slid them on and took a moment to adjust as his world retreated into darkness. "Come, Tiberius."

Tiberius came to stand at his left. Ellis took up his harness, then nodded for Jay to turn the light out. At the click, he had Tiberius lead him to the door.

"Thank you," Jay enthused once they were out on the mezzanine level once more.

Ellis shook his head. "Don't thank me. We have to tell him everything. Get it? He has to know where you've been going at night, why you've been pulling such long hours, and why you've kept this secret from your own husband. To be honest, you might be in deeper poo than me by the time we're done. You ready?"

"Yeah."

Jay offered his arm, and Ellis took it.

"Okay. Let's go wreck your marriage."

FOUR

MRS. UDDIN INSISTED on sending Randall away with a Tupperware container full of leftovers, and he balanced it in his lap on the train. He wasn't alone, either. The rest of his pack had either Tupperware or foil-wrapped packages, so the train carriage smelled delicious.

The shifters were full of cheer, relaxed and lounging in their seats as they chatted.

Randall could get used to this. This was family, and the longer he spent in their company the more they felt like they could be *his* family. This was how a pack was meant to be.

He gazed out of the window as the train rattled and shook its way toward Liverpool Street station. There was no countryside out there, only tight-packed suburbia, and in the darkness lights from flats and pubs cast out into the streets to create a jigsaw of colour and shadow. It felt so normal, like he was just a bloke who'd been to a party, and not a werewolf surrounded by twenty others as they passed through a world that had no idea they existed.

It wasn't like Briar's pack at all, but then nobody was like

Briar. If they'd known that Preeti was an Alpha too maybe things would have been better. Maybe she'd still be alive. Maybe she could have used her gift to run that pack better than Briar ever had.

It was all too late now. She was dead. Jim and Lara were dead. Only Randall, Briar and Nazim had survived the fight with Zev's pack, and Nazim had fled with Briar.

Briar must have retained his gift, Randall was sure of it. There had to be love in his heart for Preeti still. Two full moons had passed since her death and yet London's news was free of reports of hulking wolf-monsters or the rending slaughter of hapless bystanders. He doubted that Briar would lock himself away for the duration of the full moon.

He wished he could reach out and share the things the Uddins had taught him, to show Briar a better way, but in his heart he knew the big man wouldn't listen. He hadn't listened in thirteen years, why should he start now?

"So what'd mum say about you being a raging bender?"

Randall pulled his attention away from the window and stifled a yawn.

Hasan sat opposite and was stuffing a pastry into his mouth while he waited. Crumbs floated down to his t-shirt and he made a half-hearted attempt to brush them loose, but that just relocated some of them to his jeans.

"What do you say about it?" Randall asked.

Hasan shrugged. "I say we're lucky. We get to know, without any doubt, whether we're in love. Even better we know whether our partner loves us. The gift can't be fooled. Humans throw their money at dating sites to try and find that kind of certainty." He stuffed the rest of his pastry into his mouth. "You got the gift. You're in love. And because of that, you can keep us level, and those around us safe." He shrugged. "I don't give a flying monkey's whether you love a bloke or a brick. You're the Alpha, and you're treating us right."

Randall watched him and fought the urge to brush crumbs from his chest. "Thanks. That means a hell of a lot to me, you know?"

Hasan grinned. "So what'd she say?"

"Oh, I dunno." Randall rapped his knuckles against the lid of the Tupperware in his lap while he thought back to the conversation with Hasan's mum. "I know she meant well, but it still felt like my being with Ellis is a sin against Allah that I'll have to work out with Allah if I'm to be forgiven. There was that whole 'I love you and I worry for your soul' vibe. She was quite keen on telling me that it was totally okay to love a man so long as we weren't sticking it where the sun don't shine."

Hasan shrugged. "I reckon it's nobody's business but yours and Ellis' who's bumming who. And mum's, like, that generation, you know? You must've heard worse."

"Ha, yeah." Randall shook his head. "Way worse. At least nobody at your mum's took me out back for a kicking."

"See?" Hasan leaned back and watched him. "Has that really happened, though?"

"Oh yeah." Randall shrugged. "Not just from Briar's pack. They didn't beat me for being gay, though. That was just your regular bullshit bullying."

Hasan nodded. "I'm sorry. We didn't want to get close, didn't want to deal with that arsehole Briar. You were like our motivation for rescuing cubs, but we never thought to rescue *you*. I don't know why."

"I survived." Randall turned to gaze out the window, but he could still see Hasan's reflection in the scratched glass. "And I'm free now. I just wish the cost hadn't been so great, you know?"

Hasan turned to face the outside, too, and he nodded. "Yeah. I know."

They rode the last couple of minutes in brotherly silence.

THE PACK HAD THINNED out from Liverpool Street onwards. Most had headed for the Circle Line to go south. A few came with Randall to the Central Line. The further he travelled, the more of them he left behind, and they each hugged him before they hopped off at their stations. By the time he arrived at Bond Street he was alone.

It felt weird coming so far west and calling it home. He was an East End boy, born and bred. Ellis' neck of the woods was posh and moneyed, and even though he was up to his eyes in debt Ellis himself was as middle class as they came. He lived in a beautiful home with genuine antique fixtures in one of London's most expensive boroughs and he sold paintings that cost more than most people's cars. And now Randall lived in that home too. The address had even enabled him to take on clients who would pay far more for him to train their pampered pets than his regulars back in Stepney could afford.

Even the tube stations were different. Stepney Green was over a hundred years old and it looked it, with exposed Victorian brickwork and iron girders overhead to hold it all in place. Bond Street was all clean white walls and shiny escalators. Stepney Green spat you out onto an old road which had largely survived the Blitz, whereas Bond Street had three exits, one of which led into an upmarket shopping centre.

Randall took the escalator up to the Oxford Street exit and made his way down Davies Street. The pub he passed was busy, but in the cold December air everyone was tucked away inside with only a couple of smokers outside, neither of whom passed any comment on his Tupperware.

It wasn't sexy, was it? There was nothing cool about plastic containers full of leftover party food. He tucked it under one arm once the pub was behind him and hurried down the quiet street as red brick gave way to white stone.

Even the buildings looked posh. One side of the street was lined with cast iron railings behind which houses had long ago been converted into flats. On the other side, antique dealers and art galleries. It was a world away from the market stalls, pound shops, and takeaways of Stepney, and Randall's alienation felt subtly reinforced by Mrs. Uddin's gift. People in Mayfair didn't take leftovers home with them.

He hurried until he reached the warren of alleyways and mews which led past the O'Neill gallery and on toward their home. The gallery lights were off and the doors locked, so he continued onward. Ellis would take a convoluted route home every night to avoid reflective surfaces, but Randall could take the more direct path, and soon he stepped down the narrow street lined with garage doors in which Barnes had waited for Ellis.

It always made his hackles rise, coming here. Barnes had laid in wait and attacked Ellis with silver. There was no sign of it now, of course. They'd left Barnes' body in the gutter, but this was Mayfair, and the council had washed the blood away in under a day.

Randall trotted past the spot and drew his keys out of his pocket to distract himself, so it was only when he looked up again that he caught sight of the dark shape which stood on the doorstep to their building.

It could have been a neighbour, just returned home himself. It was too short to be Ellis, and besides it had no dog with it. Randall slowed himself and tried to look casual, which led to a swagger which felt strange, and he raised his chin.

The man was well-dressed. He wore a dark suit with a fine quality wool coat over it. His pale hair was parted over his right eye and not a strand of it was out of place. He made no effort to unlock the door, nor to use any of the buzzers.

Randall licked his lips and stopped a couple of feet away. "'Scuse me. Can I help you?"

The stranger turned and descended the steps. He was shorter even than Randall — five foot six at the most — and when he raised his head to face Randall the light caught his eyes. They were uncommonly pale, almost golden in the yellow of the street lamp. Randall was too far away to detect any scent, but he was willing to be the man didn't have one.

Those were a vampire's eyes.

"Randall Carter?" The man's voice was cultured, as one might expect given the area and his clothes.

Randall did his best to look nonchalant. He trained dogs. He had a website. Maybe Ellis wasn't the only vampire in town who needed his services, yeah? No. He didn't believe that for one second, but the bloke obviously knew who he was. Lying about it wouldn't get them anywhere.

"Yeah," he answered. "That's me."

"Wonderful." The other man's smile was a cold thing. "Not another word from you, Mr. Carter, until I say so. Follow me."

He turned on his heel and strode away as though he had no reason to think Randall might disobey, and Randall tried to ask who the hell he thought he was.

Tried, and failed. His feet swung into action, and Randall followed the vampire as though he were suddenly hung from wires. His eyes swivelled to the safety of his own front door as he walked past it, and the best he could do was make a strangled sound at the back of his throat as his body did as it was ordered.

FIVE

ELLIS INSISTED they take the tube, despite the enormous pain in the backside it was to use stations with ramps and lifts rather than risk Tiberius' paws on escalators. Jay was fidgety the entire way, and the squeal of the trains' wheels and brakes was enough to set Ellis' teeth on edge and make him regret going underground.

Once they were free of the tube, Ellis took Jay's arm and Jay led him along pavements and into a lobby which sounded cavernous. Their footfalls reverberated around it and bounced dully off the heartbeat in the far corner. Ellis was already blind by the time Han moved into this flat, but he hadn't been back here since he was turned, and he'd always thought Jay's description of the place might be exaggerated. The way the sound echoed, though, left no doubt: it was vast, and there was indeed a 24-hour concierge desk.

No wonder the fella could afford to patronise an art gallery. There had to be money in the app market.

Jay drew him into a lift. It was smooth and quiet. Quality machinery. No mice in the lift shaft.

"You live here?" Ellis felt his eyebrows lift. "And you work for me? Way to make a bloke feel inadequate."

"Ha." Jay huffed at him. "It isn't easy, you know."

Ellis frowned softly and tipped his head toward Jay. "How so?"

He felt Jay's shrug through his arm. "He's so... caring."

"Oh aye. I can see what a chore that is!"

"Shut it." Jay snorted. "He earns so much more than I ever can, and he likes to look after me. And I feel guilty spending his money, so I earn my own." He sighed as the doors opened. "Then I feel guilty that I'm not here, but I feel guilty that I'm not at the gallery helping you out..."

Ellis squeezed Jay's elbow and let the lanky man lead him from the lift. "Maybe you could spend a bit less time worrying about everyone else, and give yourself a bit of time too, aye?"

Jay didn't answer. Ellis heard a key and bolts turn, then he was led through onto a soft carpet so plush that Tiberius' paws were almost silenced by it. He retained his hold on Jay's arm until he heard a third heartbeat.

"Ellis!" There was an undercurrent of exhaustion to Han's greeting, but he hid it well enough that Ellis suspected Jay couldn't detect it. "Jay managed to prise you away from a busy evening at last, yeah?"

Han's sounds drew near, so Ellis offered his hand, and his fingers were enveloped within Han's warm grip.

"Oh, aye," Ellis said dryly. "A busy evening of online shopping. I was grateful to be rescued to be honest."

Han's scent had changed. He favoured a particular cologne which Ellis readily detected, but the way in which it interacted with Han's body was unique to him, and that interaction had altered. The scent was sharper now as different undertones swept to the forefront.

"So what brings you all the way out here?" Han's sarcasm

was a mild, teasing thing. His flat was only a couple of miles from Ellis'.

Except that to get here meant crossing the Thames as well as the territories of vampires he had never met. He didn't want to know what would happen if he crossed a body of running water as wide and deep as that which snaked through the city's heart, but it had been all sorts of uncomfortable when Randall had carried him over a canal and he could only imagine how much worse it would be with natural water.

Crossing beneath the river seemed to have no ill effect, but using the tube without assistance was unthinkable. Ellis hated everything about it, from the random speed fluctuations to the screeching, from the high-pitched squeaking of the mice in the suicide channels to the lingering smells of thousands of people and whatever they'd been disgusting enough to eat during their travels. Finding his way through the rabbit warren of platforms and stations was the least of his concerns.

"I reckon it's pretty obvious," Ellis answered. "I came because Jay says you're dying, and you never bloody told me!"

Han snorted. "I'm not dying! I'm fine! Jay worries too much—"

"I do not!" Jay's voice rose with his indignation. "Why don't you tell him what the doctor said?"

"It's nothing to worry about," Han murmured. "Come on, let's sit down."

"Nothing?" Jay squeaked.

"Only dolphins can hear you now, Jay," Ellis said softly as he retook his assistant's arm. "Could you do me the honours?"

"Yeah. Of course." Jay steered him further into the flat, then guided his hand to the back of a chair. "It's facing away from you. Not on wheels. Got it?"

"I've got it, aye. Thanks." Ellis walked around an armchair

which felt soft and cool to the touch, like leather. He doubted Jay would have allowed Han to buy genuine leather, though, so it was more likely to be some faux-leather fabric. He lowered himself with care until his backside contacted the cushion. "Ah, there we go. Good boy!" He fussed Tiberius' head, then released his harness. "Go lie down."

Ellis heard Tiberius settle beside the armchair. He waited for the soft sounds of more bums on seats, but only heard one.

"Well now you're here," said Han, "do you fancy a drink?"

"No, no." What he fancied least of all was having to deposit whatever he ate or drank down the loo before sunrise before it could evacuate of its own accord. "Come on, Jay. Sit down."

Han chuckled as Jay finally sat. "How do you do that?"

"He has these mother hen vibes that ricochet around whenever he isn't sitting down." Ellis smirked briefly, then ran his hands over the arms of his seat while he chose his next words. "You're my friend, Han."

"Uh huh…"

"So don't you give me any shit. I'm not going to take it from you. If Jay says you're dying, I believe him." He drew breath, then added "Let's try again. What did the doctor say?"

Han's breath escaped him in a puff. "It doesn't matter, mate. There's nothing that can be done. What's the point worrying?"

"Because I care about you. I care about you both!" Ellis frowned.

"Look. The fact is I can drop dead at any second. The only fix for this is a heart transplant, and even then something like one in ten people die due to complications from the operation itself. After that you're on anti-rejection drugs for life, which wreck your insides and take years off your life expectancy, and you *still* might just drop dead at any second. None of that matters because there are no hearts available and there aren't likely to *be* any hearts available." Han wheezed to a stop, and his breath turned ragged as he tried to recover the energy lost from speaking for twenty seconds without a break.

Twenty seconds.

Ellis grimaced and tipped his head slightly. He closed his eyes to cut out the very faint grey which crept in past his glasses and focused on the heartbeats across the room from him.

"Ellis?" Han added.

"Shh. Give me a moment."

Han and Jay's hearts beat side-by-side. With the direct comparison of one to the other he thought he could hear a slightly fainter beat in one of them, but he couldn't be certain that it wasn't his imagination.

"Tell him," Jay said.

"What else is there?" Han answered, his breath still weak.

"Not you, sweetie. Ellis, tell him."

Ellis lifted his head and pursed his lips. "What about this defibrillator thing? Won't that help?"

"It's pretty clever." Han's words evened out as he recovered at last. "It's a bit like a pacemaker, but when you go into tachycardia—"

"A what now?" Ellis blinked.

"When your heart starts going too fast," Han supplied, "it's the start of a heart attack for degenerative cardiomyopathy, so when that happens the ICD gives you this shock which cancels the electrical signals and—" he paused for breath "—lets your heart work normally again."

"And what happens to you through all this rubbish?"

"Apparently I'd just feel, like, palpitations. But if it doesn't work I'll black out."

Ellis snorted. "You're making it sound nicer than it is, I

reckon. If it doesn't work, you have a damn heart attack and die."

"Well, yeah. But first the black out."

Jay's breath hitched and his weight shifted. "Tell him!"

Ellis rubbed his forehead as he leaned his elbows on his knees. "I'll 'appen as I will have that drink, aye," he muttered.

"You don't want a drink," Jay huffed.

"Jay!" Han sounded startled.

"He's fine. He's right. I don't want it. I just want a minute to process all this shit." Ellis stood and stepped away from his chair, then stopped himself before he could collide with anything.

He had no idea of the layout of this flat. He didn't know where the tables and chairs were, where the doors were, whether there were open drawers or other hazards. He couldn't tell whether there were ornaments or sculptures in his way, or stray clothing littered across the floor. The entire room was an assault course that he couldn't see, and storming off in a huff wasn't an option for him.

Ellis stood helpless where he'd stopped. His hands balled into fists at his sides. He felt sick in a way he hadn't in weeks, not since he'd heard strangers tear each other to pieces.

Not since he'd heard their hearts stutter to a halt.

That was going to happen to Han. Not in some distant future like it should, but soon. His heart would give up, his last breath would rattle in his throat, and then the man who had been there to help him when he first moved down to London, when he first set up a small Gallery in Fitzrovia, would be gone forever. Jay was right: it *wasn't* fair. Han was a good man. A kind, thoughtful man who always had time to spare for his friends and who never treated him any differently when Ellis began to lose his sight.

If it wasn't for Han, Ellis wouldn't have a business. Han

brought his clients to Ellis' gallery. He once said that as their businesses began at around the same time it seemed only fair for them to help each other out, and as they'd both grown, Han's clients had become wealthier and Ellis was able to move to Mayfair. Jay had quit his job as Han's assistant to come help him once his retinitis pigmentosa was diagnosed, and Han had been insistent that Ellis take Jay on. He'd even kindly tolerated Jay's late nights, his night-time disappearances to help Ellis out, and not once had Han ever doubted his husband or accused Ellis of anything untoward. He was the single best friend Ellis could have hoped for, and the thought of losing him made him sick with anger.

"Hey." A hand touched his arm, and Ellis started in surprise, so lost in his thoughts that he hadn't heard Han's approach.

"I don't want to lose you," Ellis whispered.

"Shed no tears until you see the coffin," Han murmured.

Ellis scowled and felt for Han's chest, then bunched the shirt he found into his fist. "Don't you dare throw your mum's proverbs at me. Not now. Do you want to live?"

Han grabbed Ellis' forearm. "What's the point of that question? You want me to break down and cry, do you? You want me to scream at how unfair it all is? Life isn't fair, mate! But it's all we've got."

Ellis tugged his glasses off, and heard Han's sharp intake of breath. He leaned in until he could almost see Han's dark eyes.

"This is important," he hissed. "Do you want to live?"

SIX

RANDALL'S BODY marched him to the end of the mews and around the corner, where a large black Land Rover waited. He knew it waited because it came with a full complement of big, burly men in dark jeans and darker sweaters all watching his approach.

If he'd been in any doubt before, he wasn't now: he was being kidnapped.

One of the waiting men got behind the wheel. Another opened the passenger door for the vampire. A third opened the rear door for Randall.

"Get in, Mr. Carter, quietly and without any resistance."

Randall ground his teeth as he climbed into the back of the vehicle. The rear windows were dark, so once he was in there he'd be all but invisible from outside, but he sat down next to a man who felt twice his own size in the confined space, and the one who had held the door for him eased in to squish him into place.

The vehicle's interior was plush with leather and soft fabrics. Of the vampire's four henchmen, not one of them was without his own scent, yet the blond in the front passenger seat showed no compunction against using what was very obviously some kind of mind-control power in plain view of them. Either he had no issue with breaking the Council's laws, or his power gave him particular leeway.

Randall squirmed in his seat. He grit his teeth and fought to do so much as elbow either of the humans at his side in the gut, but his arms barely moved. He tried to form words, but none came. He couldn't even yell in his impotence. His body was terrifyingly obstinate, and his heart thudded at the sense of helplessness that swelled inside him. He tried to look out of the windows and caught glimpses of expensive old buildings and deserted streets, but after a few moments of that one of the guards withdrew a black strip of cloth from inside his jacket and used it to blindfold Randall.

Blind. Randall bared his teeth and dug his fingers into the sides of the Tupperware in his hands. He didn't have Ellis' senses, not in this body, but if he changed in front of these people he'd be violating his own people's rules. Worse, if he let this vampire know what he was, it would be the loss of an ace up his sleeve that might save him later.

The ride, at least, was smooth, and filled with twists and turns. Perhaps they were taking a circuitous route to prevent Randall from learning too much, or maybe they did actually travel a couple of miles. He had no way to know. All he could do was wait.

AFTER WHAT HE guessed to be around fifteen minutes they took his samosas, bundled him out of the vehicle, and across an even pavement. Up a couple of steps, in to a building. He was marched along, twisted this way and that, until heavy hands against his shoulders steered him into a solid chair.

"Stay seated, Mr. Carter."

Randall ground his teeth. He felt hands work at his wrists, and the bite of plastic zip-ties against his skin. The same was done to his ankles, though his socks offered some protection there. Once he was physically secured the blindfold was loosened and tugged free.

The light was subdued, but still far brighter than he'd adjusted to, and Randall blinked water from his eyes to take in his surroundings. The room he was in was large, bigger than Ellis' entire flat, and with a tall ceiling at least twelve feet high. There were shelves dotted with books and ornaments, sparsely placed to please the eye. The walls were covered in a deep burgundy wallpaper with a dark gold baroque pattern, then wood-panelled from around knee height to the floor. There was a vast stone fireplace which wasn't lit and was stuffed with neatly-arranged logs as though it lay ready to be useful. There was an antiquated globe in one corner, the deep red wood of it cradling a beach ball of a planet whose shapes and borders seemed thoroughly alien to him. Of primary placement in the room was the vast, gleaming mahogany desk which sat in front of him. It was massive, fully eight feet from left to right, and so well polished that Randall could see the ceiling's complex mouldings reflected in its surface.

He couldn't, of course, see any reflection from the precisely-groomed vampire who sat across the desk from him, his manicured hands resting on its surface.

"Leave us," the vampire said.

Randall heard footsteps, and the quiet click of a door behind him.

"Now. Let us have a conversation. You may speak, Mr.

Carter, but let's not have any shouting. It's quite unnecessary."

Randall sucked in a breath. He half expected nothing to happen when he tried to speak, so when sound emerged it startled him. "Who the hell are you?"

"My name is Charles Devitt." The vampire's emphasis was on *vitt*. He regarded Randall with his eerie amber eyes, and added "You smell like a werewolf. It's quite distinctive. Let's not have any shapechanging from you either, all right?"

Randall growled as he squirmed in the heavy wooden chair he was tied to. There went his ace. "What do you want?"

"Oh, how gauche," Devitt drawled. He sat back in his seat and "I merely wish to speak with you. After this you will be free to go. Don't fret so."

"Then why all the cloak and dagger shit?" Randall flexed his hands and twisted his arms, but the plastic bit at him, and he healed so fast that it was impossible to become inured to the pain. "Let me go!"

"You inverts are always so over-dramatic, don't you think?" Devitt sighed faintly. "We are going to talk, Mr. Carter, about your... boyfriend? Is that the term? It's a terrible word. Neither of you are children."

"Inverts?" Randall stared at him. "What does that even *mean*?"

Devitt snorted. "Sodomites. Homosexuals. Although what the Devil either of you see in one another is beyond me. Mr. O'Neill is a cripple and you are black. It would be amusing if it weren't so repugnant."

Randall sucked in air and held it. Anger seethed within him and tightened all his muscles. His body primed itself to fight even though he couldn't move from his seat. The moon wasn't anywhere near full, but Devitt's bigotry wasn't the casual, offhand racism he was more accustomed to. This was direct, almost antagonistic trolling. It smacked of the kind of shit he'd expect from someone's sainted grandma, not a man in his twenties.

A *vampire* in his twenties, he realised. A vampire whose idea of a globe was from some time when everything east of a very weirdly-shaped Germany was Russia.

"How old are you?" Randall said.

"One loses count." Devitt smirked. "Around a hundred and fifty years or so." He spread one hand across the smooth desk surface and watched his own fingers, then glanced up to Randall once more. "I think that's quite enough of the pleasantries. There's little point in answering any further questions from you. It isn't as though you will remember any of this when I am through with you." His smirk became a cold, calculating smile, all white teeth and humourless eyes. "Let's get down to business, Mr. Carter. You will answer my questions honestly. You will add no unnecessary commentary. You will ask no questions of your own. Tell me: are you aware that Mr. O'Neill is a vampire?"

"Yes." Randall's lips formed the word, and it slipped out with ease. He swallowed down his sudden stab of fear and tried to change shape. A wolf would slip free of bindings measured for human limbs.

The wolf wouldn't come.

He twisted in the chair. Wrenched his arms against the zip ties until his wrists bled. He tried to scream, but all that came out of him was a rush of air.

"Relax, Mr. Carter. Don't bleed on the rug. I understand it to be quite the bother to wash out." Devitt stood and circled his desk and approached Randall's sagging body. He dragged the tip of one icy finger through Randall's bloodied skin and raised it to sniff as though he were sampling a freshly-poured glass of wine. Once satisfied, he drew a handkerchief and wiped his finger clean. "Well, now I see your appeal, Mr. Carter. I've never thought to actually feed from one of your sort. All that hair and muscle is quite off-putting. But that still doesn't explain what you see in O'Neill." He sat back against the edge of his desk as he stuffed the handkerchief back into his pocket. "Where shall we begin?"

"I don't know," Randall whimpered.

Devitt nodded to himself. "Then let us begin where O'Neill would not wish us to. The man has secrets, Mr. Carter. If you know what he is, then I'm certain you know what other secrets he holds. Let those be our guide. Tell me something about him that he would not want me to know."

Randall's thoughts spun out of control. Everything that Ellis wouldn't want another vampire aware of crashed through his mind in a stampede towards his mouth, and it all fell into gridlock. His mouth opened, but nothing came out.

He felt a flicker of hope. Could this be the answer? If he simply tried to tell Devitt everything all at once, would it save him from answering any questions at all?

Devitt leaned forward like a hawk examining prey. His gaze flickered from one of Randall's eyes to the other, as though he could read something there.

Shit. Don't tell me he's a telepath too?

Randall swallowed. That couldn't be possible, could it? Would that be two powers? Or was it all part of the same ability?

No. If Devitt could read his thoughts, he wouldn't have to order Randall to speak. He wouldn't even have to go to the trouble of a kidnapping.

"It seems," Devitt murmured as he straightened, "that Mr. O'Neill has far too many secrets under that ridiculous hair of his. Very well. We shall go through them one at a time." He grinned. "Tell me how he killed Tomasz Jasiński. You may know him as Peter Barnes."

Randall's horror that Devitt knew about Barnes escalated as his own mouth obeyed without question. "Barnes had a silver knife. He cut Ellis' shoulder and Ellis' arm turned to dust. He started cutting Ellis' chest, so I bit his arm and dragged him clear. Then Ellis found the knife and stabbed him with it."

He felt sweat bead across his forehead, and his gut twisted with his betrayal.

"You bit him..." Devitt's eyebrows lifted, then he added "Ah! You were a wolf at the time?"

"Yes."

"I see. Where is the knife?"

"I don't know. Ellis got rid of it."

Devitt nodded to himself. "See? Isn't this pleasant. We're getting somewhere. Now, Mr. Carter. Do you know how Mr. O'Neill killed the vampire who created him? His name was Jonas."

Randall bit his tongue. Blood welled in his mouth, sharp and coppery, all warmth and salt. "Yes," he spat.

"Wonderful. Tell me."

SEVEN

HAN SNORTED INTO ELLIS' face. "Of course I want to live! It's literally nobody's dream to die when they're twenty-nine years old, Ellis! Or have you come all the way over here to take the piss?"

"No. I wouldn't." Ellis relaxed focus. The strain was uncomfortable, so he let it go. "You two are my best friends, Han. You've been right here for me ever since I came down south."

"Too bloody right we have. So what the hell are you trying to do here?"

Ellis sighed faintly and lowered his head. He relaxed his grip on Han's arm. "I'm trying to save your life," he muttered.

"Oh, you're a cardiologist now?"

Ellis shook his head. "No. Don't be so bloody facetious. I'm a vampire."

Han paused. His heart stuttered, and for a moment Ellis worried that he'd triggered some sort of tachy... cardy... whatever the hell it was.

"Bullshit," Han hissed. "What the fuck, Ellis? You finally

bother to visit, and it's to give me some weird-arse crap? If this is to try and distract me from my own imminent death it's kinda working—"

"If I could get here without crossing a ruddy massive river, I would," Ellis snapped. "You couldn't have bought something on the north bank, could you? I have to use the tube to get here, and I can't get around it without help!"

"What the hell's the Thames got to do with anything?" Han stepped back from him and tugged his arm free. "Let me guess, you can't cross running water? Is that what you're saying now?"

"It's true, sweetie," Jay whispered from the direction of the couch. "It's all true."

Han's breath rasped in his throat. His heart stuttered again. "This isn't funny, Jay."

Ellis spread his hands slowly. "Calm down. Han, please. You need to stay calm—"

"Show him," Jay insisted.

"Show me what?" Han's clothes swished with some sort of swift movement.

Ellis pressed his lips together tightly. He knew exactly what Jay meant, and Ellis had to agree that it was the sort of evidence which tended to work best. It was the only overt display of what he was, but it also primed his body to feed, and the hunger that came with exposing his fangs without intention to use them was an uncomfortable distraction, like sporting a hard-on during gym classes at school. Well, maybe not quite *that* bad. At least showing his fangs wouldn't get teenagers yelling *poof* at him.

Would it calm Han, though? Or just agitate him further? He had no idea whether Han's distress placed him at any greater risk from heart trouble, but he didn't want to drag things out either.

"Fine," he grumbled. "Hang on."

"Hanging with bated breath," Han said. He oozed sarcasm.

Ellis shook his head, then raised his chin and parted his lips. He felt like a bloody idiot every time he did this. That wasn't to say it was a common occurrence: showing off what exactly he was was the antithesis of keeping a low profile, but it seemed to be that people would only believe it if they saw it. It didn't seem unreasonable, but it was slightly silly standing around with his mouth open like he had some impressive dentures to show off. He willed his fangs to descend, and felt the tell-tale itch of his gums as they did so. He opened his mouth a little further to avoid jabbing himself in the lip with them.

Han gasped slightly. He stepped closer, and Ellis became almost fixedly aware of how close the other man was to him. Warmth radiated from his body and buffeted through Ellis' clothing. His pulse thrummed just below the readily-punctured surface of his skin. He smelled less like Han and more like food, and if Ellis were to turn him he'd have to drink every last drop he could from this live, vital body. It was so close. So very, *very* inviting.

"How'd you do that?" Han's warmth grew closer. "Are they implants? How much were they? It's a bit mental for cosmetic dentistry. Can I touch 'em?"

Ellis groaned at the thought of any part of Han's body getting near his mouth.

"Uh." Jay's voice came closer. "Maybe that's not such a great idea, sweetie."

"Seriously?"

Ellis could only guess at what happened next. He felt pressure against his teeth, and then he heard a weak moan from Han, and Jay swore like a sailor. Had Han poked him with a finger and impaled himself?

He tipped his head and took a breath. It brought with it the delicious aroma of fresh, live blood, so he ran his tongue forward and found a thumb pressed up against one of his canines.

"Ellis!" Jay moved, and the digit was torn from his mouth.

"Oh my god!" Han's exclamation was soft, and his breath trembled.

Ellis ran the tip of his tongue over his teeth and gathered the faintest smudge of Han's blood from them. It was like waving scotch at an alcoholic, and he stepped forward instinctively.

"Put them away!" Jay shoved against his chest. "Now!"

Ellis tried another step, but Jay's hand was firm, and he sounded angry. Angry Jay was a rarity indeed — rare enough that the scarcity of it penetrated the bloodlust which had overtaken him, and he withdrew his fangs as swiftly as he could. "Oh god. I'm sorry. I didn't take anything, I swear!"

"Fucking hell." Han stumbled away from them both and fell hard against the sofa.

"You're bleeding," Ellis said. "I can stop that."

Jay's hand remained where it was. "You back in the room with us?"

"Aye." Ellis grimaced as he nodded. "I won't bite. But if you want it closed I have to breathe on it."

"Or I can put a plaster on it," Han whispered. "Rather than have you going all weird on me again."

"I'm weird?" Ellis scowled and stalked toward Tiberius' heartbeat, one hand outstretched. His shin found the chair before his fingers, though, and he turned to lower himself carefully so as not to end up on the floor. "You're the one who jabs his fingers into people's mouths."

"Oh come on!"

"For god's sake!" Jay yelled. "Stop it! Stop it! You're

bickering like bitter old queens, for crying out loud! Han, I had to *beg* Ellis to come here and offer this to you, because I can't lose you! Do you understand me? I can't live without you! I love you! I married you because I want to be with you forever, not for three bloody years! This is a *secret*! We could get killed just for telling you what Ellis is, and you'd be bumped off for hearing it."

Jay's voice seemed to reverberate around the vast apartment, and Ellis heard the rasp of his breathing as his tirade ended. He was upset again, but it didn't take a vampire's hearing to work that one out. He'd have to be a monster to *not* be upset.

He heard flesh rub against flesh. One hand against another, or against a face or arm. He heard clothes swoosh, and the faux-leather of the sofa creak faintly. One body muffled the pulse of another, and then came the distinct and faint smack of a soft kiss.

Ellis slid his glasses on. He couldn't see what was going on, but it might be a bit less unnerving to Han not to have Ellis staring at him from across the room.

"Okay," Han eventually said. "I'm sorry."

"You better be." Jay moved until the path to Han's heart was clear again.

"As am I," Ellis muttered. He didn't feel sorry, but it would be childish to cling to that.

They sat as awkward silence descended. The longer it dragged on, the more he became aware of the flats all around them: the faint throbs of pulses above and below; the chatter of distant televisions and beeps from phones and tablets.

"The eyes," Han finally said. "They aren't contacts, are they?"

Ellis shook his head. "No."

"So when I saw them and I thought they were... That was like a year ago or something. Is that when you got... made?"

"Pretty much. A bit over." Ellis nodded. "I thought Jay was pulling my leg when he said they'd changed. It was only when you asked if they were contacts back then that I realised he wasn't."

"And that's why the sunglasses?"

"No." Ellis pushed his hair back from his face. "Remember I shut the gallery down when I went properly blind?"

"Of course."

"Yeah, I went on a bit of a bender. Got right rat-arsed pretty much all week. That's when I got turned." He sat forward and rested his elbows on his knees. "Vampires have heightened senses. All of it. Sight, hearing, touch, temperature, balance, you name it. It wasn't enough to give me my eyesight back, but it was enough to give me a bit. I can just about make out bright things in strong light if I get up close and personal and squint at 'em. Otherwise it's just like my sight was a couple of years back before it all completely went, and it's—" He broke off and shook his head.

Han took a sharp breath. "A bit of a slap to the face, right?"

Ellis laughed bitterly. "Yeah."

"Can't you fix it?"

Ellis lifted his head. "Eh?"

"I dunno. I mean, vampires, right? Don't you just ignore injury and stuff?"

He couldn't help but smirk at that. "Not so much, no. We heal fast, but not ignore it altogether. But this isn't an injury. When you get turned, you're like... pickled for posterity. Everything about your body becomes this physical absolute. Every hair you had, every scar you had, every mark on you, every nail, every eyelash, it becomes fixed in place. If you want to go through with this make sure you've got the haircut you want, your nails are trim, and you've got your facial hair the way you like it, because you're going to get stuck with it and you can't ever change your mind."

"Oh." Han sniffed. "Is that why you've sported that shitty stubble for so long?"

"Hey!" Ellis scowled and leaned back. "I was drunk for an entire week. I'm impressed it wasn't even more of a mess."

"Heh." Han shifted in his seat. "Shouldn't mock the afflicted, I suppose. That's what you're offering, then? To make me a vampire?"

Ellis nodded slightly. "I can't fix your heart. But I can make it irrelevant."

"Uh huh." Han paused, then added, "What's the catch?"

"What, other than drinking blood?" Ellis' eyebrows climbed.

"I figured that's a given. What else?"

Jay laughed weakly. "I guess the big one's going to be electronics."

"Because..?" Han asked slowly.

Ellis reached into his jacket and fished out his phone. "The trouble with being a vampire is that you have no reflection. You don't create body heat either. You kind of just default to the ambient temperature, which makes it difficult to offer a handshake in winter without someone thinking you've got a circulation problem. Your voice doesn't get picked up by technology, and nor does your image. You don't appear in photographs, you can't be heard over the phone, and—" he faced the screen toward Han and ran his fingertip over it "—electronic devices do not recognise you."

Han's breath came sharply. "You *do* know what I do for a living, right?"

Ellis gave a curt nod. "Yeah. You remember that sexy biometric security system we used to have at the gallery?"

"Of course!" Then Han groaned. "This is why you took it out?"

"Aye. It wouldn't let me into my own business. Wouldn't read my fingerprints. Jay had to arrange for a contractor to come in and swap it out for something older."

"God, they were so confused," Jay sighed. "Obviously thought I was crazy. Got a good discount by letting them take the biometric system away with them, though."

"A *discount*?" Han sounded irate. "That system was worth three times the one you've got now!"

"Yes, but I couldn't very well ask you for your help, sweetie," Jay murmured, "or you would have thought I was crazy too."

"So you knew? You've known all this time? This is why you keep working late, isn't it? This is why you disappear at all hours?"

Jay swallowed. "Yeah."

Ellis reached down to scratch between Tiberius' ears. If this was about to erupt into an argument he didn't want to be involved.

Han took a moment, then huffed. "Arsehole," he grunted.

Ellis put his phone away. "There's more," he said. "And you really need to know it all before you make a decision."

"Okay," said Han. "Hit me with it."

EIGHT

"I DON'T KNOW EVERYTHING," Ellis was forced to admit. "All I can tell you is what I've figured out in the last year or so."

"Then that's what we've got to work with." Han sounded like he wanted to urge Ellis on.

"Aye, you're right." Ellis gripped his knees a moment. "Okay, where to start? Um. You need blood. You can eat and drink the usual stuff and still taste it just fine, but you have to get rid of it by sunrise or it'll all come up without your say-so."

"Wait, stop." Han took a breath, then exhaled slowly as though he were deflating. "You have to, what? Fingers down the throat or something?"

"No." Ellis shook his head. "You can just, like, *make* it come up. Find yourself a sink and, er. Yeah. It's pretty disgusting, but if you're ever forced to ingest something at a social you can at least fake it. People get weirded out if one of their friends suddenly stops eating and drinking altogether."

"Right. That's gross."

"No, what's gross is learning the hard way."

"Oh, no!" Jay cut in. "Eww!"

"Yep. That's pretty much how it went." Ellis shrugged. "Anyway. Once you're turned, anything you had in you will come out by sunrise, so there's that indignity to endure too. I don't know if you can make that happen. That's the kind of thing you only ever get one chance at."

"Uhh." Han sounded less than thrilled.

"I think that's largely it for the disgusting bits, though." Ellis mustered a smile. "Like I say, your senses will be keen. You'll hear your neighbours' televisions, every car that goes past your building, every appliance in your home. You'll hear the heartbeats of everyone around you for fifty yards or so. You might hear the tube going past underground if you're right over it — it depends on how deep the line is. It'll only hurt if the sound is louder than you can tolerate. I wouldn't get up close to speakers at a gig or anything like that."

"And I suppose it'll work for everything else that way too," Han mused.

"Exactly. It's all amplified. But the weird thing is that you don't really seem to feel pain. Not unless it's something that could really do you some harm. You can stand boiling water, freezing cold, getting hit. I mean, you *feel* it, but it's like you're aware that it can't really injure you. You just feel your body healing itself and it's gone. But silver—" He shuddered at the memory. "God, silver hurts. It hurts like hell, and any part of you that gets silver in it will just turn to ash and drop off."

"That sounds like personal experience," Han said with care, "but you seem to have all your parts."

"I healed. It took a lot of blood, but I healed." Ellis winced. "And speaking of that, healing does use your reserves. It drains you. You should be able to go two or three weeks with just a little blood, but once you start getting yourself beaten up it'll dwindle away and you get hungry. Don't get hungry, Han. It's not pretty."

"Uh," Han said again.

"Mm." Ellis nodded. "Anything in you that shouldn't be there will get pushed out when you heal, and you can't stop yourself from healing, so I reckon it isn't very subtle. The more you heal, the hungrier you get, and you reach a point where nothing will stop you from feeding from anything, or anyone. You can't do anything weird like stock up, either. Once blood's out of a living body it's useless to you. You have to take it straight from the source."

"No collecting a fridge full of blood bags." Han gave a weak little laugh. "Got it."

"Yup." Ellis sat back. "If your head comes off, you die. If you're turned to ash, you die. If you get stuck with wood to the heart it will paralyse you, and that makes it easy to kill you in my book. Other than that, if you cut your hair it'll regrow. If you shave, it'll be back. If you trim your nails they'll be right where you started before you even finish. The more well-fed you are the more you pass for living. You have to remember to breathe if you want to talk. You'll go insane if you try to cross over a body of running water, but you can pass under it fine. You still need to sleep for your usual amount of hours. Sunlight is a no-no."

"And putting your fangs in someone is the most obscene thing they can have happen to them with their clothes on?" Han offered.

Ellis grimaced. "Aye. And they can't resist once you're in. All you have to do is break the surface and they're helpless. It's grotesque, if you stop to think about it."

"I wouldn't say no," Jay piped up. "Uh, for Han. I mean, you know. If that's what you need, baby."

Ellis pressed his lips together.

"Wait." Han stood up. "Have you two, uh... Have you ever—"

"No!" Ellis and Jay answered at once.

"Then—"

"Jonas used to bring volunteers to me," Ellis grunted. "Then once I was out on my own I'd just, you know. Pick people up in bars. Give 'em a good necking."

Han's breath hitched. "Random people?"

"Yes."

"But—" Han sat again. "What about, I don't know. What if they were ill? What about blood-borne diseases? Parasites? You don't have any idea what a stranger could have!"

"It doesn't seem to matter." Ellis rolled his shoulders slowly. "I haven't caught anything, I haven't been ill. If I've ever bitten someone who was infected with something it hasn't seemed to pass on to me."

"But you don't know."

"No." Ellis shook his head.

"Fine. Okay. What else?"

Ellis rubbed slowly at his stubble, then dropped his hand. There was no nice way to phrase this, but it wasn't fair to leave it out of the equation either. "You might go insane."

"What?" Han laughed briefly.

"Apparently there's a small chance that when someone gets turned it can drive them insane." Ellis bit his lip. "Vampires aren't human any more. The blood does something. It interacts with everyone in a unique, unpredictable way. Most of the time this results in some kind of supernatural ability, beyond just the senses and healing. I can see the past when I touch objects people have been emotionally invested in. I know of others with different powers. One can scale walls or walk across ceilings. There's a bloke who can control minds, and another who is impossibly fast. But sometimes what happens is that the new vampire just breaks." He grimaced. "And I don't think it's in some kind of treatable way, or in a way which they can live with. From what I've heard it's full-on psychosis."

"Oh my god!" Jay's words rushed out of him. "That's horrible!"

"What are the odds?" Han asked.

"I don't know. I can try to find out."

"Might be a good idea, yeah?" Han deadpanned. "But then I suppose even asking the question would be suspicious. I figure if you can't tell people this stuff, you can't go around turning them willy-nilly?"

"Aye, I'd be risking us both if we do this," Ellis admitted.

"Which means there's some kind of government, yeah?"

Ellis rose to his feet and pushed his hair back again. "God, yeah. There's the Council, their Vassals and Thralls, the Constabulary—"

"Stop."

Ellis pursed his lips and crossed his arms.

Han stood and began to pace the room, his footsteps light against the carpet. "How many vampires are there?"

"I don't know. We aren't allowed to travel outside our own territory unless it's at the Council's behest."

Han sniffed in disdain. "You're penned in? Why the hell do you tolerate it?"

"It's not by choice!"

"Okay. Who's in charge of this bullshit?"

"The Council." Ellis crinkled his nose a little. "Five elders. All post-war as far as I know. No democracy to it. Age is the only entry condition."

"And, what? They just make up rules as they go along?" Han was nearing the flat's front door now.

Ellis swivelled on the balls of his feet to track Han's

movement. "I don't know. I think they just maintain older rules, from what I've heard."

"But they're the oldest?"

"Extant. Before the war there were others, but what I'm told is that between two wars most of them were either bombed or moved away. Now most of them who's left are baby boomers and the like." Ellis turned a little more as Han's stride took him around behind the armchair.

"Right. So they've seized power and clung to it for seventy years, and nobody's got a problem with that?"

Ellis couldn't help but smirk slightly. "They do. There's a movement in play to overthrow the Council and install a democracy. If that weren't on the table I wouldn't risk making you this offer. You wouldn't stand a chance. But if the Council gets ousted, I suspect there'll be a few unsanctioned turnings in the chaos, and by the time things sort themselves out I expect that one way to earn the favour of the voters will be to forgive them for getting a bit eager during the mess."

"The only way you can influence that is to run for office yourself," Han argued. "Otherwise it's just assumption and guesswork."

Ellis froze. "Er, no. No, I'm not—"

Jay sucked in air and bounced to his feet. "It's perfect!"

"Eh?" Ellis turned to face him. "No it isn't!"

"Don't be daft," Han muttered. "It *is* perfect. If we're all to survive any of this, you need to hold some sort of position of authority so that you can protect us, at least during the early days. You know there's a revolution coming, right?"

"Well—"

"And that means someone trusts you enough to have told you, otherwise you would've told this Council, right?"

"Aye, but—"

"Perfect. And it's them you'd go ask about the number of vampires who go bonkers when they're made, yeah?"

Ellis frowned and didn't answer. Christ, no wonder Han and Jay got along so well — they were both far too bloody clever by half. He'd always known it, but never been on the receiving end, and it felt a little bit like an interrogation.

"Right." Han came to a halt in front of him. "I'm going to need some time to think this through and talk it over with Jay. You talk to your contacts in the revolutionary underground or whatever is going on out there and find out what the chances are that I'll go utterly insane if we go ahead with this."

Ellis unfurled his arms and lowered them cautiously. "You'll consider it?"

"Yeah. But there are going to be a few things I'll need."

"Name them."

"I need Jay back."

Ellis opened his mouth, then couldn't find anything to say.

"Me?" Jay stepped in. "Why?"

"I don't have the luxury of tearing out my security systems and replacing them. I'll have to add you to our databases and give you my access levels to everything. And if rogue users who don't actually exist are found in our servers they'll get removed, so I'm going to need you on the payroll to stop that happening."

"You can't hire him without a vacancy or jumping through all the hoops," Ellis countered. "It's illegal."

"Yeah, I'll have to sort that out. But you've got Christy now, right?"

Ellis scowled. "She's only just started."

"Bullpats, she's been there two months. I need Jay."

"Uh," Jay cleared his throat. "I'm right here."

Ellis rocked his jaw and tipped his head toward Jay. "It's your choice."

"I think," Jay murmured, "that it's a good idea. I know what a vampire needs, I can help him with work, and I can answer most of his questions without the need for you two to go back and forth across town all the time."

Ellis flexed his fingers slowly, then gave a faint nod. "All right. That seems logical. But I'll miss having you around."

"Oh, sweetie!" Jay stepped in and suddenly the taller man's lanky frame wrapped around him in a tight embrace. "I'll miss being around. But we're just a text away, and maybe one day you can tell Christy what's going on and she can fend Edison off for you instead!"

"Ha." Ellis leaned against him and hugged him. "Right. Balls to this. Take me away from here before I get all emotional."

"Sure thing!" Jay pulled back, and Ellis heard another kiss. "I won't be long."

"No problem," Han answered. Then he added "Good luck, Ellis."

"I'll bloody well need it."

NINE

THE TUBE HAD BEEN as horrible as ever, and Jay spent the journey in an agitated state, fidgeting and checking the time every few minutes. Ellis could hear the slip of plastic against cotton every time Jay pulled his phone from his pocket, then the snap of its case as he closed it.

"If I'm keeping you," he'd offered at one point.

"Hush," Jay huffed. "Do you know the route?"

Ellis shook his head. He texted Barb to get her permission to visit, and she'd given him her address a while ago, but he'd never been there. It meant leaving Mayfair. "No."

"Then I'll walk you."

Jay wouldn't brook any argument, so when they reached Green Park and used the step-free slope up to street level, Ellis took him by the elbow and recited the address.

The air carried with it a distinct tang of ozone as Ellis was led along the pavement. "It's going to rain," he muttered.

"Thanks for coming this evening," Jay said. "And thanks for telling Han."

Ellis shook his head slowly. "What was I going to do? Tell you to stick it?"

"It might be safer for all of us if you did." Jay sighed faintly. "Would they really kill him if you did this?"

"Yes." Ellis winced at the all too persistent memory of Constable Hughes' questions after Jonas' death. "And they seem to have very perceptive Constables to root out the facts."

"Shit." Jay walked on, effortlessly steering Ellis around unknown obstacles. "Oh," he said after another couple of minutes. "91, yeah?"

"Aye."

A tremor ran down Jay's arm, and Ellis was about to ask what was wrong when Jay burst out in peals of laughter. "Well then!"

Ellis bit his lip. Doubt clutched at his insides. "It's a brothel, isn't it?"

Jay's laugh grew louder, and shook him so hard that his arm jerked free of Ellis hold. His body lowered, or he'd bent almost double, and he started to gasp for air. "Oh god. Ohhhhhh god! I reckon you two'll get along great!"

Ellis narrowed his eyes. He felt Tiberius' harness tremble rhythmically — a sign that the dog's tail had begun to wag. "It isn't funny."

"Oh it is!" Jay spluttered as he straightened up again, then he clapped a hand on Ellis' shoulder. "It's not a brothel."

Ellis raised his eyebrows. "Then what is it?"

"This is brilliant." Jay snorted. "It's a chocolatier."

JAY LED him to the door and then stranded him there, and Ellis heard his fits of giggles as he hurried away.

Ellis felt for the door and his hand darted across glass until he found the metal frame. No handle, so he skipped his fingers across to the other side and found it protruding from the opposite frame, cold and smooth. A tug, a push, but the door was firmly locked.

He tipped his head and listened. Barb had already responded to his text to say that a visit was fine, so it was reasonable to expect her to have heard his and Jay's arrival unless there were something louder near her. He couldn't make out anything like that, though; no nearby television or music other than that from a pub down a side street. Otherwise it was late, and most people in the flats above the shops here were already breathing in the slow, deep tempo of slumber.

"Barb?" he murmured softly.

He heard boots clump heavily down carpeted stairs. A door opened and closed, but it wasn't the one he stood by.

"Sorry," she said as she hurried over. "I thought you still had company. Totally forgot about Tiberius. Hey, boy," she added. "What's so funny about a chocolatier, anyway?"

Ellis smiled dryly and offered his hand to her. She took it and held on to it like she wasn't sure why it had been given to her. "I need you to show me where we're going?" he explained.

"Oh! Right! C'mon!" She pulled his hand, and Ellis grimaced as he was dragged along the pavement, Tiberius hurrying to catch up with the sudden change in direction.

He didn't feel inclined to try and dissuade her from it, but he did keep his head down, just in case the area was prone to low-hanging pub signs or planters.

She let go of him to unlock the door, and her hand took his again, but he smiled tightly. "I can manage from here. Thank you."

"Wicked! There's no step, but it's stairs after a couple of feet once you're in."

"Great. Thank you."

He followed her up the stairs and into what had to be a flat. He didn't know whether it was directly above the chocolatier's shop, or just nearby. "Tiberius, chair," he said, and Tiberius took a few steps before he stopped.

Ellis felt around until he found the back of a velour-covered sofa, and he pressed his lips together, not wishing to sit just yet. In his experience velour was usually rife with crumbs and hair, and while this particular seat's owner was too undead to drop either that didn't mean she never had guests 'round.

"I reckon he finds a vampire chocolatier about as funny as a blind art dealer, you see," he finally said in the direction of her footsteps.

Barb snorted and flopped into a seat. It floofed beneath her. "He knows?"

Ellis lifted a shoulder. Let it fall again. "Jay's always known."

"He's your cutie assistant, right?"

"I'd rather the Council not find out, obviously."

Barb laughed abruptly. "Ellis, I wouldn't tell 'em fuck all, let alone about your beautiful assistant. What can I do you for?"

"How's this revolution coming along?" He ran his hand slowly along the back of the sofa. It felt clean, if a bit faded in places. The chocolate business paid about as well as the art business if the furniture was anything to go by.

"I can't tell you a whole lot. I would if I could, but you're too close to Westminster. Sorry. Why do you ask?"

"I understand." Ellis smiled. "But if he's going to invade my mind at any point he'll know I know you, and he'll know to come invade your mind for details. Can you at least tell me how soon things are going to move?"

"If you're worried about Jay—"

He shook his head. "No. I've got... a bigger problem."

"You'd better sit, then. Don't worry, the place is clean. You won't leave here with stuff all over your arse."

Ellis bit the inside of his cheek at being caught out so easily, and he released Tiberius' harness so that he could move around the sofa and settle himself into it. The cushion beneath his rear let out air under his weight and he sank a further two or three inches before it was done.

"Right. What's the problem?"

Ellis planted his elbows on his knees and clasped his hands together. "I have a friend." At Barb's wolf-whistle he laughed and shook his head. "No. I mean, yes, I have one of those friends too. But that's not the problem here. My friend has some serious heart problem. Doesn't sound like he can get a transplant, and it's going to kill him sooner or later."

"Shit." Barb's leather clothes creaked as she moved. "How long's he got?"

"No idea. They don't know. He could drop dead tomorrow, he could be fine for a few weeks, I don't know. They were talking like it's days and weeks, though, not months and years." He disengaged his fingers from one another and balled his hands into fists instead.

"They?"

"It's Jay's husband," he breathed. "He's a good friend. A very dear friend. Together they've been my bedrock ever since I came to London. Since before I was turned."

"Oh god," Barb groaned. "So you wanna turn him, is that it?"

"I don't *want* to," Ellis muttered. "But there's no other way. He's going to die, and the longer I leave it—"

"The more likely he is to just kark it," she finished. "Fuckin' 'ell." She blew what sounded very much like a raspberry, then added, "Wouldn't he be better off that way, though?"

"I've left the choice with him." He flexed his fingers, then wove them together again, palms together. "He's going to discuss it with Jay and they'll work out what they want to do."

"Right." Her knuckles cracked in unison. "Is there anyone in London you ain't told what you are?"

Ellis leaned back and crossed his arms loosely. "Three people. That's all."

"Three too many if you're on the Council. Or a Constable. Or almost anyone else." She paused. "Jay and his bloke, and who else? Your other half?"

Ellis nodded. "Aye."

"Pillock," she grunted. "I can't say we'll move fast enough for your mate's heart, if he chooses to let you bite him. You know how to do it, right?"

"Take everything out, put some of my own in, isn't it?"

"Eh, pretty much. You can't do it once someone's already dead. They've got to be living when you go at it, and once their heart stops you've got a couple of minutes to finish the job or they're just a corpse." She hesitated before adding "He knows the risks, yeah?"

Ellis nodded grimly. "He wants to know the odds that he'll go insane."

"I dunno. It's not the kind of thing studies have been done on." She chuckled. "Last one I heard of was back in the Eighties. They had to put him down. Went crazy, started murdering people. Mortals. Just straight up drinking 'em dry in public and dumping 'em wherever they fell."

Ellis sat up sharply. "Christ!"

"Yeah. Nasty shit. But your mate can't play the odds. He's

got certain death or he's got certain death. It's just that our flavour of certain death leads to an uncertain future, and the other flavour leads to an absolutely sure one. If he goes mad, we kill him. If the Council finds out about him, they kill him. If he manages to stay hidden long enough, he can sneak in post-revolution and claim he'd been there all along and we probably won't give a shit because I guarantee the moment the Council's gone you won't be the only one to make a quick unsanctioned newbie."

Ellis raised his chin. "You've got someone in mind?"

"No way. I'd be a shitty parent. But I guarantee there's enough chafing at the bit out there that yer man won't be the only one to crop up. Enough that I reckon there'll be a bit of hand-waving to let the whole lot stay while we figure out new rules."

"Right." Ellis eased forward in his seat, then used the arm rest as he stood. "Tiberius, here." When the dog came to his side he dropped his left hand to find the harness, then straightened up once he had it. "Got a rough estimate of your timescale, at least?"

"January, maybe February. Nights are longest, we can move easy if we need to." Her voice rose too. "I'm sorry. We can't rush it forward. But at least you only gonna hafeta keep your boy safe a couple of months, tops."

Ellis laughed at the idea of being Han's protector. He offered his hand to her, and she shook it firmly. "Thanks, Barb. Let me know if it takes off earlier, aye?"

"Cross my heart," she said. "Come on. Let me get the front door. It's got a weird lock on it."

"Thanks." He followed her thudding boots. "And if you can point me toward Mayfair I'd appreciate it."

"You're on!"

TEN

RANDALL WANDERED, samosas clutched to his chest. None of these streets looked familiar, but when he found a junction and squinted up at the road names each one had a red W1 in the corner.

He rubbed at his close-cut hair and tried to work out how he'd got here. It was dark, but the street lights were still on. The night buses were running, and there were a few cars out. He pulled his phone to check the time.

Ten to two.

He winced. They'd left Ilford before the trains shut down, so he must've hit the city by midnight. Then... He definitely got onto the tube, not a bus. Ameera and Hasan had hopped off after only one stop and the rest had trickled off here and there until Randall reached Bond Street.

He turned and tried to figure out which way was north, but he didn't know the area too well, so he pulled up the maps on his phone and turned GPS on.

He couldn't have spent close to two hours just standing around in Mayfair, right? And Mrs. Uddin wouldn't have laced the drinks with any booze. They weren't strict about alcohol, but it did bugger all for shifters anyway so why waste the money?

His phone finally worked out where he was, and he squinted at the bright light of the little screen. He wasn't far from Ellis' — *their* — flat. "Oh. Right."

Randall walked along and followed the little dot on his phone until the compass oriented itself properly, and it wasn't long before he began to recognise the rabbit warren of alleyways and mews'. He turned off GPS, put his phone into his pocket, and patted himself down.

No blood. He still had his wallet, keys, and phone. He even still had Mrs. Uddin's Tupperware and its full complement of goodies. He couldn't have been mugged.

Maybe he'd misjudged the time he left Ilford. That made more sense. And maybe they'd messed up and taken the Circle line, or perhaps it wasn't a mistake and that's just the way they had to go for half of the pack to get home. Most of them lived further east than Tower Hamlets.

Rain began to fall lightly. A spot here and there at first, and then it gathered pace.

He must've got it wrong. And he was tired. As his feet continued toward the flat it became increasingly obvious to him that he'd got his times all jumbled up. After all, he totally remembered getting to Bond Street. He'd clearly taken a wrong turn, since he usually came up from Charing Cross or Green Park.

Yeah. That had to be it.

Couldn't be anything else.

He tucked the box under one arm to fish his keys out, and forgot about it.

HE SNUCK QUIETLY UP the wide marble stairs and let himself into the top-floor flat he shared with Ellis.

"Are you home?" he whispered.

"Aye. Do you want the lights on?"

"Yeah, if that's okay?"

He heard a slight movement, then Ellis answered "Go ahead. And what's that smell?"

Randall felt for and flicked the light switch. When he headed through to the living room he found Ellis on the sofa with his fingers splayed across a book, and Tiberius fast asleep in his bed in the corner. "Party goodies. Ameera's mum gave me some samosas to take home."

Ellis slid a bookmark between the pages and closed his book. "They smell amazing! Did you have a good time?"

Randall crossed to the fridge and slid the container into it. He nudged a box of eggs aside to make enough room. "Yeah. It was pretty good. How about you? What'd you get up to?"

Ellis was quiet. He placed the book on the coffee table as Randall returned, and his expression was grim as he did so.

"Ellis?" Randall kicked his boots off and put them neatly up against the skirting board, then used his t-shirt to pat rain from his face. "What happened?"

Ellis leaned back and beckoned Randall over, so Randall hurried to his side and settled on the sofa. He leaned against Ellis' body and snaked one arm behind the slender vampire's waist and examined his features.

The glasses made him harder to read, but not impossible. Not now that Randall knew him. The press of his lips when he was frustrated, the angry furrow of his brow, the way that he tolerated stray hairs if he was in a good mood and fussed with them if he wasn't...

His lips were firmly clamped together now. They formed a thin line so tightly pressed that Randall couldn't see their surfaces at all. His eyebrows were almost entirely hidden below the frames of his glasses, which left the crease between them deep and shadowed. Yeah. There was no mistaking that face. Ellis was pissed off, and maybe a little upset, too.

He leaned closer to kiss Ellis' shoulder. His lips pressed against the dark cotton shirt, and he waited.

Ellis' chest lifted as he drew breath to speak. "Jay came to the gallery."

"Uh huh." Randall chose not to interrupt. Ellis would get there in his own time.

"Han's dying." Ellis' voice croaked, and he leaned into Randall. He wrapped both arms around the werewolf's shoulders, and Randall clung to him more tightly. "He has a problem with his heart."

Randall listened as Ellis explained the situation. He murmured softly and kissed his shoulder while Ellis talked about the offer he'd made to Han, and ran fingers over the back of his neck as he outlined the conversation he'd had with Barb.

Ellis sighed and tugged his glasses off so that he could burrow his face against Randall's shoulder.

"I'm sorry," Randall breathed. He took the glasses and held them safely so that Ellis could wrap arms around him again. "God, you should've texted me. I would've come straight back."

"Don't be daft," Ellis murmured. His hands slid gently across Randall's spine, but his touch was gentle and exploratory, nothing more. "There's nowt you could've done."

"I could have been there for you." Randall kissed Ellis' soft, thick hair, just behind his ear. "You silly sod. Don't ever think I wouldn't be by your side for stuff like this."

Ellis' muscles shifted beneath Randall's arm. His spine curved as his body began to relax. "You had bums to sniff."

Randall grinned at that. "Yeah. Well, it was just a social. Not like we were out fighting for our lives or anything. I can leave that kind of thing whenever you want me to, okay? There's no full moon, they don't need me to keep 'em on the straight and narrow. Everything's nice and calm." He turned his head, and this time his kiss lingered against Ellis' ear. "I know it's a pain having to keep coming and going halfway across town, but I can get here pretty quick when you need me, okay?"

Ellis exhaled through his nose in a little huff, then he withdrew and raised his head. His ice-coloured eyes fought to focus, and Randall faced him to try and make it easier for him. "When'd you get to be so bloody wise?"

Randall laughed at that and rested the glasses on his thigh so that he could caress Ellis' jaw in his palm. His stubble prickled softly, a little too long to be rough. "Nah. It's not wisdom. It's just common sense, innit?" He tipped his head to the side and leaned in so that he could kiss Ellis' lips. They were soft and welcoming, but cool to the touch. Either Randall was warm from the walk, or Ellis would need to feed soon. "Are you hungry?"

"Nah, petal. I'm fine. Thanks for asking." Ellis held his hand out, and Randall returned his glasses to him. "This common sense thing. I'm not sure it's as common as you claim."

"You're an artist at heart." Randall smiled slowly and trailed his fingers over Ellis' thigh. "You're passionate. You're quick to listen to your heart. You trust your feelings. I don't think those things are all that common either."

Ellis laughed. "Randall Carter," he murmured. "Is this your new way of saying it?"

"Nah. I love you." He grinned. "You just remember that the next time you've got people dropping heavy stuff in your lap." His grin faded, and he kissed Ellis' cheek. "You're not alone any more. I'm here, and I love you."

Ellis closed his eyes and leaned forward until his forehead came to rest against Randall's. "You're right," he whispered. "I should've. I will next time, I promise, petal."

Randall gave his thigh a light pat. "That's enough for me." He traced the outline of Ellis' hip. "Are you tired?"

"Aye."

"Then let's go to bed. C'mon."

He turned the light out and followed Ellis through to the bedroom and had the niggling feeling that he'd forgotten something. Something he'd meant to talk to Ellis about when he saw him.

If it was important, it'd come to him.

ELEVEN

ELLIS WOKE to the warmth of Randall's flesh pressing against his body. The shifter's hand was on his stomach, and one leg was coiled around his own. His cock was half-hard as it prodded Ellis' hip.

He wondered if he could pretend he was still asleep. He didn't breathe, he didn't have any autonomic functions which could have given him away. Maybe Randall's morning horniness would fade if it got left unattended.

Ellis grimaced a little at his own thought process.

"El?"

Ellis crinkled his nose. There wasn't any graceful way to shorten his name, and El made him sound like a fashion magazine. "Morning, petal."

"Morning." Randall's fingers played with the trail of hair below his belly button and he leaned in to kiss him.

Ellis turned to the kiss and parted his lips, but his hand found Randall's and rested over it.

Randall's lips curved against his own. "Not feeling it this morning, beautiful?"

"Sorry."

Randall chuckled at that and gently slid his leg free. "You don't have to apologise. You're not obligated to fuck me all day every day, you know."

Ellis lifted his chin and offered a half-hearted smile. "Any other day, petal. I don't know."

He really didn't know. It was a horrible feeling, this realisation that despite Randall's naked body pressed to his own and the werewolf's obvious eagerness, Ellis couldn't dredge up any arousal.

"You're worried," Randall said gently. "That's all it is. Until you hear from Han what he's decided you're probably going to stay worried." His lips brushed over Ellis', and then his fingers combed through his hair. "It's *fine*."

"Is that fine as in I'm an arsehole, or fine like actually fine?" Ellis' lips twitched into a dry smile.

"Actually fine." Randall chuckled, then his warm body slid across Ellis' as he climbed out of bed and landed on the carpet. "I've got clients after lunch. Want me to walk with you to the gallery before I go?"

Ellis propped himself up on one elbow. "I'd like that."

"Better join me in the shower first, then."

Ellis rubbed at his stubble as he swung his legs free of the sheets. "Deal."

THE AFTERNOON FELT like something more normal. A day just like any other, where Ellis could sit at his desk and engage in idle chit-chat with Christy while they both worked. Not one of those days where the world was falling down around his ears.

Randall had walked with him to the office and stolen a

kiss, then reminded him to text if Ellis needed him. He reckoned he'd be back by around eight at the latest, and Ellis had shooed him away.

He was one lucky bastard, and he knew it.

"You're grinning again," Christy said.

"Uh huh."

She chuckled to herself and went back to her typing.

Christy wasn't a bad sort. She'd settled in well under Jay's tuition and her hands weren't anywhere near as clammy anymore. She wasn't Jay, but Ellis would have to get used to it. He knew he couldn't keep Han's husband forever. He just didn't really want to face the day that it would end.

The gallery door opened, and footsteps entered. One heartbeat came with them. Ellis took a breath, then let it go and returned his attention to his email. He couldn't tell Christy they had a customer. She *wasn't* Jay.

Could he tell her some day? Was she the kind of person he could trust? She seemed reliable, he'd never heard the tremors or pauses of a lie in her words, but who knew how someone might react to the news that their employer was a vampire, or who she might tell? No, he'd have to wait. He'd known Jay for years by the time he was turned, he knew Jay wouldn't tell anyone — not even his own husband.

The thought of waiting years for an assistant he could be honest with made him miss Jay all the more.

"Oh!" Christy broke into his thoughts. "Customer! I'll be right back."

"Tell you what," Ellis said. "Take me with you and we'll see if we can't convince them that art makes the perfect Christmas gift."

"OH MY GOD! THAT WAS AMAZING!"

Ellis laughed as he settled in behind his desk again. "It was areet," he said, feigning humility.

"Forty-three grand? All right?" Christy flopped into her chair and it squeaked in protest.

"Eh. December's usually one of our better months. And half that goes to the artist, so we only made twenty-one and a half." He shrugged.

"But—"

"That's not enough to cover your wages for a whole year." He chuckled at her. "It'll do our rent for three months though. But that's not including insurance, utilities, wages—"

She groaned. "I didn't know it all cost so much."

"Yep. Let Gerard's agent know we'll have a few bob headed his way, would you? I'll contact the courier."

"With pleasure!"

He smiled as he went back to his emails. Today was looking up at last. Maybe later he'd be up for taking Randall to bed for more than just sleep later.

IT WAS a little after eight when Randall entered the gallery. Christy had been gone a couple of hours, leaving Ellis with his Christmas shopping all evening, and even after two hours at it he still hadn't managed to buy a bloody thing.

He might have to cave and ask for help. But not from the man he was having so much trouble buying for.

"Hey," Randall said as he breezed into the office. "Sorry I'm late. Central Line was held up just past Holborn for a bit. Any news?"

Ellis pushed his chair back from his desk and waited for Randall to perch in his lap before he shook his head. "Not yet." His arms fit comfortably around Randall's waist, and he lifted his head expectantly.

Randall obliged him with a warm kiss which bore lingering traces of something spicy.

"Samosa?" Ellis chuckled.

"Busted." Randall ran fingers slowly through his hair, and Ellis leaned into the touch. "I've been thinking."

"About?"

"What if Han says no?"

Ellis grimaced. His fingers slowly worked at Randall's t-shirt and eased the hem free of his jeans, and he slid fingertips against soft flesh once he had access to it. Randall gasped briefly at the touch, then rested against him as Ellis' fingers warmed against his skin. "I don't know," he finally admitted. "He can't. He wouldn't." He rested his cheek against Randall's shoulder. "Bastard. He probably will."

"You'll have to ask him," Randall murmured. "Can't let it hang about. Unless you can just turn him if he drops dead all of a sudden?"

"Nope. It has to be while he's still alive. Apparently it won't work on someone who's already dead."

"That's a pain in the arse," Randall grunted.

"Aye. But even if it worked, I still wouldn't have his permission. I don't know." He closed his eyes briefly. It felt oddly comforting. "I don't know if I could do it without him giving me the go ahead. I don't think I could."

"I can understand that." Randall's hand rubbed slowly over Ellis' ribs. "Jonas didn't ask you if it was okay. I suppose he couldn't with the laws and all that." He hesitated. "I guess nobody gets asked, right? I mean, nobody's supposed to know about vampires. Going around offering to turn people and waiting for them to give you a yes or no is like the exact opposite of keeping it quiet."

Ellis laughed a little. "I suppose." His laugh died in his throat. "That's horrible, isn't it? Or is that just me being artistic about it?"

"No," Randall said quietly. "It *is* horrible."

Ellis spread his fingers further across Randall's skin. "Every vampire I've ever met, and none of them had the choice. God, that's awful. Who could do that to someone without asking them first? I mean, it's not the worst existence ever. I imagine it's probably reet great if you've got working eyes. But to just... be told you can't travel, you can't ever go abroad, you can't even leave the city you live in... To find out that suddenly there's this whole new set of rules to live by that you never signed up to..." He paused for breath. "I hated it. And I hated Jonas for doing it to me. How many of them hate each other out there? How many regret that they never got to—" The gallery door opened and he broke off.

Footsteps. They were sure and calm, and they approached the stairs, but they didn't come with a pulse.

Ellis quickly sat back and drew a fingertip across his throat.

"Then she wanted to tell me that her dog's behaviour was all my fault," Randall snorted, effortlessly taking the hint and switching to a far safer subject. "Can you believe it? She feeds him at all kinds of hours, she barely walks him, and then it's my fault that her poor dog's aggressive?"

"Petal, I don't know much about dogs, but I know they need routine."

"Right? But can I get this through to her?"

Ellis listened as the vampire outside came up the stairs, and he cursed inwardly. There was no way whoever it was hadn't overheard at least some of their extremely illegal conversation before they'd pushed open the door, and there was no way to know how long they'd stood out on the pavement eavesdropping. Randall was doing a sterling job at the fake conversation, but if this wasn't Barb coming up the stairs they'd be in serious trouble, and it didn't sound like Barb's boots.

Whoever it was wore shoes: flat shoes, not heels.

There was a knock on the office door. "Ellis O'Neill? Mind if I pop in?"

Ellis grimaced and tugged Randall's t-shirt down into place. He knew the answer already. The man's voice, his accent, it was all etched into his memory. But he called out "Of course. Who is it?"

"It's me." The door creaked on its hinges as it opened. "Hughes," he added as he entered the room.

Constable Hughes. A bloody *Constable* had caught him talking about vampires with his ostensibly human boyfriend in his lap.

Shit. Double shit. Double shit with cherries on top.

TWELVE

"WHY DON'T you run on home, petal, and I'll catch up in a minute?" Ellis had to force himself to relax his grip on Randall's t-shirt.

"Just a minute?" Randall placed a lingering kiss against his cheek. His pace had quickened, and Ellis knew damn well that Hughes could hear it every bit as well as he could.

"Well we won't be long. It's just work stuff, I'm sure."

He waited for the Constable to try and stop Randall from leaving, but it didn't seem about to happen. Randall stood and leaned down for another kiss, and murmured a light-sounding "Catch you later, then" on his way out of the door, but Hughes didn't move.

Randall closed the door after himself, and both Ellis and Hughes were silent as they waited for the footsteps to retreat and the gallery's front door to open and close.

Why would Hughes let Randall go? He'd bloody caught them at it, there was no way Ellis could hope he hadn't, so why would he let the man he thought to be human walk out of the room?

"I could nick you for that," Hughes announced.

Ellis schooled his expression and pulled his chair back in toward his desk. "I'm sure I don't know what you mean, Constable," he answered smoothly. "Why don't you have a seat?"

Hughes snorted. "Nice. Subtle. But yeah, for what it's worth, nobody asked me my bloody permission either. I reckon you're right there." He moved over and sat in the chair which faced Ellis' desk, and dragged it out of the little dents it had made in the carpet as he did so. "Seems like a proper philosophical conversation to have with yer fella, dunnit?"

"I'm afraid that I'm not really about to agree on that point in any manner other than purely hypothetical," Ellis said. He ran his fingers nervously along the edge of his desk to check that he was squarely aligned with it, then put one hand over the other and leaned his elbows on the wooden surface. "And I'm sure you're not here about philosophy. How can I help you?"

It was a dangerous game. He was throwing all his chances on there being some hidden motive for Hughes to have let Randall go. Maybe Hughes had bigger fish to fry, or perhaps he was sympathetic to the fact that Ellis was young, but if the Constable wasn't going to drag them both off to be sentenced right away Ellis had to hope it might be something Hughes was willing to overlook.

"You remember that bloke who rocked up dead near your place a few months back?" Hughes said.

"I do." Ellis spoke levelly. To deny it would be pointless: Hughes had already questioned him about Barnes' — Jasiński's — death.

"I been goin' over the forensics report. Funny story this, but apparently it was a dog what attacked him. Tore his arm to shit it did. It was a right fucking mess all the way down to the bone."

"Mm." Ellis remained still. He didn't even want to know how Hughes got hold of a police forensics document.

"I gave you a chance to cop to this once already. So here it is again. And I ain't gonna tell the police if you say yes, O'Neill. Nobody's gonna take your dog away, okay? I promise you that. Cub scout's honour."

Ellis pursed his lips and spread his fingers slightly. "When were you a cub scout, Constable?"

"Ha. Fine, okay. My personal honour. Which I'm pretty keen on, yeah?" Hughes' chair shifted. "What happened, eh? Did he come at you and yer dog 'ad a go at him for you?"

Ellis narrowed his eyes. Hughes had indeed offered him this get-out before. Why go to the trouble of doing it again? *Was* it a matter of personal honour to him, to solve these things even if nobody else ever knew his findings?

"Aye," Ellis finally said. "I was on my way home and he came at me with a knife. Tiberius grabbed him off me, and I found the knife and stuck it in him before we ran. I had no idea it would kill him. I'm not a fighter, I've never stabbed anyone in my life, and I sure as hell couldn't see what I was doing. I'd no way of knowing whether I hit a leg, an arm, his stomach or anything else. I just wanted to protect Tiberius and stop the fella from following us."

Like all the best lies it was almost all true, and Ellis had no autonomic functions to give him away. He had to hope that was enough.

"Yeah I figured that might be what 'appened. You remember I told you there was silver in the stab wound, yeah?"

Ellis grimaced. "Yes."

"Didn't cut yourself on it, did you?"

He dropped his head faintly, then murmured "All right. Cards on the table, Aaron. He cut my fucking arm off with the damn thing. He stuck it in me and the whole lot just turned to ash and—" he shook his head bitterly. "It was terrifying. That's when Tiberius got stuck in. I think he must've realised I was in trouble. I heard the knife fall and I just grabbed it and damn well had a go at him before he could hurt Tiberius. And then we bloody ran. I pocketed the knife, I had to get Tiberius' harness in the wrong hand, and it was hellish, and yes. I left the man there to die in the bloody gutter."

"Why didn't you just tell me this when I asked?" Hughes didn't sound unkind.

"Because I was terrified you'd think Tiberius was a dangerous dog and have him destroyed." Ellis raised his head, but remained hunched over his desk. He didn't need to fake any of that statement at all.

"Sounds fair. I'm sorry, mate. I should've given you more assurances back then. Would've saved me a load of running around. Where's the knife?"

"Gone." Ellis shook his head. "I washed it and gave it to my assistant. As far as I'm aware he broke it down and sold it online as scrap silver."

"As far as you're aware?"

"That's what he said he'd done. He's got no reason to lie."

"Hm." Hughes shifted in his chair again. "Shame, but never mind. I was hoping to try and pull some identifying marks off it. It ain't every silversmith who's willing to make something so useless as a knife out of solid silver, and it ain't every weaponsmith willin' to make a blade that won't work proper against anythin' living."

"I'm sorry. I didn't think." Ellis shook his head. "I just thought it was dangerous and should be destroyed."

"Yeah." Hughes sighed. "I s'pose you're right there." There

was the sound of nails scratching against skin. "Did he know what you were?"

Ellis blinked and held himself still. "If he did," he said carefully, "I didn't tell him. But why else would he use a knife of pure silver?"

Hughes grunted at that. "See, that's what I'm thinking too. You don't need to go to those lengths to stab some random bloke on the street. And you said he was the one who came at you. That suggests he was waiting for you. Did he say anything? Tell you why he was trying to kill you?"

Ellis shook his head faintly. "He said something, but it wasn't in English. I don't know what it was. He sounded angry, though."

It was one thing to lie to Briar's face: the werewolf had been angry, not in full control of himself, and he didn't seem like the sharpest tool in the box to begin with. But lying to Hughes felt like a dangerous game. He was a Constable. They didn't dish that job out to anyone, and it would be dangerous to underestimate the man just because Ellis had got away with murder twice already. Well, not strictly murder — both times *had* been self-defence, after all — but it still made him distinctly uncomfortable to tell an outright fib to someone who had practice in spotting such things.

"Yeah. He was Polish, so that'd make sense," Hughes mused. "You wanna know what I find weird, though?"

"I have a feeling that you're about to tell me," Ellis said dryly.

Hughes chuckled. His chair creaked. His voice was a foot closer when he spoke next. "Tomasz Jasiński was a failed artist. Apparently his work was okay, but not commercial. He was living in poverty. Rented space in some old Polish woman's loft, you know? She hadn't even had a conversion done on it. Apparently he had to take pallet wood up there and build himself a floor. One light bulb, no windows, had to shimmy up and down a ladder whenever he needed to take a slash, and she still charged 'im a couple 'undred bob a month for the pleasure. The loft 'atch was so small he had to take the ladder up to get canvasses through it, and they'd only fit one at a time."

"Um." Ellis frowned slowly. "Well, that's... not too unusual a story, I'm sorry to say. But I don't see—"

"Yeah, I'm gettin' there," Hughes cut in. "See, funny thing is that 'bout a year or so ago 'e started earning a bit more. The lady wot rented him the loft says he found 'imself a patron or whatever it's called, and the bloke loved his work, bought everything he did. Then that dried up 'round a year or so ago. And what's *really* funny is the police took 'er statement back when Jasiński rocked up dead, but I didn't read it. Now that's pretty slack of me, but I made a mistake. I wrote it off as irrelevant, because I was pretty sure you'd killed Jasiński and that it wasn't any more complicated than that. But then I 'ad it drop through my letterbox this morning, and I 'ad a read of it."

"Areet?" Ellis sat back and slid his elbows to the armrests of his chair. "And what'd it say?"

"She says Jasiński's patron was a fella. She never met 'im, he never came 'round, but Jasiński was pretty smitten with him. She reckons 'e were 'one of them', as she put it, which is kinda outdated but she's old so whatever. She says she never remembers Jasiński call the fella anything other than Jonas. She didn't know whether that was a surname or first name, but she was right sure the name was Jonas."

Ellis rocked his jaw slowly. "Do you think," he said with the levelest tone he could muster, "Jonas told Jasiński what we were?"

"I reckon they were lovers. And we all tell our lovers what

we are sooner or later, don't we?" Was there a touch of anger to Hughes' voice? Or was it bitterness? "I reckon Jonas told Jasiński he was coming over 'ere to do you in, and when Jonas never returned, Jasiński 'ad it in for you. What I don't understand is why it took him a year to get cracking."

"Maybe he couldn't find me?"

"You've got a soddin' website, mate," Hughes snorted. "No, I reckon something else was goin' on. I reckon something spurred him into action. 'Is landlady reckons he was working on some big piece for months, but it ain't in his loft. I reckon he wanted to finish some, like, magnum opus or whatever it's called before he came after you."

Ellis sighed slowly. "Either way, hopefully it's all dealt with now."

"You killed Jonas," Hughes stated. "Did you cannibalise him?"

Ellis froze.

Speak! For god's sake, say something! You look guilty!

"What?" he breathed. "No! Christ, Aaron, you were the one who investigated it! He came in here, he reeked of blood, he threatened my assistant, my dog—"

"And I hate to be the one to point it out, but you're blind as a bat, ain't you?"

"Obviously!"

"And you ain't a fighter. If you were, you would've been able to handle Jasiński. The guy took your arm off, but you knew it'd grow back, and if he'd stuck you in the heart it would've been game over. Instead your dog 'ad to savage him, and the best you managed was a lucky shot at the bloke's liver. If you'd been at all capable you'd 'ave got him somewhere that wouldn't give him time to call himself an ambulance. You'd go for the throat or the spine, you'd go up through the diaphragm or into the groin. Major organs or arteries, not a twenty-minute bleed-out. You can't fight, O'Neill. So how did you destroy Jonas?"

"I already told you!" Ellis grit his teeth and curled his fingers around the armrests. "I lost my temper and I beat his head against the floor until he turned to dust in my hands!"

"You're lying." Hughes stood. "You broke the law. You ate him. You knew Jasiński was connected to Jonas and that's why you tried to fob me off first time I questioned you about Jasiński's death. Not because you didn't want me to know you'd killed Jasiński, but because you didn't want me to find the connection between him and Jonas."

"This is nonsense!" Ellis rose slowly and pushed his chair back with his calf. He leaned his hands on his desk. "Hughes, I swear to you, I didn't bloody eat Jonas!"

"I think you did. And I'm going to prove it. You're under arrest for the cannibalism of the vampire known only as Jonas, and if you try and eat me I will rip your fucking head off."

THIRTEEN

JAY HATED HOSPITALS. They were always filled with such
solemn people, and you never knew how far away you were
from a person who had just taken their last breath. Guy's and
St. Thomas' may be one of the city's best, but it was still a
hospital, with that dreary hospital ambiance.

He sat on a tired old plastic-coated chair in a tired old
linoleum-floored corridor. It smelled of antiseptic and piss,
even though he doubted anyone really had a pee right there in
the corridor. It was just this stench that pervaded the entire
hospital so far as he could tell.

They'd been here so often over the past few weeks that
he'd lost count. The nurses on the cardiac ward knew him and
Han by name without checking any paperwork. As if to
remind everyone what this corridor was for there was a rickety
old crash cart against one wall with a laminated sheet of paper
sellotaped to the side which read "PROPERTY OF CARDIAC
UNIT. DO NOT REMOVE." Who the hell wanted to steal a
crash cart anyway? This was London. Most people just nicked

stuff out of shops rather than come into the bowels of hospitals to do it.

He checked his phone for the fifth time. Gone ten at night, yet they were still sitting in the damn corridor waiting for a bed. And Jay had the horrible notion that a bed would mean someone had finally died. They wouldn't discharge a patient so late at night, surely?

Han sat patiently to his right. He didn't fidget, he didn't play with his phone or read a book. He simply waited and cast the occasional smile to a nurse.

"This is ridiculous," Jay scowled. "Do they have a bed or not?"

"It doesn't matter," Han said.

"Fuck this." Jay pushed to his feet and strode to the nurses' station. He leaned on the desk and stared directly at the nurse who was busy checking a file, and waited. He breathed slowly and tried to calm himself. The poor nurse didn't deserve Angry Jay to the face.

"Mr. Newfield?" The nurse looked up after a moment and offered a polite smile. He was in his early thirties, and had a broad body that suggested he hit the weights when he wasn't at work.

"Is there a bed?" Jay blurted it out, then sighed. "I'm so sorry. This isn't your fault. But my husband's been referred up here after his check-up this afternoon and we've been sitting here in the corridor for like six hours. My arse is numb. His arse is probably numb. We can't sit out here all night, can we? We haven't even had dinner, and the restaurant's closed—" He broke off and affected a tired version of his most winning smile. "Does he have to stay overnight? Is there any point to him sitting in the corridor until nine in the morning when the consultant arrives?"

The nurse glanced up at the clock behind the counter, then

frowned. "I'm really sorry. Take a seat and I'll call around and see if I can find a bed in another ward."

"And if you can't?"

"Then I'll call a porter to bring a gurney up."

Jay stared at him. "You want Han to sleep in the corridor?"

"No," the nurse answered. "I want him to sleep in a bed. But if it comes down to it a gurney's got to be better than one of our chairs."

Jay cracked his knuckles, but he nodded. "Thanks. I mean it. Thank you." He strode back to Han, but found he couldn't sit. "They're going to see if they can find you a bed in a different ward for the night."

Han looked up at him and smiled gently. "Okay."

"No it is *not* okay!" he hissed, trying to keep his voice down. "You shouldn't be here! We already had to wait two hours for your bloody appointment because he was running late, and now we're here all night just because he wanted you in for observation. What observation are they doing with you sat out in the corridor all night?"

"Why don't you sit down, baby?" Han reached out and ran a hand along Jay's thigh.

Jay huffed and crossed his arms in a sulk.

"Tell me about Ellis," Han prompted. "Do you think he really can do what he's offering?"

"Of course!" Jay sat right away and took Han's hand. It felt a little cold, and Jay rubbed it to try and warm it up. "I really think you should accept his offer, sweetie. I know the electronics will be a pain, but they're only worse for Ellis because he can't see. You could use a stylus just fine for most devices. It's just the biometrics we'd have a problem with, but if I'm in the system I can let you through doors and everything."

"That's not really a viable long-term solution, is it?" Han

mused. "We'd need something for emergencies, or times when I need to pull an all-nighter. Will I have to sleep during the day or something?"

"No. Ellis usually gets up around lunchtime and works from home until it gets dark." Jay didn't want to go into recent developments. It was one thing for Han to know what Ellis was now, but to tell him about Randall and the werewolf's blood really wasn't his secret to give away.

"Okay, so that's viable and proven." Han nodded to himself. "I won't be able to talk to clients on the phone though. That's a big problem."

"Maybe," Jay said slowly, "you can take some time off. Christmas is slow anyway, right? People don't really get back to work until the new year. We can tell people you've been in and out of hospital, and come up with some... I dunno, some throat problem, and say you've had to have an operation and..."

"You want to tell people I've lost my voice?" Han laughed at him, but with that fondness in his dark eyes that meant it wasn't mocking. "Wow. That's pretty hardcore, isn't it?"

"Your PA can tell people you're busy. That's how Ellis handles it."

Han shook his head and leaned against Jay. He raised a hand to yawn into, then his stomach gurgled. "Urgh. I'm sorry."

Jay kissed his forehead and slid an arm around him. He really did feel cold. "I can go home and grab something warm for you?"

Han let out a dirty little laugh and slid his hand up along Jay's thigh. He let his thumb bump up against Jay's balls and grinned. "You've got something warm right here, baby."

"Ha ha. You know what I mean." Jay grinned and rubbed

Han's shoulder slowly. "And I can grab us something to eat, too."

"Nah. I'm fine. Thanks." Han turned to kiss Jay's jaw. "So no phones, no biometrics, no mirrors. No shaving, no manicures, no haircuts. No travel. How's this even tolerable?"

"It's better than being dead." Jay winced at how blunt it sounded. It was better in his head, but once it was out of his mouth it was ugly and honest, and he hated it.

"My nan would call it worse. She'd say I'd become a hungry ghost or something like that. Doomed to exist by feeding on the chi of the living." Han smiled wistfully. "It's kind of accurate, right?"

"You'd be here," Jay whispered. "With me." His arm tightened. "Tell me you'll say yes?"

"I dunno, baby. I don't fancy being lost for the rest of time, fumbling around biting people while I forget what life was like." Han pulled away and fidgeted with the crease in his trousers.

Jay made a strangled sound and launched to his feet again. He paced up and down the corridor. His trainers squeaked on the dreary grey linoleum every time he turned.

Why couldn't he make Han understand? His husband wasn't religious, he didn't believe in anything that couldn't be proven through repeatable testing or experimentation, so why the hell was he willing to just sit here and die when Ellis had the solution?

"Jay," Han said gently. "I know it's hard."

"You're *damn right* it is!" Jay snapped. "What would you do if it was me with the dicky ticker? What if I was the one they couldn't help, and I could drop dead any second, eh? What the hell would *you* do?"

"Shh. People are trying to sleep." Han stood, and even that

small movement seemed to tire him. His shoulders were low, and he took a couple of breaths before he continued. "I'd probably do what you're doing," he admitted as he took Jay's hand.

Jay stopped his pacing and pouted down at his husband. The man he loved. The man he'd married, for god's sake. There were dark circles beneath his eyes, and his skin was pale even in the washed-out light cast from the nurses' station.

"Everyone's gotta go sometime, though," Han sighed. "We've got to face that. They're not going to—" he paused for breath "—find a donor."

"Then you *have* to say yes to Ellis!"

Han rubbed at his chest and took a loud gasp of air. "May... be."

Jay's cheeks heated and his eyes stung. He was pushing too hard. It was late, they were hungry, and Han had a bloody heart condition, for crying out loud. "I'm sorry, sweetie," he whispered. "Why don't you sit down again? They'll find a bed soon."

Han nodded.

And then he collapsed.

"NURSE!" Jay screamed at the top of his lungs. He dropped to Han's side and tried to find a pulse. "Nurse! Help!" He pressed up against Han's throat and noticed with a sickening lurch that Han wasn't breathing. His skin had turned a sickening shade of grey.

He didn't hesitate. Jay tipped Han's head back, pinched his nose closed, and clamped his mouth over Han's. He heard footfalls and the rattle of wheels, but he just kept on rescue breathing, then pumped at his chest while the nurses prepared the crash cart. He used to think the endless practice on the Resusci Anne was a waste of an entire day's first aid training, but now that everything came to him on auto-pilot he couldn't be more grateful for it.

The nurse had to pull him away from Han. Only then did his voice break through Jay's focus. "You need to get back, Mr. Newfield. We're going to attempt to resuscitate."

Jay nodded, numb, and skidded back from them on his arse. The shiny linoleum accommodated him, but the further back he got the more clearly he could see the cluster of nurses around Han's cold, lifeless body. He saw them cut Han's shirt away. He saw them peel backing from stickers and attach them to Han's chest. Then he heard the whine from the crash cart and a horribly impersonal recorded voice as the machine checked Han's heart, issued a warning to stand clear, then discharged.

One nurse walked away. Did that mean Han was dead? No, the machine was still counting, charging, warning, discharging. Han's body didn't flop around like it did in films. He just laid there. His chest twitched slightly. The nurse was talking quickly into a phone, her voice clipped, urgent. The other nurse was still at Han's side, checking the machine, waiting for some response, pressing the buttons when required.

Han's chest moved. Not in some sort of spasm. It rose, and colour quickly flushed back into his skin.

"No shock indicated," the machine droned.

Jay butted up against a wall and hugged his knees tightly to stop himself from rushing in and getting in the way. He ached. He wanted to hold Han in his arms. He so desperately wanted everything to be all right. The clatter of wheels against the floor accompanied hurried footsteps, but he couldn't look away from Han. He *wouldn't* look away. His cheeks were wet and he had to blink to keep his vision clear, but he was going to stay right here. Right by Han's side, where he belonged.

"Is he—" he whispered as more nurses arrived. They were

lifting Han onto a gurney. Jay sniffed and wiped his cheeks before he tried again. "Is he okay?"

"We're going to have to take him down to the ICU." The ward's own nurse came over to offer Jay a hand. "Would you like to go with him?"

Jay nodded numbly. "Yeah. If I can?"

"Of course. Come on. Up you get."

Jay grabbed the hand and heaved himself to his feet. Only then did he notice how badly he was shaking.

Han was on the gurney with a sheet over his legs. They were beginning to wheel him away already.

Jay whimpered and hurried after them, and as he went he pulled his phone out and fumbled off a text message.

He couldn't take it anymore. Ellis had to come and *make* this happen, whether Han wanted it or not.

FOURTEEN

RANDALL CHECKED HIS WATCH. It hadn't been a few minutes now. It hadn't even been half an hour. He'd been home forty minutes and Ellis still wasn't here.

He flicked through channels on the television. Ellis' TV was so old it had a nearly-as-old freeview box attached to it, and he didn't subscribe to any cable or satellite channels, but even so there were still endless-seeming channels of dross to flick through and almost all of them at this time of night were either on closedown or offered teleshopping rubbish. His abs were just fine, thanks, and he didn't need a hundred pound blender just to make smoothies. Maybe these advertisers required their target audience to be half-asleep.

He checked his watch again.

The other guy who had shown up barely looked older than Christy. He was lean and pale, with spiked hair and sharp cheekbones. There was something kind of New Romantics about him in that way: all sharpness and dark lips, androgynously beautiful with his alabaster skin. He even dressed a bit like it was the Eighties with his leather thong necklace and bracelets.

Randall had no doubt the guy was a vampire. He even dressed like he was in the Lost Boys, but it was more than that. The lack of scent, the way he didn't breathe unless he needed to speak, and the way Ellis had shooed Randall away quickly. God, if the guy had heard them talking...

Randall turned the TV off and paced the flat. Then he grabbed his jacket and his keys.

Sod this. He had to find Ellis.

RANDALL JOGGED TO THE GALLERY, but he slowed down once he reached Claridge's. If he went charging up like a rhino it might give away that he knew something, but on the other hand after Ellis had said he'd only be a few minutes surely it would be acceptable for his boyfriend to be worried about his absence?

He sent yet another text. Still no answer.

Randall growled and slid his phone into his pocket. His irritation was growing, but thankfully now that he was an Alpha it was just that and nothing more. By god it'd turn into something else if the vampire had laid a finger on Ellis, though.

He tried the Gallery's door, but it was locked. The heavy wood didn't budge. He banged against it a couple of times and listened with his ear to the door, and he heard a bark.

Randall's teeth clenched together. He stepped out of the little alcove the door was tucked away in and examined the gallery windows. The blinds were closed and there was no light escaping around the outer edges.

He returned to the door. "Tiberius?"

Another bark. It sounded like the dog was just the other side of the door.

"Fuck." Randall rubbed his head quickly and tried to work out what to do.

There was no way Ellis would leave Tiberius behind. Either he'd been forced to do so, or he was still in the gallery and unable to answer.

Or he was dead.

Randall's growl became a soft snarl. Had he walked away and left Ellis with his murderer? He'd never forgive himself if that was the case. But if it were true, who had locked the gallery? Why would his attacker have done it? Had this Hughes guy come here to kill Ellis and steal art, and didn't want any of his crimes discovered until Christy arrived in the morning?

It made no sense. The only way to work anything out would be to get into the bloody building, but if he tore the door off its hinges he'd set off the alarms and risk being caught on a camera somewhere. Ellis' own cameras didn't cover the doors, but out here in the street who knew what CCTV had coverage of this porch?

He banged his head gently against the door. "Think, Rand," he muttered. "Come on. Think!"

Tiberius let out another worried-sounding bark. The poor dog was alone in there, and if nothing else Randall had to get him out and taken care of. He needed someone who could get in without triggering the security systems.

"Jay!" He yelled the name like a swear word and grabbed his phone, cycling through for Jay's number.

It bounced straight to voicemail.

"Jay! It's me! Uh, it's Randall! I think Ellis is in trouble. I need to get into the gallery, but it's locked. Tiberius is in there, I can hear him. I just... This... bloke came to see Ellis and now he's gone. Can you call me as soon as you get this message? Okay. Thanks." He hesitated, then hung up. The quicker he got off the phone, the faster Jay would get notification of the voicemail.

He paced up and down the mews, avoiding the weak light cast from the single Victorian street lamp up the far end. He bombarded Ellis' phone with texts, then sent almost as many to Jay, too.

His phone rang. He snatched it up and groaned with relief when he saw it was Jay. "Jay!"

"Randall!" Shit, Jay sounded even worse than Randall felt. "Where are you?"

"I'm at the gallery. Did you get my message?"

"Yeah. I mean, I got texts, and your voicemail, and—" Jay cut off. "Sorry, I'm babbling. Gallery. I can be there in ten minutes. Can you wait?"

"Yeah. Yeah, of course! Are you okay?"

"No." Jay's voice cracked. Randall heard his breath shudder. "Ten minutes. Stay there."

Then he hung up, and Randall returned to his frenetic pacing.

TRUE TO HIS WORD, Jay was there within ten minutes. A black cab pulled up at the entrance to the mews and Randall saw the skinny assistant throw paper money at the driver then leave without waiting for change. He came jogging down the mews, and the closer he came the worse he looked.

His skin was so pasty Randall had the fleeting panic that Jay had been turned, before he noticed that Jay was breathing hard. His eyes were reddened, and his cheeks bore isolated spots of colour while the rest of him was drained of it. His hair was limp, lank. He looked ill.

"Jay?"

Jay shook his head and grabbed a bunch of keys out of his coat pocket. He fumbled through them until he found the one he wanted, and his hand shook as he tried to unlock the gallery door.

"Let me—"

"I've got it," Jay snapped.

Randall bit his tongue, and was flooded with a bizarre moment's deja vu. Hadn't he done this recently? Bitten his tongue?

Jay shoved the door open and Tiberius yelped in surprise, and the sound jerked Randall back into the present. The eerie sensation sank away.

"Tiberius, baby! Where's your harness? Where's Ellis?" Jay crouched just inside the door and fussed the dog.

Randall stepped around them. He paused to check that Tiberius was unharmed, but the dog seemed fine — if harness-free. "I'll check upstairs."

Jay sniffed and nodded. At a beep from the wall he stood and turned to tap a code into the alarm system.

Randall ran up the stairs in the dark and used the hand rail to guide him. He was halfway up when the lights came on and blinded him, but he pushed on and shouldered the office door, lashing out for the light switch. "Ellis?"

Nothing. Ellis wasn't here.

Randall rubbed his eyes and moved around the room quickly. Tiberius' harness was neatly folded and laid in the centre of Ellis' desk, but there were no signs of a struggle. Everything was neat and tidy. There was nothing else left behind. The chair which faced Ellis' desk wasn't quite seated properly in the carpet dents, and Randall moved it back into place automatically. The unmoving placement of the furniture enabled Ellis to walk around his own office without fear of stumbling into something, and a chair out of place was a hazard.

Someone had moved it. That suggested maybe the vampire Hughes had indeed come to talk. He'd sat down, they'd talked, and then Ellis had removed Tiberius' harness. That told Tiberius that he was no longer working.

Would Ellis have done any of this if he had expected to be back?

Jay hurried into the office, and Tiberius padded in after him, his tail hung low. "Nothing downstairs."

Randall shook his head. "Nothing here, either. I think he's been taken."

Jay's hands balled into fists. "Shit. No. Not now. We have to find him!"

"Yeah. But vampires don't leave a scent." Randall studied Jay.

In the light, Jay just looked even worse. His skin was the pallor of shock, and he had a thin sheen of sweat which gave his skin a dull gloss to it. He hadn't shaved since the morning, and his stubble was a dark shadow across his jaw which only served to accentuate his terrible paleness. Even his lips looked pasty.

"Jay," Randall said as gently as he could muster. "What's wrong?"

"It doesn't matter. We have to find Ellis. Oh, god, Randall, *please*." Jay's shoulders hunched, then he folded into a chair and began to sob.

He cried like a man who had already cried himself empty. His tears were sluggish, sparse, and his throat sounded raw with anguish. He slumped, defeated, against the back of the chair and did nothing to try and hold himself up.

"Jay!" Randall sprang forward and grabbed his shoulders to prevent him from falling out of the seat altogether. "What's going on? Something's wrong. Tell me!"

"We have to find Ellis," Jay whimpered. He managed to lift his head, and his reddened eyes beseeched Randall more powerfully than his voice could.

God, was Jay secretly in love with Ellis? That would explain why he pulled all those late nights, why he was willing to accept that his employer was a vampire and do all he could to make life easier for Ellis, wouldn't it? Was that why Jay had really taken against Randall back when they'd met?

Randall's jaw rocked. That couldn't be right. It didn't *feel* right, and it didn't make any logical sense. He'd seen Jay talk about Han. His eyes lit up in a way that nobody could feign. Jay loved his husband, and he loved him so utterly that it broke through like sunlight breaching clouds every time Han's name was spoken.

"We'll find him," Randall said, calming himself so that he could project authority into his words. "Jay, I need you to take a breath and calm down, okay? We are going to find Ellis. But first I need you to tell me what's wrong."

Jay hiccoughed. "It's Han," he whispered. "He's had a heart attack."

Randall sank to his knees by Jay's side, and suddenly he understood.

They had to find Ellis.

FIFTEEN

THE GRIP ON ELLIS' arm was tight and unwavering. Hughes steered him without any hint as to where he was being taken, and with no understanding of how to do the job.

Ellis loathed being steered. It was bad enough to be led by someone who didn't think to walk around cracks in the pavement or warn him when there were kerbs, but getting dragged along like a recalcitrant child made it so much worse. What little independence was left to him was stolen by that single act.

That was the point, he supposed. But Hughes had been kind enough to allow him to remove Tiberius' harness once Ellis had explained that without doing so the dog would still consider himself to be working. He'd even let Ellis lock the gallery so that Tiberius wouldn't roam the streets and to prevent strangers from wandering in and stealing the stock. Both those things were decent of him.

Releasing Randall had been decent, too. Hughes had come to arrest him for one crime, caught him committing another, but hadn't added it to the list. His decency could well save

Randall's life. And if he were decent enough to do all those things…

Ellis drew a breath and murmured "Constable, would you mind if I took your arm? This is extremely unsettling for me."

"Yeah, getting nicked is unsettling for most people," Hughes said.

"Aye, true," Ellis agreed. "But most people aren't relying on your eyes when you arrest them, are they?"

Hughes didn't answer. Ellis had no idea whether he'd been ignored, or Hughes was just thinking that through.

"I promise you that I won't try to run," he added. "I can't. I don't know where we are, which direction to go in, or whether there are any obstacles."

Hughes stopped, and jerked Ellis to a halt too. "I should warn you I'm armed, and I'm the fastest thing on the planet. It takes me seconds to get to your gallery from Bond Street, and nobody sees me do it."

Ellis' lips parted in shock. "Bloody hell!"

He knew Hughes was fast. He had no idea he was *that* fast. No wonder the fella could be on his doorstep ten minutes after sunset even though Hughes lived in Battersea. Nine of those minutes were probably down to crossing the Thames by tube.

"Fine," Hughes groused. His fingers were gone, then he awkwardly took Ellis' hand and touched it to his own forearm. "How do we do this?"

"Hang on." Ellis felt his way up Hughes' arm. It was thin, like he'd been woefully undernourished when he was turned. "There," he said, once his fingers were settled around Hughes' elbow.

"And I just walk?"

"I don't have a stick with me, so you need to walk me

around cracks and bumps. And warn me when there's a kerb, aye? I've had enough of those already."

"All right," Hughes relented. "Let's go."

He made a passable guide, once Ellis had corrected him a few times. He was alert and attentive, and he only needed to be told once to take something in. All skills which probably made him an excellent Constable.

"Hughes," Ellis said quietly.

"What?"

"What's going to happen?"

They took several steps before Hughes drew breath. "I'm taking you to a holding cell," he finally said, his voice so quiet that it'd take a vampire to hear him from three feet away. "You'll be questioned while I gather the evidence I need, then we have to get the Council together to hear the case."

"And how long's all that going to take?"

He felt Hughes shrug. "Could be anything up to a week. Depends how busy the Council is with other stuff."

"A week?" Ellis' grip tightened, then said the only thing that came into his head. "I haven't even done my Christmas shopping yet!"

Hughes laughed. It wasn't a cruel sound, just an amused one. "You're worried about that?"

Ellis huffed at him. "Constable, if I'm going to get executed on whatever evidence you manage to concoct, it would at least be nice to know that my fella's going to have something to remember me by."

"Yeah. About that."

Ellis slowed to a halt, and felt Hughes turn to face him.

"I'm gonna hafeta pull him in." Hughes sounded apologetic. "You know that, right?"

Ellis withdrew his hand and jabbed a finger at Hughes with it. It wavered in empty air. "You let him go earlier," he snarled.

"Yeah. Because I'd come to get you. One job at a time, eh? I'm not gonna take my power for granted against multiple opponents. Never know what might 'appen. Slow and steady wins the race and all that shit. I'll get you safely stowed, then I'll go pick up yer fella. He shouldn't be too hard to track down."

"Why not?"

"'Cause by now he'll be wonderin' where you are, so he will go to the Gallery, find your dog, and take it 'ome." As if on cue, Ellis' pocket buzzed. "'Ere we go. Willin' to bet that's him. No," he added as Ellis reached into his pocket. "None of that."

Ellis took a step forward, but too many things happened at once for him to keep track of: his pockets lightened; there was an odd drumming sound; a hand slammed against his chest and stopped him going any further.

He bared his teeth as he heard his phone buzz again. But he didn't feel it this time, and the sound didn't come from his own clothing.

"Hughes, for god's sake!" He grabbed at Hughes' arm, but it was already gone by the time he got there. He felt like a slug trying to wrestle a snake.

"I can't let you answer, O'Neill. C'mon, we're not idiots here. You'll warn him."

"Have a bloody heart! Are you really going to stand here and tell me you've never made a mistake?"

Hughes' silence was all Ellis needed.

"Are you telling me," he added more gently, "that you've never fallen in love?"

"That is *none* of your business," Hughes hissed.

Ellis clamped his teeth together and furiously tried to assemble what little he knew about the Constable. It wasn't much. Had his actions been decent, or all part of a trap to ensure Randall's whereabouts when Hughes went back for him? Had Ellis misjudged him so thoroughly? He didn't have any living clues to hone in on, no pulse to hear or skin to feel, but even so he thought he'd seen some sign that Hughes wasn't completely heartless.

We all tell our lovers what we are sooner or later, don't we?

Ellis sucked in air. "Oh my god."

"Stop wasting time." Hughes took Ellis' hand and guided it to his elbow. "We're leaving."

Ellis took it and let Hughes lead him. "You've done it, haven't you? You had a lover, and you told her what you are."

"Him," Hughes corrected. Then he added "Fuck."

"Let Randall go," Ellis pleaded. "He won't do anything." Well, he probably would. "He doesn't know there are more of us." Apart from Hughes and Barb and whatever other rumours Ellis had shared.

"Oh, he don't?" Hughes laughed briefly. "I 'eard what you were talking about when I got there, numbnuts."

Ellis swore inwardly. "Fine. Please, just let him go. Don't go after him for my mistake, aye? You got me." He hesitated. "Tell you what. I'll confess to whatever you want me to if you'll promise me you'll leave him be."

"You what?" Hughes' pace faltered. "Is that what you think I want?"

"I don't have the foggiest idea what you want." Ellis shook his head. It wasn't possible to negotiate from a position of such utter lack of knowledge. He didn't know what Hughes wanted, why he did this, why he was going to go back for Randall even though he already had Ellis on a far bigger charge. His lack of contact with almost every vampire in the city left him out of the loop on whatever gossip there was out there, and the scraps Barb shared weren't enough to provide the information he needed desperately to talk himself out of this situation.

Hughes had to want *something*. Why else do this job? Was it for money? If so, Ellis was shit out of luck. Bribery wasn't within his power. Hell, paying Christy and Jay was barely within his power. If Hughes' lover knew what he was, had he already been killed, or would Hughes do whatever it took to keep his own secret even while he arrested Randall for the same crime?

They marched onward. Ellis heard animals. Mostly bats, but the occasional rodent or fox too. They could be passing any of the major parks which surrounded Mayfair, but no traffic passed them. It was most likely that they travelled west, then, through Hyde Park.

"I thought the Council convened in Aldwych?" he ventured.

"They do."

"This doesn't sound like Aldwych."

"Probably not," Hughes agreed. Then he added "Look. I... I'm not a total arsehole, all right?"

Ellis pursed his lips. "I don't think that you are," he said with caution, curious as to where Hughes was going with this.

"I'm just doing my job."

"Ah, the Nuremberg defence," Ellis said.

"You calling me a fucking *Nazi*?" Hughes' snarl was enough to make Ellis wish he'd kept his mouth shut.

"You're going to kill a man," Ellis said with care, "because it is your job. Since when was that *ever* okay outside a war zone? Or are we actually at war with the living? Did I miss that memo? Let me guess, nobody bothered getting it transcribed into braille."

"We have to protect ourselves. This in't the dark ages, is it? It's not like the biggest human town 'round 'ere has a thousand people in it. There's eight and an' 'alf million people in London. You've got no idea how much they outnumber us by."

"Enlighten me."

"It's something like forty thousand to one. That ain't a mob with burnin' torches and pitchforks, O'Neill. It's a fuckin' *landslide*. If they get enough of a whiff that we're here we are *toast*."

Ellis tried to work out the numbers. He was much more used to working on a slightly smaller scale, but after a few moments he realised "There's only a couple of hundred of us?"

"And that's including the Greater London area," Hughes muttered. "You lot got it easy here in the middle. Some people gotta make do with a couple of streets or a handful of tower blocks."

"The Council keeps the numbers down to protect their own land." Ellis stumbled, and gripped Hughes' arm more tightly to keep from falling. "That's why they're so set against unsanctioned turnings."

"Yeah," Hughes said bitterly. "Anyway. Mind yer 'ead."

Ellis ducked, then Hughes paused. A heavy key scraped in an even more cumbersome lock, and the tumblers which rolled aside sounded thick and ponderous. It was no modern lock, that was for certain.

"Stairs down," Hughes said as they moved forward.

Ellis felt for a handrail, but there wasn't one. There was only stone, smoothed with age but still bumpy and uneven. The steps beneath his feet were solid as stone too, and his shoes *clip clipped* against them, but they weren't flat. The more they descended the more he could tell by the angle of his feet against each one and the way they curved at the forward edge that they were worn down with centuries of use.

Wherever Hughes was taking him, it had been here since long before either World War. Hell, it might even be older than Hyde Park itself.

There were more doors, each as old as the first if their locks were anything to go by, but the last opened on a creak of hinges, and rather than being led through it Ellis was firmly pushed.

He grit his teeth and turned on his heel. Hughes' hands patted him down, and he heard his keys go, as well as the slip of leather over silk when the Constable removed his wallet. Everything else had already been taken from him.

"What's the point of this?" he breathed.

"You'll be safe from the sun down 'ere," Hughes said.

Ellis bit his cheek. "Is that really going to matter?"

"No." The door clanged shut and the key turned again. Heavy bolts sealed it shut. "Not really."

Ellis reached out and found cold metal. Round, vertical. He gripped it.

Of course it didn't budge.

"Hughes—"

"I'll come back when it's time." Hughes cut him off. Ellis heard thuds as items — presumably his own — were deposited against a hard surface, but then Hughes' footsteps retreated, and a door swung shut.

SIXTEEN

"WE GET A CAB," Jay hiccoughed.

Randall stood and placed a hand on Jay's shoulder in an attempt to calm him. "Shh. It's going to be okay. Why do we want a taxi?"

"Basic search pattern. We'll comb the area. It's faster in a car this time of night. I've done it loads of times. It always works."

Randall sighed and gave Jay's shoulder a gentle squeeze. "If he's been taken somewhere," he countered as softly as he could, "we'd do far better to have some idea of where."

Jay pulled himself upright and grabbed for his phone. He thumb-typed as swiftly as any teenager Randall had ever seen. "I hate that he can't answer phones," Jay keened as he typed. "Texting's shite in emergencies!"

"Yeah." Randall withdrew and took out his own phone. There was no response to his earlier message, but it didn't hurt to try again. *Where are you?* he sent.

"Okay. Okay, uh." Jay rubbed his eyes with the heel of his

hand. "They don't leave a scent, so you can't track them, right?"

"Right." Randall nodded.

"They won't be on the CCTV, so we can't tell what way they went." Jay took a shaky breath, pulled a hankie from his jeans, and blew his nose. "We can split up and ask around."

Randall ran a hand over his head and wandered slowly toward the office door. Tiberius' eyes followed him, but the young German Shepherd's tail remained attached to the floor. "Okay. So, this vampire arrived while I was here earlier. Said his name was Hughes. Does that mean anything to you?"

Jay shook his head. "What'd he look like?"

"Uh. Tall. Like, your height, roughly. Spiky hair. All angles and limbs."

Jay narrowed bloodshot eyes and said slowly "I think I've seen him. Really pretty, kinda bishie-looking?"

"I dunno what that is," Randall said.

"You know. Bishounen? All androgynous and beautiful?"

"Yeah!" Randall snapped his fingers. "That's the guy! You saw him?"

Jay nodded and wrapped his arms around himself. "He stopped by a couple of months ago. Came in like he knew where to go, you know? Most people walk in here and they linger around looking a bit lost, or they dawdle toward the art, but he came in and went straight for the stairs. He said he was a friend. Ellis texted me to say he knew who it was, so I figured the bloke had been here before and he was a vampire."

Randall nodded. "Yeah. He came straight on up when he got here earlier, too. But Ellis wouldn't tolerate someone on his territory unless they were—" He broke off. "When was Hughes last here?"

"Um." Jay stood and went to the desk he time-shared with Christy and turned the computer on. "It'll be in my diary."

Randall followed and sat on the corner of the desk as they waited for the machine to boot up.

Jay tapped in his password and fired up his email, then entered another password. Finally he had his calendar, and scrolled through it until he found it. He tapped at the screen. "September. A few days after that crap with the guy who was trying to kill Ellis."

"Shit." The word burst out of Randall in a rush of air.

Jay blinked up at him. "What?"

"The only vampires Ellis would put up with in here," Randall said, "are either people in this revolution he's getting dragged into, or representatives of the Council on official business."

Jay shut his machine down and stood straight. "He's a Constable," he said, with mounting horror spreading across his features. "Oh, god. We have to find him!"

"Yeah." Randall eased off the desk edge and peered up at Jay. There seemed to be something more to Jay's urgency all of a sudden. Some depth that hadn't been there a moment ago. "What is it?"

"This revolution thing." Jay cracked his knuckles and stared at Randall. His breath was quick and shallow, and what colour had been returning had disappeared again. "They want to overthrow the whole Council. They want to replace it with a democracy."

Randall gnawed the inside of his cheek a moment, then a cold dread settled into his chest. "Ellis told you."

"Yeah." Jay nodded. "Get it?"

"Yeah." Randall hurried to Ellis' desk to grab Tiberius' harness. "C'mere, Tiberius. We need to get you home." He crouched by the dog and began to wrap the harness around him, taking care to make sure the Velcro was fastened.

If Ellis knew about this revolution, then he had contacts

in it. One of them was probably Barb, the blond vampire with the biker leathers and the distinctive perfume. If Hughes had taken Ellis for interrogation, he might lead the Council to Barb, and then the whole thing would come crashing down before it had had a chance to get off the ground.

"Right," Randall said decisively as he stood, Tiberius' harness in hand. "We take Tiberius home and get him tucked away safely, then we try to find this woman Ellis knows. If she's one of the revolutionaries she might know where Hughes has taken Ellis and how we can get him back. It should be far more efficient than driving up and down the West End all night. Come on, boy. Let's go," he added to Tiberius, and urged him toward the door. "She had this perfume. I could pick it out easy. We'll drop Tiberius, then I can change in the privacy of Ellis' flat and we can sniff it out. It might take some time to find the trail, but—"

"Hang on." Jay hurried after him and turned out the office light, then followed him down the stairs. "We can save a lot more time than that."

"How's that?"

"'Cause I think I know where she lives," Jay said. "Ellis came over last night to talk to Han about turning him, and he told us about this revolution. He said he'd have to talk to someone to see whether there could be some way Han could survive being turned without the Council's sanction. I think he's hoping that the revolution will come soon and Han can kinda slip in under the radar. He went to see her straight after he was with us."

"Ellis gave you her address?" Randall waited on the doorstep while Jay armed the security system and locked the gallery door.

"Han and I live on the south bank. Ellis has to take the

tube to get to us. He can't go over the Thames, he's gotta to under it."

Randall stared at him. "So when he left your place last night," he said slowly.

"I escorted him," Jay finished. "Right to her doorstep."

"Holy shit, I could kiss you."

"Oh, sweetie. You're gorgeous, but I already have one husband. I don't have time for another."

Randall snorted, and a small grin crept across his lips. They hurried through the warren of streets toward the flat, and even though Tiberius had to stop to relieve himself things were still looking up.

RANDALL RAN his keycard through the front door's reader, then led Jay and Tiberius up to the flat and unlocked the door. He had a flutter of hope that Ellis might he inside and bemused at their panic, but no such luck.

Jay got the lights, and it was a little weird to note the familiarity another man had with Ellis' home.

"You've been here a lot?" Randall said lightly as he released Tiberius and set his harness on the shelf where it belonged.

"No threat," Jay said as he raised his hands.

"No," Randall agreed. "It's just weird to me." He offered a slight smile that he hoped was reassuring. "You two are such good friends, and I kinda feel a bit like an intruder at times."

Jay mustered a weak smile. "I'm gonna go freshen up."

"Sure."

Jay disappeared off to the bathroom.

Randall fed Tiberius and refilled his water bowl. He tried

texting Ellis again, but didn't hold out any hope it'd be answered, which was lucky, since it wasn't.

Would Barb appreciate two people arriving on her doorstep who knew she was in on this revolution *and* where she lived? Hell, even just that they knew she was a vampire could be enough to put the wind up her. What if she decided to cut her losses, dispose of the evidence, and wash her hands clean of everything?

Randall didn't doubt that he could handle her if it came down to a fight, assuming that her power wasn't something like obscene strength or speed. Just so long as she didn't bite him.

He grimaced. That was the ultimate vampire defence. Their bite immobilised immediately, albeit while providing intense pleasure, but it would bring him out of the fight and leave Jay defenceless. But the fangs of a vampire weren't especially long, either. If they failed to penetrate, say, a thick layer of protective fur...

Randall nodded to himself and kicked his boots off. He emptied his coat pockets and hung his coat, then peeled his t-shirt off over his head.

"Uh." Jay cleared his throat as he stepped back into the living room. "This is... not what I expected."

"Have you got keys to get in here?"

Jay nodded. "Yeah."

"I'm going with you to keep you safe," he explained as he pulled his socks off. He balanced on one foot then the other and tossed the socks onto the sofa. "But I don't want her to know what I am. And if I do end up revealing werewolves exist, I don't want her to put a face to it. You okay doing all the talking?"

"Ohh!" Jay's head bobbed. "Yeah. That's fine."

Randall unfastened his jeans and turned away, then pushed

his briefs down and began the shift once they were past his thighs.

Jay gasped — most likely at the brief glimpse of his arse and more private parts — then exhaled in an awed "Oh my god!"

Randall fell forward onto all fours and shrugged free of his jeans. The world had lost some of its colour, but what he'd lost was more than made up for by the precision of his sight, the keenness of his hearing, and the sheer breadth of his sense of smell. He had no doubt that in this shape his senses were more than a match for a vampire's.

"That's so amazing," Jay breathed. "Do you get it from a bite?"

Randall blinked at him. "Rrff."

"I'll take that as a no." Jay did one last check of the flat, then added "Do you need a collar or something?"

Randall bared his teeth. Absolutely nobody was putting a collar on him. Well, nobody but- No, no, don't start thinking like *that*!

"Another no. Okay." Jay went to the door and opened it, then turned out the lights after them.

———

JAY LED ON FOOT, and had a conversation on his phone as they hurried toward Soho. Randall didn't mean to eavesdrop, but it was impossible not to.

"Mr. Xie is stable," the voice on the other end of the line said, "but resting."

"And you'll call me if that changes?" Jay insisted.

"Of course, Mr. Newfield. Your contact details are right here on Mr. Xie's records."

"Okay. Thank you." Jay hung up and glanced to Randall.

Randall gently bumped his shoulder against Jay's knee to show some sort of solidarity, of understanding, and Jay drew himself up fully.

"Thanks," Jay whispered.

"Rr," Randall answered.

Soho at night as a wolf was a frightening experience. There were people everywhere, and as much as Randall glued himself to walls and shadows he couldn't help but draw the occasional glance or gasp. They mostly reeked of alcohol, but if too many of them all Tweeted at once about the "wolf in Soho" it might be enough for some sort of rumour to start.

Jay seemed on the ball. "Oh that's my dog," he'd say. "Yeah, part Husky, part Malamute. I think there's a little German Shepherd in there too! He was the only one that colour in his litter! Isn't he adorable?"

Jay was a genius. No wonder Ellis had entrusted his secrets to this man. He was so deft at defusing and deflecting attention that he had to be a bloody godsend once Ellis had been turned.

Randall began to relax. He wagged his tail at people who oohed at him, and looked up at Jay like a dutiful hound who loved his owner. It seemed to help the ruse, though he would have appreciated if fewer people had drunkenly patted his head. It was weird. And smelly.

Jay led on, past the bars and clubs, and to a street dotted with boutiques: cake shops; estate agents; cafés. As they walked, Randall picked up scent after scent, until he picked up on the odour of Barb's perfume.

When Jay stopped, it was outside a chocolate shop, as closed as all the other boutiques along this street. Randall flicked his ears and sniffed along the edge of the shop, then stopped at a discreet little door which sat between the shop and another retail unit. There was an array of intercom buttons up at human chest-height which were numbered, not named.

Jay turned and hurried after him, then nodded slightly. "Barb?" he said quietly. "If you're home, I really need to talk to you." He ran his fingers along his lower lip while he considered, then added "It's about Ellis. I think he's in trouble."

Randall swivelled his ears toward the door to focus his hearing, but he needn't have. Barb's boots were like a herd of elephants.

The door wrenched open and there she stood, the perfume rolling from her in almost-visible waves. She looked Jay over, then regarded Randall briefly.

"Barb?" Jay said hesitantly.

The vampire ran the tip of her tongue along her upper teeth, then stepped back and beckoned him inside. "Hey cutie. Nice dog. Why don't you and me take this conversation upstairs, eh?"

Jay eased past her, and Randall bolted in in case she felt like shutting the dog out. The way she looked at Jay's arse in passing couldn't be good, but the gaze she gave the back of his neck seemed so much worse.

God, he hoped they weren't making a huge mistake.

SEVENTEEN

ELLIS FUMBLED his way around the cell as he assembled a mental map of this new environment. He was hardly overburdened with entertainment, and he was buggered if he was going to sit on his arse and do nothing.

The walls were stone, but rougher than those of the stairwell. That wasn't a surprise to him. If the stairs were well-used but the cells not then there were likely other rooms down here, another purpose for this place. More than just a prison for doomed vampires.

He found a simple bed. It was metal, with springs beneath the mattress which would probably be illegal under modern health and safety laws. From the curved shape of the head and foot ends it seemed reminiscent of the metal beds he'd once seen in photographs of air raid shelters from the Second World War, and the mattress was so thin he wouldn't have been at all surprised if that was exactly the source of this furniture.

The bed had thin sheets on it, but at least it did have sheets. He wasn't sure whether that was a good sign that showed his captors cared for comfort, or whether it meant they were used to incarcerating humans down here just as much as vampires.

He found a bucket in the corner and grimaced. Apparently they *were* amenable to storing living people down here.

The cell was small. Wide enough for the bed and bucket, and just as long. About eight feet by eight, by his reckoning. He reached overhead and found the ceiling. Another eight feet. That put him in a cube.

The walls weren't damp, and he found no windows. The only opening was his door, which was a medieval thing of solid metal bars and stone surround. He pulled on the bars and yelled for help, but the very walls seemed to muffle his shouts, and the door was resolutely unmoved. He tried to snake an arm through them, but there was nothing beyond but air.

Ellis rested his forehead against the cold metal. There wasn't a damn way he would get out of here on his own. He couldn't budge the door, and there wasn't any other way. Hughes had taken his phone, so he couldn't even text for help.

"Shite," he breathed.

There had to be something he could do. He wasn't a man to sit around and do nothing. Nobody ever got anywhere in business through inaction, and he wasn't going to bloody stay in this cell without finding a way to be productive.

He lifted his head from the bars and ran his fingers across them, then gripped them and closed his eyes. He focused, and tried to feel for any impressions that may have been left here. Had someone held these bars before him? Was there-

There was a vampire. She was screaming bloody murder as she wrenched at the bars. Her hair was pure copper, dull in the dim light from the solitary bulb out in the corridor beyond her cell.

She was pretty, Ellis supposed. He'd never been drawn to women,

but he was a man who could appreciate beauty. Her eyes were true green, made pale and apple-coloured by her undeath.

She was furious. Upset, but also livid. Her screams were mostly curses. She damned the Council, their puppets, and a slew of names Ellis had no familiarity with.

She only gave in when they came to take her away.

Ellis' fingers flicked apart to release the bars and break contact. With the vision over, he was in darkness again, and he took a moment to re-acclimatise to it.

He wasn't convinced that he'd learned anything more than he already knew. This was a cell. The Constables put their prisoners here, then those prisoners were taken to the Council for their sentencing. Ellis felt his way along the wall to the bed, then sat slowly and curled one hand around the metal of the headboard. The other he slid down beneath the mattress.

There was a flood of loathing. Hatred. A man lay on the bed, beautiful and unbreathing. He stared at the ceiling with ice-blue eyes and he seemed peaceful, calm, yet the feelings which flooded Ellis were at odds with his outward mien.

Ellis watched. The vampire was dressed in a khaki-coloured shirt with a pencil-thin red silk tie. The shirt was open at the neck and the tie knotted loosely. There were dark stains across the khaki material which were brown and smelled of dead blood. He wore dark brown suspenders over the shirt, and black trousers. His hair was full and short, parted over one eye, and it fell back against the pillow in a gentle wave.

There was something vaguely New Romantics about him. His shirt was a little too big and overhung his waistband, except where the braces kept it in place. Nobody had done that with their shirts since the Eighties. Coupled with that tie, Ellis was sure this vision was old, the emotions so strong that it lingered despite the decades which had passed.

A key rasped in the door and a figure entered the cell. He was short — around Randall's height — and the solitary light behind him gave his blond hair the appearance of a halo.

"Marcus," the newcomer said.

"Get fucked," Marcus answered.

The vampire with his back to the bars snorted and stepped toward the bed. "Get up, you Bedlamite."

Marcus swung his legs from the bed and leaped to his feet as though he had no choice. The calm expression shattered, and he bared his teeth at the shorter vampire. His fangs descended.

The other vampire snapped his fingers. "Focus. Stand still. You will not attack me."

"What do you want, Devitt?" Marcus snarled. His fingers spasmed, but he was pinned in place.

Devitt. Ellis knew that name.

Barb had warned him about the vampire who controlled Westminster. Charles Devitt. The one with the mind control power. The one who could destroy them all if he found out about the revolution.

Devitt stepped aside. He circled the trapped vampire as though Marcus were a butterfly pinned under glass. The light caught his eyes fleetingly and they seemed like chunks of pure amber, lit from within.

"I want you," Devitt whispered, "to tell the Council that it was Aaron Hughes who turned you."

Marcus' expression fell. His anger collapsed in on itself and became something else.

It became fear.

"Please," Marcus whispered.

"This whole mess has been unfortunate," Charles stated calmly. "For what it's worth, I'm sorry about that." His voice was smooth, his accent cultured. He sounded like an Eton boy if ever there was one. "But this happens from time to time. There is no cure. Nothing can be done."

"You did this to me," Marcus cried, his voice strangled. "You promised—"

Charles waved a hand to cut him off. "And it didn't work. You can't run around killing the humans in public, boy. And you certainly cannot *fling their corpses onto a dance floor while screaming 'I am a vampire'. That is the antithesis of secrecy, would you not agree?"*

Ellis' gaze was drawn to the blood on Marcus' shirt. He felt sick.

"Not Aaron," Marcus begged. "Please. Anyone else. Not him."

"This is how it has to be." Charles stepped in and gazed up into Marcus' eyes. "I did not come to see you tonight. Once I leave this cell you will forget that I was here, and you will be free to move again. When they parade you in front of the Council you will tell us that Hughes turned you. You will tell him that you are lovers, and that he did this without seeking our permission first."

Marcus screamed. "You can't do this! They'll kill him! Please, I'll do anything! Leave him alone, please!"

"Goodbye," Devitt said. He turned his back on Marcus, and only Ellis was there to watch the young vampire sob wretchedly yet unable to move from his spot.

And once Charles was gone, Marcus slowly stopped crying and sank back down onto the bed, confusion creasing his delicate features.

"Oh, shit," Ellis coughed as he dragged his hands from the bed frame. "Oh *god!*"

What the hell had he just seen?

The darkness clamped around him and he pushed his hands into his hair. His elbows rested on his knees and he sat there, propped up, stock still while he tried to process the vision and push down the sharp hunger it had aroused within him. Jesus, even the scent of dried blood from three decades ago was enough to trigger his need.

Was this who Hughes had revealed his nature to? The man he had loved? Marcus said that Devitt had done this to him. Did he mean the turning, or something else?

A horrible feeling settled over him like a shroud.

Marcus had been one of the unlucky ones. The ones who weren't gifted with some sort of power once they turned.

He'd been one of those who were driven insane by it.

Ellis clutched his hair and tried to remember what Barb had told him about Devitt. The way the blond vampire had spoken in his vision suggested that Devitt was a part of the Council at the time. Barb had said some incident in the Eighties had forced Devitt off the council.

He hadn't referred to Hughes as Constable, either. Was that an omission due to Devitt's superior status, or because Hughes had yet to be given the job?

Ellis smoothed out his hair. The gesture helped to calm him and steady his nerves. If Hughes returned he might be willing to negotiate based on Ellis' information. If Marcus was the person Hughes had revealed himself to, and Devitt had turned him — whether as a favour as he implied or to gain some kind of control over Hughes — it had all gone wrong in the worst possible way. Marcus was driven insane, he killed innocent people, and heads had to roll.

There was no doubt in Ellis' mind that Marcus had done exactly as Devitt ordered. Sooner or later he must have told the Council that it was Hughes who had turned him without permission.

So how the hell was Hughes not only still alive, but also a Constable now? And how had Devitt lost his seat on the Council?

Ellis stood and used the wall to guide him back toward the bars, and shook the door as hard as he could. "Hughes!" he yelled at the top of his lungs. "Hughes! We have to talk!"

His voice didn't reverberate the way it might in a normal room. The thick walls deadened it and left it oddly muffled.

"Hughes!" he screamed.

Nothing. Not even the sounds of life up above.

Ellis sagged against the bars, too drained to continue. He couldn't bring himself to return to that bed.

EIGHTEEN

RANDALL STOOD by Jay's side as the lanky human stopped in the middle of Barb's tiny flat.

It was clean. There were none of those odours which came from human habitation: no fecal matter, no slight rot emanating from the fridge or a fruit bowl, no remains of dinner or of crumbs fallen to the floor and long since vacuumed up. Every scent left a trace, often for many days, and humans were completely unaware of the wealth of data they littered around themselves with every shed skin particle or hair, with every stray biscuit crumb or grooming decision.

Barb's perfume was strong in here. Was she aware that she had no scent, or was perfume a habit she'd been into while alive that she stuck with as some sort of reminder of where she came from?

The flat was maybe a third of the size of Ellis'. There were others up here, above the shops below, so whatever business Barb conducted at home she probably kept quiet. That gave him some hope that she wouldn't murder Jay.

Not loudly, anyway.

The furniture was dated. Faded and threadbare, the flat looked like it had been decorated in the late Seventies and left that way ever since. There was a velour-covered three-piece suite, a G-Plan coffee table, and the sort of cabinets Randall would expect someone's Nan to have, not a revolutionary vampire who wore leathers and Doc Martens everywhere she went.

"You're a cutie-pie," Barb cooed as she slunk her way toward Jay. "Where'd Ellis find you?" She brought her hands up to Jay's chest.

Jay took a quick step back. "Hey, hands off, lady. I'm married! And even if I wasn't, I'm gayer than Christmas on acid!"

Barb laughed, but she withdrew her hands, palms up to show them to Jay. "You're adorable. Sit down and tell me what this is all about?"

Jay watched her warily, then grabbed the armchair and sank into it, and Randall put himself in front of Jay's legs in case Barb wanted to climb into his lap.

"You," she said to Randall, "aren't Tiberius."

Randall wagged his tail in the hope of looking like any other dog receiving attention from a stranger.

Barb chuckled and scratched between his ears, then sat on the couch. Her attention went back to Jay. "Let me guess. He only hangs out with people who also have dogs?"

"He's in trouble," Jay stated. "I need your help."

Barb pursed her lips. "All right. I'll bite. What makes you say that?"

"Some bloke called Hughes came to the Gallery earlier, and now I can't find Ellis and he isn't answering his texts."

Randall laid down. Despite the hammering of Jay's heart and the sharp scent of terror he exuded, the assistant was doing brilliantly, and his fear could be passed off as worry over

Ellis. Hell, maybe that's what it *was*. Jay had far more on his plate than worrying about being in a room with a vampire he didn't know.

All of Barb's good humour wiped itself from her body language. She sat forward on the edge of her seat and glared intently at Jay. "Yeah. Okay. Ellis is in trouble. How long ago was this?"

"About an hour? Maybe two?" Jay shook his head. "I wasn't there at the time."

"Then how do you know that he's missing?"

"He stopped answering his texts," Jay said without so much as a pause to think something up. "I needed to talk to him, so I came to the Gallery and he was already gone. He's still not answering texts."

"Then how do you know it was Hughes?" Barb narrowed her eyes at him.

"Ellis' boyfriend told me," Jay answered.

God, Randall thought. *He's good!*

"He was there when Hughes arrived. He heard the guy give Ellis his name. Ellis said he'd be home soon, but he isn't there."

"Right. Where's the boyfriend now?"

"Out searching on foot."

Barb nodded. "Okay. Well… You're going to have to leave it with me. Go home. Get some rest, okay? I'll see if I can find him."

Jay snorted. "Not bloody likely. I'm sticking with you."

Randall's ears flicked faintly, but it wasn't any use. Jay wouldn't be able to understand him.

"I can't work effectively with you on my arse," Barb snapped. "Do you want Ellis found or what?"

"I know you're vampires," Jay retorted. "You, Ellis,

Hughes. If that's what you're worried about, don't. I already know. Okay?"

Barb stared at him. "Are you the bloke Ellis wants to turn?"

"No." Jay shook his head. "That's my husband. He's dying. That's where I was earlier. I've been at the hospital with him all day and half the bloody night. I came to find Ellis because he's had a heart attack. I don't think he can wait much longer. Okay?"

Barb stood and wandered toward the window. She nudged the curtain aside and peeked out onto the street, then drew it closed again and walked toward the sofa, but she didn't sit. "Why would you trust me with this?"

"Because Ellis trusts you," Jay said.

"He's an idiot." She sighed. "If Hughes has taken him away it's because he's arrested Ellis. Probably for telling humans what he is, which means Hughes will be coming to arrest you, too."

Randall laid down slowly. Guilt gnawed at him and made his stomach churn.

Ellis had been arrested because Hughes *had* overheard him talking to Randall. And Randall had walked away from the place without any hesitation. A growl of anger rumbled in his chest.

"Oi," Barb said. "Yer dog's getting feisty."

"Shh." Jay leaned over and placed his hand on Randall's shoulder.

Randall's ears sank back, and he rested his chin on the ground. *Stay calm. Keep it together. You are an Alpha. You can do this!*

"What happens next?" Jay asked as he took his hand away.

"Ellis'll be held until the Council's ready to see him, and then they'll interrogate him and pass immediate sentence. If Hughes has assembled his evidence it won't take long, especially if that evidence includes the human he's spilled the beans to. Well done. You're an endangered species! And they won't be so gentle when it comes to interrogating you."

Jay gripped his knees. "Why not?"

"Because you're living, and that makes you disposable. You can be tortured into a confession and it doesn't matter if it breaks you so long as the Council gets what it wants out of you."

"What the fuck?" Jay shot to his feet.

"Hey, this isn't *my* opinion. It's theirs. This is the kind of crap you tell yourself once you're old enough to have seen everyone you grew up with die of old age. 'There's no need to treat them kindly, they'll all die sooner or later'." She crinkled her nose in disgust. "Shit, kiddo, why do you think we want to overthrow those dickheads?"

"But—"

"If he's told you who I am, he's told you what I want. I'm not naive. What's your name?"

"Jay."

"Hey, Jay. I'm Barb." She gestured to the armchair. "Sit down, you're making the place look well untidy."

Jay sank slowly, and Randall stood up to lean against his leg in a show of solidarity.

"They can't torture Ellis," she explained calmly. "Pain's weird for us. We kind of know it's there, but it's not something we have to pay attention to. We only get serious agony from the shit that runs the risk of killing us."

"Silver," Jay realised.

"That, sunlight, fire. The usual suspects," she agreed. "So having a human to torture is doubly effective, because if he gives a shit about you he'll spill the beans just to stop them hurting you. Anyway," she added, "this all becomes moot if the Council's feeling particularly malicious. Or lazy."

Randall's ears span forward again, and he watched Barb closely.

"Because torture isn't malicious?" Jay squeaked.

"Eh." Barb shrugged and finally sat again. "There's worse." She rubbed the back of her neck and looked away a while before she said, "If the Council wants the matter dealt with quickly they'll see if Devitt is available to assist."

"Never heard of him," Jay muttered. "Or her."

"Him." Barb looked Jay over and sucked air between her teeth. "He can make someone tell them whatever he wants to know. He controls thoughts. He gives orders and you follow and you ain't got a choice in the matter. If the Council wants to force a confession without any mess *and* if Devitt deigns to use his power over such a minor matter, then you might find yourself telling the Council everything Ellis has ever told you, and you'll be stuck there in your own body listening to all this stuff come out of your mouth, and there won't be a damn thing you can do to stop yourself."

Randall flexed his toes, then sat up. This was all taking so long. He itched with the need to take action, but they had no action to take.

"Where're they holding Ellis?" Jay bounced to his feet too, as though he took Randall's movement as a cue. "We have to go get him."

Barb laughed. "Are you mental? We can't break in there! No way!"

"So you *know* where he is?"

"You can't get in there," she said more slowly, like she thought Jay might need things spelled out for him. "Look. Maybe they'd be willing to let Ellis turn you to make sure no human knows about us, but then there's this husband of yours, so they'll question *him* to see whether you or Ellis told him any of this, and I'm guessing the answer's yes. They aren't going to let him turn two people. Then there's the boyfriend. If he knows as well that's three. They'll see this as out of hand and they'll just wipe the lot of you. If Hughes had a better nature we could maybe appeal to it, but he's seriously hardline. Has been ever since some shit in the Eighties."

Jay frowned. "What shit?"

"I dunno."

"Then it's useless." Jay shook his head. "Thanks for your time."

He strode for the door and Randall trotted after him. They were halfway down the stairs before Barb caught up.

"Fine. Fuck, I don't know what happened. It's only what I've heard," she said, her boots clattering down the stairs behind them. "He fell in love with some bloke he met in a nightclub and couldn't bear to be without him. You know, the usual bullshit you get with vampires. Sooner or later someone realises their mortal lover is gonna wither and die, you know?"

Jay slowed down, but he wouldn't stop. Randall had to dart past him or risk bumping into his legs. "So, what. Hughes turned this bloke?"

"Yeah. But he didn't get permission from the Council, so the Council destroyed the guy."

Jay stopped at the front door and finally turned back to look up at Barb. "I don't get it. Why didn't they kill Hughes too? Hell, isn't he a Constable now?"

Barb shrugged. "The way I heard it the Council offered him a deal. They'd let Hughes live if Hughes was the one to execute his lover."

"Oh my god!" Jay stared at her. "That's barbaric!"

"That's the fucking Council for you," she snapped.

Jay shook his head numbly and wrenched the door open. Randall scooted back as it swung toward his face.

On the doorstep stood Hughes. His colours were muted and shifted with Randall's wolf eyes, but the hair, the lean frame, the slightly outdated look were the same.

Jay froze.

"No," Hughes said idly. His eyes were cold, even though his voice was light. "That ain't what happened."

"Uh." Jay glanced quickly to Randall, then up to Barb.

Randall bristled. His hackles rose, and he stepped forward to bare his teeth to Hughes.

"Christ, you lot. You're like a fuckin' disease. You tell one guy what you are and suddenly the whole world knows it. You," he added, jabbing his finger toward Jay, "are fuckin' nicked, me ole china. And so are you," he added as he swung the finger to point at Barb. "I ain't a fan of makin' two arrests at a time, but let's see if we can get this done nice and neat, eh?"

NINETEEN

ELLIS BRIEFLY GAVE some consideration to the bucket, but he really didn't want to see whatever memories might be attached to it, so he remained at the bars. He shouted now and then, or tried to shake the door, but the futility of his situation was not lost on him.

"Hughes!" He yelled. He'd have to stop soon. His throat grew hoarse and healed itself, and he really should conserve his energy.

Did he hear something?

He stopped everything. He stood stock still and left his lungs empty. His head leaned against the bars as he strained to listen.

There.

A door. A lock.

Then there were footsteps. More than one person's, and not a single heartbeat between them.

Was Hughes coming to take him to the Council already? Ellis bit his lip. He'd hoped for more time, even though he didn't know what he might do with that time.

More doors. The footsteps came closer. Then they were in the chamber beyond his cell door, and the heavy door swung shut behind them. Metal scraped against metal and the door's lock thudded into place.

Ellis didn't speak. If Hughes was one of them he would identify himself.

He hoped.

"Ellis O'Neill."

It wasn't Hughes' voice. It was a man, and his voice was calm and indifferent, with a somewhat indefinable London accent to it. It wasn't east enough to be Cockney, and it wasn't west enough to be Sloane Ranger. It was more south, if anything, with a comfortable working-class flatness to the vowels.

Ellis had heard that voice before, but he was having a bugger of a time putting a name to it. "And you are?"

"Mark Dickens."

Ellis winced. Dickens. The name, the accent...

A Councillor. Dickens sat on the Council. Every year Ellis had to report to Aldwych to confirm that he existed, that his territory was Mayfair. He'd only done it once so far, after Jonas' death. He'd be due to do it again in a month or two.

"Councillor Dickens," Ellis said warily. "I was under the impression that I would be taken to the Council, not the other way around."

"Mr. Devitt has kindly offered to chivvy proceedings along for us. There's little point assembling the entire Council if Hughes has got the wrong end of the stick. Back away from the door, Mr. O'Neill."

Devitt.

Ellis tightened his grip on the bars. "Councillor—"

"Back away from the door," Devitt said.

Ellis jerked away from it. His body obeyed, and he took

three steps back even while his thoughts still reeled from the familiarity of Devitt's voice.

A key rasped in the lock and the hinges creaked as the door was pushed inward.

Devitt. Oh, Christ. The man who had forced Marcus to lie to the Council, and he was *here*. Ellis tried not to panic, but it was proving damned difficult.

Randall. Han. Jay. Barb. *Everyone* he knew was in danger now. One wrong word and they'd be tossed under the bus, and Ellis couldn't do a damn thing to stop it.

Except the door to his cell was open. He couldn't see it, but he'd built his map of the cell now. He knew where everything was.

He bolted. He sprang toward the door and ducked his head low to try and keep himself from falling if he bumped into anyone.

An arm like steel coiled around his waist and scooped him off the floor as though he were nothing more than a child's toy. For a moment he had the distinct fear that they had a werewolf with them, but the arm he grabbed at was clothed, not furred.

"This is Victor," Devitt said. He sounded bored. "Of our peculiar little smattering of gifts, his was the most absurd strength I have ever seen. Put Mr. O'Neill down, would you, Victor?"

Ellis found himself hurled at the ground, and had no time to prepare for impact. He smacked against the stone floor so hard that his shoulder dislocated and his arm broke. A stab of pain accompanied both, though it was abstract. Unimportant.

"Get up," Devitt ordered.

Ellis staggered to his feet. His arm knitted itself back together. His shoulder realigned itself, muscles dragging the bones back into place with a grotesque scraping sound.

"I am here as an impartial observer," Dickens explained, distaste and boredom in his voice.

"For?" Ellis croaked. Deep down, though, he knew the answer.

"Stand still, Mr. O'Neill," Devitt murmured. "Tell me what Constable Hughes arrested you for."

Ellis grit his teeth, but it was no use. He screamed, but nothing came out. He tried to move, but he was rooted to the ground. He tried to keep air from his lungs, but his chest rose regardless.

"Cannibalism," he hissed through clenched teeth.

"My god!" Dickens breathed.

"Is that so?" Devitt sounded intrigued. "And who does he propose that you partook of?"

"Jonas." Ellis grimaced as the name slid past his lips.

"And is he correct?" Devitt's voice was closer. Triumphant.

What the hell does he have to be so pleased about?

"Yes," Ellis groaned. "But *you* turned Marcus without the Council's—"

"Silence!"

Ellis' words dried up.

"Charles?" Dickens sounded confused.

"He's lying." Charles' smooth voice was confident. "My apologies, Councillor. Mea culpa. I won't allow him to speak out of turn again."

"I want to hear it." Dickens spoke quietly. "Make sure he tells the truth."

Ellis' insides clenched with hope. If a Councillor could hear the truth of what Devitt did, maybe he wouldn't need to speak to Hughes after all. He might be able to negotiate some sort of deal.

Maybe. But probably not. He *had* just admitted to eating Jonas.

"Very well." Charles paused. "Mr. O'Neill, be truthful. Tell Councillor Dickens why you believe I turned Marcus."

"The Council is aware of my power. Marcus was detained in this cell after he murdered someone in a club and threw their body onto the dancefloor." The words poured from him, but Ellis was grateful for them this time. This needed to come out. "Charles Devitt entered the cell and used his mind control on Marcus. He ordered Marcus to tell the Council that Aaron Hughes had turned Marcus. Marcus argued that it was Charles who had done it. He begged for Hughes to be left out of it, but Charles made him do as he was told. He made Marcus forget Charles ever came to his cell. I've seen it, Councillor. What I am telling you is the truth. I cannot lie."

"Yes, yes. Enough editorialising," Charles drawled.

"Devitt?" Dickens had stepped back. Keys jangled. "You're under arre—"

"Silence. Stand still."

Ellis strained to hear anything, but it was as though Dickens had ceased to exist.

"Well. This has become tiresome rather quickly, hasn't it?" Charles stepped closer to Ellis, and Ellis felt the glasses tugged from his face. It was too dark down here for their removal to make any difference.

He heard the swish of fabric. The air was disturbed an inch or two from his nose.

"Absurd," Charles muttered. "Tell me, how did you manage to defeat Jonas? You can't even see what's right in front of you."

Ellis bared his teeth. "He reeked of blood. He threatened my staff, my dog. The scent was maddening. He attacked me. We struggled. I couldn't possibly win. He smelled like he'd eaten half a dozen people before he turned up. I hadn't eaten in weeks. He would win a war of attrition. There wasn't any doubt." He drew a sharp breath. "Our bite paralyses humans. I wondered if it would work on our own kind, so I bit him."

"And you found that it does, I assume?"

"Aye." Ellis grimaced. "But I couldn't hold him there forever. And if I let him go he'd start on me again. It was a stalemate, unless I fed from him. I thought I'd take enough to even the odds, but the smell of the blood, and the taste of it... It wasn't like human blood. It was far more potent. And I just kept going, and then he was dust and that was almost the end of it."

He screwed his eyes shut. For fuck's sake! Everything he'd fought so hard to conceal and one conversation with this bastard was dragging it all out.

"Almost?" Charles was quiet a few moments, then added, "Explain what you mean by that."

"I have his power," Ellis blurted. He groaned and opened his eyes, begging silently to be allowed to stop. "Languages. I speak them all. Understand them all. I didn't have it until I consumed him, and now I do."

He heard a hiss from the far side of the room. Dickens? It had to be.

"Is that so?" Charles mused. "Fascinating. How long before this power manifested itself?"

"I don't know. I can't control it. It happens automatically. If someone speaks a different language it sounds like English to me, and when I answer *that* sounds like English too. Or... I don't know. I only worked it out when Barnes attacked me. He was speaking Polish the whole time and I never knew."

Ellis had a moment's clarity. He had held Barnes' painting in his hands and watched the man paint it. Now and then he'd seen a figure, a shadow in the darkness behind him while he worked.

"That was you," he breathed. "You sent Barnes to kill me."

"You are far too clever for an Irishman," Charles sniffed.

"Yorkshireman," Ellis corrected.

"Your name is Irish. You no doubt hail back to undesirable stock sooner or later. And crippled, to boot. What sort of fool turns a cripple? No, don't answer that." Charles sighed faintly. "You have Jonas' power," he added quietly. "Could it be so simple?"

"What?" Ellis whimpered.

"Is that why it's against the laws?" Charles stepped back again, then laughed. "All these years! All these years, and I never questioned it." Ellis heard a hand pat against a body. "Well, Councillor. It's been a pleasure. But please, allow me to express to you my fondest gratitude for stealing my seat, won't you?"

The sounds which followed were unforgettable. Wet. Sounds Ellis had heard before; sounds he had *caused* before, with Jonas' unresisting body beneath his fangs, and his blood gushing down Ellis' throat.

The reflexive swallows as mouthful after mouthful was consumed. The quivers of the victim, helpless to defend themselves as they were murdered one ounce at a time. And *god* it took so long. Ellis fought to move from his spot, to do *anything* to stop what he could hear, but he was still under Charles' sway.

Bodies thudded against stone. The feeding continued. Ellis tasted Dickens' blood on the air.

"Please," Ellis whispered. "Stop. For god's sake you're going to kill him!"

It was no use. Of course it was no use. The swallowing was insatiable. Unstoppable. Continuous.

Then in a single instant it was over. The last swallow. The rush of dust like falling sand, like the sound Ellis' arm made when it fell from his body, like the terrible end of Jonas' existence.

Then silence.

"No," Ellis sagged. "Oh, god, no!"

Dickens had been his hope. His one way out of this bloody hellhole. Whatever may have happened to Ellis, at least Charles would receive justice at last. But now that was gone. Turned to ash on the cold stone floor.

Charles' footsteps came closer. Ellis tried to recoil.

"When you go before the Council," Charles murmured, "you will confess to the cannibalism of Jonas *and* to that of Councillor Mark Dickens. You will tell them that Victor protected and evacuated me and that by the time he returned for the Councillor you had already destroyed him. You will tell them nothing else. You will not mention Marcus to them."

Ellis snarled. "You're a bastard, Devitt!"

"I am a survivor," Charles sneered. "And there appears to be a vacancy on the Council now. I think it is about time I recovered my seat. I look forward to seeing you again, Mr. O'Neill, and I look forward to hearing your confession."

TWENTY

RANDALL SNARLED. He didn't care whether it looked suspicious now. He couldn't let Hughes take Jay.

"Awright. Easy, tiger," Hughes muttered.

Barb clumped up the stairs at Randall's back. Jay shoved at the door.

Then Hughes wasn't there anymore. Jay thumped against the wall. Randall felt something clip his back, and his legs buckled. There was an almighty racket on the stairs.

By the time Randall whirled around, Hughes had Barb in a half-Nelson, and her face ground against the stair carpet.

"The fuck do you want, Constable?" Barb snarled into the worn pile. She writhed and bucked, but Hughes coiled around her like a snake.

"You," Hughes spat as he stared down the stairs at Jay. "Shut the door."

"You have got to be joking," Jay snapped.

"Shut it, or I'll pull her damn head off, then I'll catch you before you get a single foot outside this building."

Jay glanced down at Randall.

Randall hunkered down and lowered his tail. They needed Barb. She knew where Ellis was, yeah, but more than that she was Ellis' only ally in this viper's nest of vampires he was surrounded by. That made her Randall's only ally, too, and if they were to find Ellis before he got executed he needed her. He swivelled his gaze apologetically up at Jay and dipped his head.

Jay let out a frustrated little sound, like a toddler's tantrum, then he slammed the front door. "There! Now let her go!"

"Right." Hughes nodded. "Let's not have this out in the bloody stairwell, yeah? Think we can all get some privacy without drawing too much attention?"

Barb swore, so he dug his knee into her back.

"If you die resisting arrest," Hughes warned, "I am totally covered. There's provision for that in the laws. Get the fuck up and stop being such an arsehole."

Randall chuffed and slunk his way up the stairs. He picked his way past the vampires in the middle of the ascent and continued up to Barb's flat. She'd left the door ajar, so he nudged it fully open and stepped inside.

He heard Jay come up the stairs and stop. Then they all moved at once: the vampires scuffled to their feet and came clomping up to the flat, and Jay hurried after them. Hughes pushed Barb into the flat, and Jay nudged the door shut with his foot.

"The fuck are you doing here?" Barb snarled when he released her.

"Looking for the other one." Hughes approached Jay and nodded. "Where is he?"

Jay scowled. "Where's Ellis?" he snipped.

"The little black fella," Hughes said, speaking slowly. "Where is he?"

"I don't know who you're talking about." Jay raised his chin.

"You're both breakin' the fuckin' law in here," Hughes sighed. "Don't make like you haven't got a bloody pulse. I can 'ear it a mile away. You want me to break you just to get one little piece of information? Is that what it's gonna take 'ere?"

Barb glanced to Hughes, then toward the curtains. She sprinted for them like greased lightning.

Hughes was faster.

He was *impossibly* faster.

Randall's wolf eyes could see in more detail than his human ones, but they also saw more quickly. It wasn't that it made a huge difference, but it made looking at slower television screens with his wolf eyes a surreal experience of flashing still images, like some bizarre flip-book made of light.

He couldn't see fast enough to track Hughes, that was rudely apparent. Barb ran for the curtains, and then she was crashing to the ground again, with Hughes on her like an angry wildcat.

"Oh my god," Jay whispered.

The vampires wrestled, but Hughes had Barb's arms bent up behind her, and when she kicked out all she hit was the sofa.

"I'm gonna find him sooner or later," Hughes muttered. "You know that, right? Protecting him ain't gonna do him or you any good."

"What do you want him for?" Jay's voice shook as he spoke, and the poor man looked on the verge of collapse.

Randall wasn't surprised. Jay had been to hell and back, and he still hadn't slept. His husband was in the hospital, and the man who could save him had gone missing. He was in a small flat in Soho surrounded by monsters. But he still stood. Randall's admiration for the man climbed another notch, as did his determination to keep him alive.

"Because 'e's 'eard all this too. 'E knows stuff he shouldn't. Christ almighty." He climbed off Barb and hauled her to her feet.

"How'd you find us here?" Jay tried to look nonchalant. The dark circles under his eyes didn't help.

"Funny story, that. I dropped O'Neill off and came back, and there was you and the little bloke prancing around with O'Neill's dog. I follow, but you two go into a flat and only one comes out." Hughes looked to Randall. "And there's this ruddy great dog out of nowhere. I have a sniff 'round but the other bloke's disappeared, in't 'e? Not 'ide nor 'air of 'im. So I leg it after you, and you come right 'ere, to Applegate's flat. I stands around outside listenin' to you bang on about everything you really shouldn't know, as well as some prize idiot plan O'Neill's got for turning some other bloke, and I realise you lot are gettin' well out of hand."

Randall sat with a soft thump. His gut twisted. It couldn't be true, could it? Had Hughes been able to move so fast that they hadn't seen him in all that time? What the hell had he done? Run up and down like a lunatic just to keep within earshot of people who must have seemed like snails by comparison?

Jay shook his head weakly. "We'd've noticed you," he muttered. "You can't have."

Hughes snorted. "Nobody ever looks up in this city."

"You were on the *roofs*?" Jay blinked. "What the hell?"

Hughes shrugged. "Doesn't matter, does it? I'll ask one last time. Where's the little bloke?"

Randall stood and shook himself out. This would go

around in circles until Hughes dragged one or both of them away to wherever Ellis was imprisoned. Someone would probably be killed, and it was likely to be Barb, because Jay was more useful as a torture victim.

He wasn't going to let that happen.

He shifted. His muscles tore and healed. His bones splintered and realigned. His vision became fuzzy and filled with colour. His skin itched as his fur retreated through it. And then it was done.

Hughes stared at him with his lips parted. Barb's eyes were wide as saucers. Jay looked about ready to faint.

Randall pushed himself to his feet and raised his head. "Right," he said. "Why don't we sit down and talk this through like adults?"

"WELL," Hughes said faintly. "There's that, I suppose."

Barb's gaze roved down Randall's body and lingered. "You, er. You know you're butt naked, right?"

"Randall," Jay whispered loudly. "What are you doing?"

Randall raised his hands. He moved with care, as though he were addressing cornered animals. For all he knew, that might very well be the vampires' mindset right now. "Come on," he said gently. "Let's talk." He gestured to the sofa, then stepped backward toward it until he felt it against his calf.

"What exactly are you?" Hughes said, eyeing Randall warily.

"That's obvious, isn't it?" Randall slowly sat, then crossed his legs and gently eased a tatty old cushion into his lap, since Barb wouldn't stop staring. Now that he was in human form he could see that the sofa was a dreary shade of red. It might have been bright and bold thirty-odd years ago, but now it just looked tired. "I'm a shifter. I'm a werewolf. There. Now I've broken my rules too. Except you aren't human, and neither am I." He smoothed his hands across the cushion. "Tell us where Ellis is, yeah?"

Hughes narrowed his eyes and regarded Randall, then Barb. Finally he evaluated Jay.

You're outnumbered, Randall prayed he'd realise. *Stand down. Please.*

"You said Barb was wrong," Randall prompted. Perhaps if he could get Hughes talking about something else they could come back to Ellis' location. "Set the record straight, then."

"That's none of your business," Hughes scowled. But he moved over to take the armchair, and sank into it with a scowl on his face.

"Oh, shotgun!" Barb sprinted to the sofa and plopped down beside Randall.

Jay sidled around the sofa to Randall's side of it, evidently willing to use him as a shield against the vampires.

"Come on," Barb cajoled. "If I've got the wrong end of the stick about whatever happened with this Marcus bloke it's only fair you set me straight. You know, before you cart us all off for execution." She grinned. "Juicy deets, Hughes. Share 'em."

Hughes grit his teeth, then cracked his knuckles. "All right. But if I tell you, you come quiet. Deal?"

"Deal," Barb said, smiling sweetly.

Randall ran a hand over his hair, then nodded. "Okay, yeah. You've got a deal."

"Randall?" Jay said uncertainly.

He looked up at Jay and gave a slight nod. "Trust me."

Randall was ninety percent sure that whatever cell could hold Ellis wouldn't be able to hold him. Not in his biggest shape. He was a monster, without any doubt. He could tear doors from their hinges with barely any effort. Hughes arresting them and locking them up with Ellis was almost as good as Barb just telling them where to find him.

Jay's shoulders sagged. "Okay. Deal."

Randall mustered a brief smile, and turned his attention to Hughes.

"I met a guy," Hughes said quietly. "I was a right little shit when I was turned. I was all punk this and anarchy that. Middle finger to the Council, you know how it goes." He eyed Barb.

"I like where this is going already," she said.

"Yeah, well. Back then Charles Devitt ran everywhere from Covent Garden down to Westminster. He owned half the city, and he'd like sublet little parcels of his turf out for others to manage on his behalf. There was this club in Covent Garden. I loved the place. Proper decent vibe it had, and Charles would always be pissy that I was entering his territory without permission, but I was like 'fuck you, arsehole' and I kept going anyway." Hughes ran one hand along the arm of his chair, and gazed at his fingers blankly. "I met a lad there in 1983. He was... so beautiful. So absolutely perfect. And he was smart, too. Bright and quick and funny, and I loved him."

"Marcus?" Randall said softly.

"Yeah." Hughes looked to the curtains and his hand fell flat against the armrest. "I was an idiot. I told him what I was. I mean, that's just the kind of thing that comes out sooner or later when you love someone, innit?" He glanced pointedly across at Randall.

"Yeah," Randall admitted. "It is."

"Yeah." Hughes looked away again. "Then one night, Marcus got turned. I only found out last year what happened. It was Charles that done it. He reckoned he felt sorry for us, that Marcus'd get killed for what he knew just because we loved each other. Since Charles was on the Council, and he's got that mind control shit, he decided he'd turn Marcus, then convince the Council he'd had permission. Except—" Hughes broke off and raised his chin. "Marcus lost the lottery, din't 'e? It drove him 'round the bend. He went out to clubs and he'd just slaughter people right in the middle of 'em. Tore their throats out and drained 'em dry, started yelling 'e was a vampire there to kill them all. It was horrible." He closed his eyes a moment and rubbed at them.

"Oh, god," Jay whispered. He stepped around the sofa and over to Hughes' side. Then he placed his hand on Hughes' shoulder and squeezed. "I'm so sorry."

Hughes blinked up at Jay in shock, and Randall's heart went out to him at the look on his face. The poor thing suddenly seemed so fragile, like a man to whom compassion was almost alien.

"Thanks," Hughes whispered. He gripped the chair and shook his head slowly. "Um. Anyway. The Constabulary took Marcus in, and when he got dragged up in front of the Council he screamed that it was me what turned him. Swore point blank I was the one. I get hauled up there too, and my poor Marcus—" He faltered, then continued on. "God, he was in so much pain. Screaming, crying, he begged me to kill him, to put an end to it. Then in the middle of it all he screams it was Charles that turned him, and not me."

"Fucking hell," Barb muttered.

Hughes shrugged. "Marcus insisted it wasn't me. Then he was back saying it was. The Council ruled that it was just his insanity that made him blame me, and they said I should prove it wasn't me by being the one to execute him."

"What?" Randall blurted at the same time as Jay and Barb demanded the exact same thing.

"Marcus begged me to end his pain." Hughes shrugged. "I

had to. After all that, the Council decided that made me extra loyal or some shit and they promoted me. Made me a Constable. Charles lost his seat, 'cause Marcus had been so convincing, but he had enemies there who'd wanted an excuse to punt him off anyway so they took their chance."

"But this is bullshit!" Barb stood. Anger lined her features. Anger, and upset. "Why the hell would you take that promotion?"

"I'd just murdered the only person I loved," Hughes whispered. "I had to. I couldn't sit home every night just replaying..." He trailed off.

"What I don't follow," Randall said more kindly, "is why you would arrest Ellis for the crime you yourself committed. Why don't you tell the Council what you know? Tell them it was Charles who turned Marcus without their permission."

"Because he's got me by the short and fuckin' curlies," Hughes snarled. "I've bloody done it again, because I'm an idiot. I've got a human lover, and Charles bloody *knows*. He tried to kill him already, so we struck a deal. Charles leaves Jude alone, and I don't tell the Council what I know he did."

"Jesus," Randall murmured.

Barb leaned forward and planted her elbows on her thighs. "What if things were different?"

"Eh?" Hughes stared at her.

"What if it didn't have to be this way? Listen." She shook her head. "What if there wasn't any Council. Not like this. What if we had democracy? What if we had modern, fair laws? Laws that change with the times? What if the Council was voted for regularly, and it was their job to look after all of us, not just themselves?"

Randall bit his lip. Barb was taking a huge risk, but it wasn't his place to stop her.

Could it possibly pay off?

Hughes regarded her warily, then sat up slightly. "Sounds like anarchy," he said cautiously.

"I'm willing to bet it will be for a while, yeah," she agreed.

Hughes pressed his lips tightly together, then raised his chin. "I like anarchy. What're you suggesting?"

TWENTY-ONE

WITHOUT HIS WATCH Ellis had no idea how much time passed. He was so exhausted that he'd finally retreated to the bed, but even once he curled up on it with his back to the wall he didn't dare sleep.

The longer his incarceration dragged on, the less able he was to force himself to stay awake. The first time he caught himself dozing he'd started awake in a panic. By the third time he decided he might as well get some rest. Hughes couldn't take him during the day, but more importantly Charles couldn't come back to fuck with his head while the sun was overhead either.

Back when he'd been able to watch films and appreciate their cinematography he'd been particularly fond of a French classic, La Haine. It was starkly shot in black and white to emphasise the alienation of the protagonists from the city of Paris in which they lived, and one of the characters had told a joke which Ellis found of little comfort to him now.

Heard about the guy who fell off the skyscraper? On his way down, past each floor, he kept telling himself: so far, so good. So far, so good.

Well, Ellis thought grimly. Every hour which passed without a visit from either Devitt or Hughes? So far, so good.

Dozing made it even more impossible to keep track of the time. The temperature seemed constant, too, protected from being sun-warmed by the earth around it. He drifted in and out of awareness and kept his hands tucked up inside his jacket, trapped under his armpits in case he had another vision from the bloody bed while he wasn't prepared for it.

When he heard cautious footsteps, Ellis couldn't tell at first whether they were real or a dream. They were distant and faint, as though he were underwater, and he struggled toward consciousness because they were just too odd to ignore.

There was a pulse, too. Quick, and ever so quiet.

Ellis warily swung his legs from the bed. Was this someone who belonged here, or an intruder? He stood and made his way as quietly as he could to the cell door, and tipped his ear toward the sounds.

He heard a thud. Then a heavier one. Before he could work out what they might be, the next sounds were even more bizarre. There was a lot of rustling.

If he didn't know any better, he'd think someone was getting naked out there.

He considered backing away from the door, but then there were new noises. Sickening ones. Familiar, grotesque sounds of a body tearing itself apart and pulling itself back together.

"Randall?" Ellis strained to hear. "Randall!" he yelled. "I'm down here!"

He had a horrible thought for a moment that somehow it could be a different werewolf. If Briar had found him instead, shouting had just been his last mistake. But there was a growl of a response before that train of thought could go too far.

It's me.

"Thank god." Ellis sagged against the bars.

Wood cracked, and metal twisted. When the footsteps moved this time they were clearer, but also softer. Barefoot now, the boots abandoned somewhere.

Ellis brushed his fingers against the wall as he stepped away from the door, and continued all the way back to the bed as the sounds came closer. It was like a wrecking ball tore through the centuries-old structure, bearing inexorably down on his prison. He didn't want to be in the way when it finally arrived.

The footfalls were finally in the same room as him. Claws clicked against metal. The monster at the cell door growled a soft sound of triumph.

Ellis nodded. "I'm all right." To certain degrees of 'all right', but he didn't want to delve into that now. "Do whatever you need to, petal."

A growl rumbled in Randall's chest, deep and angry. Metal grated in protest. The growl slowly became a snarl, and Ellis winced as he heard muscles strain and tear.

And then, suddenly, with a sound like a distant crack of thunder followed by a rain of dust, something gave way. Metal clanged against stone and skipped over it before it ground to a halt.

"Christ." Ellis felt his way toward the door. There was grit underfoot as he reached it. He raised a hand, and Randall's massive paw brushed across his palm.

He sagged and hurried out of the cell, leaning against Randall's powerful forearm and feeling for the door in passing. It felt intact, and Ellis supposed that instead of the metal it had been ancient stone and mortar which had given way.

Randall tugged him away from the cell and over uneven floor made even more treacherous by broken wood littered across it. Then he paused and shifted back down to something more human and panted "I thought we'd never see you again."

"We?" Ellis gripped Randall's elbow, then drew him into a tight hug. "Later," he added. "And as much as I'm enjoying pressing meself up against your naked self, maybe we should get to wherever you ditched your clothes?"

Randall laughed faintly. "Yeah. It's daylight out. Are you ready for it?"

"I could use a top-up. They knocked me about a bit." Ellis grimaced. "Have we got time?"

"Do what you have to." Randall's voice was tight, and his arms curled around Ellis' body as though the werewolf could protect him from whatever he'd gone through during the night.

"I'm sorry." Ellis bowed his head to Randall's shoulder, then kissed his way toward the werewolf's neck.

Randall's chest heaved. His fingers clutched at Ellis' jacket, and his cock stirred against his thigh. He groaned — such a sweet, desperate little sound — and tipped his head to the side to give Ellis room.

God, the shifter was a horny little minx. Ellis hadn't even pierced the skin and he was already getting himself worked up.

"Quickly," Randall whispered.

Ellis' fangs descended as though they were responding to Randall's plea more than Ellis' own will. They sliced through skin and kept Randall's body from healing itself around the intrusion, and he pressed his tongue against flesh, lips over skin, and began to suck softly.

Randall's ragged breath was his only sound now as he stood helpless. This powerful creature succumbed to Ellis' mouth and the only response from him was a rapidly increased hardening of his cock until it dug against Ellis' body, proud and insistent.

The blood was exquisite. Ellis had no other word for it.

Randall's blood was vital, full of power and life, thick like honey and every bit as sweet. It took only a handful of swallows to make Ellis feel as though he too were still living.

But there was no harm taking just a little *more*, was there?

Ellis groaned and pressed against Randall's hard, stocky frame. He traced his hands over perfectly-formed biceps, smooth and warm yet curved with underlying muscle. His touch drifted to Randall's chest and pressed against his pectorals, where the shifter's nipples were tight and hard against his palms.

He dropped a hand down between them and curled fingers around Randall's shaft. It was hot and heavy in his palm.

Randall's breath carried a weak moan.

Rescue, some small part of Ellis' brain screamed at him. *This is supposed to be a bloody rescue! You can't fuck in the corridor!*

Ellis snarled softly, then withdrew his fangs and exhaled across Randall's skin. The shifter didn't need Ellis' help to close a wound, but it was habit now, and not one to forget.

"Jesus fuck," Randall whimpered. "I want you."

"I'm going to fuck the living daylights out of you," Ellis whispered roughly. "But not here, eh?" He unfurled his fingers with a great deal of reluctance.

"Oh, god. Yeah. We've gotta go!" Randall pulled back from him and Ellis heard him grunt as he dressed as fast as he could.

He bit his own lip and kept his hands to himself. The mental image of two people fleeing through Hyde Park with raging erections didn't help him any, though.

HIS SKIN ITCHED in the morning light, which was bright

enough to make Ellis' world a dim grey as they hurried through the park.

"Ah, shit," he hissed as he tried to push up sunglasses which weren't there. "My phone, my watch... Everything's back there!"

"We can't stop," Randall whispered, his voice strained. His mind was no doubt still on Ellis' declaration of intent.

"It's a few hundred bob's worth of kit—"

"No," Randall interrupted. "Hughes said we'd only have a fifteen-minute window of opportunity. We can't go back, the porters'll be there by now."

None of that made any sense, but Ellis had a bugger of a time choosing which part to pick on first. Finally he went for "Where was I being held?"

"It's a church. W8," he explained.

Ellis squinted as he tried to place the postcode. "Kensington?"

"Yeah. There's like this whole underground part to it. During the day the hall down there gets used as a community centre, so pretty soon someone's going to find their ancient doors have been wrecked."

Ellis snorted a brief laugh. "You mean if I'd stayed there all day I would've heard yummy mummies doing their morning yoga?"

"Yeah, probably. I didn't stop to check the schedule, though." Randall chuckled. "Hughes says it used to be a monastery a few hundred years ago. One of those weird Orders who liked to have their monks sleep in tiny windowless cells way underground. The Council's got places like it dotted all over the city that they have access to, apparently. That one was the nearest to where he picked you up, so that's where he took you."

"Areet." Ellis nodded to himself. "That leads nicely into my other question, then."

"Hughes?" He heard Randall snort. "Git tried to arrest us."

"I get the feeling there's a long story here." Ellis grit his teeth as he heard an early morning commuter talking loudly into his phone from a hundred yards away, and tried to shut out the chatter about meetings and sales targets. "How'd you go from that to him telling you where to find me?"

"Barb's recruited him." Randall sounded like a man whose grin could only be described as shit-eating.

Ellis listened intently as Randall outlined the evening's events: Ellis' failed return, Randall and Jay's search for him, their talk with Barb, and finally Hughes attempting to arrest them all for talking about vampires.

"Wait." Ellis rubbed his forehead, but it made his skin itch all the more, and he forced himself to stop. "You were a wolf?"

"Yeah, uh. I had to change back and get them all to stop fighting," Randall muttered.

"So now Barb and Hughes both know you're a werewolf," Ellis concluded.

"Yup. But I think that's what tipped Hughes over into talking things through. I reckon he didn't fancy the idea of trying to take three of us at once."

Ellis tipped his head. "Aye. He doesn't like making multiple arrests at once." He swore, and added, "I need to speak to him. There's something he should know."

"It'll have to wait," Randall said. "He won't be up for hours yet. Which gives you more than enough time to screw my brains out."

Ellis had to admit that Randall's reasoning was highly persuasive.

TWENTY-TWO

WHEN THEY REACHED THEIR FLAT, ELLIS' skin had
gone from itchy to downright uncomfortable. The air outside
had that cold, crisp feel to it that suggested a very bright
morning winter sun was in a clear sky, and he hated to think
what this might be like when summer rolled around.

Randall ushered him inside and closed the front door, and
Ellis hurried to the stairs, only to be forced to wait outside his
own front door for Randall's keys.

Once inside, he picked out Tiberius' heartbeat and smiled.
"Tiberius!"

The dog clamoured across the floor, his heavy tail swishing
as it wagged, and his wet tongue was on Ellis' hands. Ellis
sank to his knees and wrapped his arms around the German
Shepherd, half hugging and half making a fuss of him. "Good
boy! You're such a good boy! Did they look after you? I bet
they did!"

Tiberius wriggled and whined in his excitement.

Ellis listened to his dog's happiness and let it surround
him. Forced to trust Tiberius' safety to Hughes, and then to

Randall's ingenuity, it was an enormous sense of relief to find that neither had let him down. Tiberius wasn't only a working dog. He was a friend, a protector, and part of the family. The thought of losing him had already driven Ellis to kill once before.

When had this happened? When had he become someone who genuinely thought that the death of his adversaries was a valid option?

Ellis sat back on his heels and petted Tiberius' ears. "What time is it?"

Randall's clothing swished softly against itself. "Just gone eight. In the morning," he added. The werewolf stepped closer. More of his clothes swished, then landed softly against the floor.

Ellis urged Tiberius to go back to bed, then stood and patted himself to try and dislodge dog fluff. He had no idea whether he was successful. "Are you stripping off?"

"Yeah." Randall moved closer, and the more distinctive sound of denim bunching together before it, too, hit the floor. "Question is why aren't you?"

"Well, I—"

He was cut off by Randall's lips crushing against his. The werewolf's body pressed into him, and his breath poured into Ellis' mouth, flowed across his cheek. Hands grasped his shirt and tore at the buttons, and he stumbled back into a wall, where Randall pinned him.

The effect on his cock was instantaneous. He hardened under Randall's insistence, and the echoes of his earlier desire flooded through him, sweeping his jumbled thoughts and tired fear aside.

Randall's lips broke free as the shorter man shimmied down his body. Fingers hooked into his waistband and unbuttoned it, then dragged down the zip of his fly, and by the time Randall's lips passed over Ellis' belly button his trousers and boxers had been yanked down to his knees.

"Jesus, El," Randall whispered. His breath coursed over Ellis' shaft. "You've got a beautiful cock."

Ellis felt for Randall's shoulders, but before he could find them Randall's tongue flicked the tip of his slit, and his knees buckled. Only the wall saved him from collapse.

"How long have I got to wait before you'll fuck me with it?" He slid his lips over the head and wrapped them tightly around Ellis' shaft, and his tongue pressed against the underside as Randall's mouth took him in, inch by inch, all heat and wetness and eager little breaths.

Ellis growled and finally found Randall's shoulders. His fingers dug in. He eased a foot back to regain some measure of stability, then began to slowly thrust over Randall's tongue. "Not much longer," he managed to spit, "if you keep this up."

Randall's whine of desperation clenched at Ellis' insides. That a man as wonderful, as beautiful, as downright *powerful* as Randall would be on his knees begging to be fucked did things to him he couldn't begin to understand. This man had ripped an iron door out of solid stone. He'd torn through doors hewn from solid hardwood and which had stood for centuries. All that strength, and here he was with his lips nestled in Ellis' pubic hair and Ellis' cock rammed deep down his throat, and he wanted more. He *begged* for more.

Ellis dragged a hand up to Randall's hair. It was wonderfully textured, so short and dense, so completely different from his own. His fingers cupped the back of Randall's head and — just for a moment — he held tight.

He could feel Randall's throat swallow around his head. He could even feel the pressure against his tip as Randall tried to exhale.

That was the last straw. He released his hold and let

Randall breathe, then pulled free of his mouth and sank down before him.

"Get on your front," he snarled.

He heard Randall swallow, and his heart thud. "Right here?" There was such an adorable quiver to his question.

"Right here," he agreed.

"Oh, god." Randall moved, and Ellis followed the motion with his hands.

He leaned forward as his touch trailed first down Randall's arms, and then to his back as the shifter rolled onto his front.

Ellis crawled over Randall's prone form and pushed his knees apart.

"Fuck me," Randall whined. "Do it hard, El. Please."

Ellis couldn't wait to be asked twice. He took his cock in hand and found Randall's crease with it, then bowed over him and kissed his shoulder as he teased and taunted himself as much as he did Randall.

Randall pushed himself back. He didn't wait. He didn't give Ellis the chance to get any more lubrication than the saliva which coated him. His ass engulfed Ellis' head in one swift motion, and it was all Ellis could do to stay still, to resist the need to thrust into that eager arse.

"Ellissss!" Randall continued to push. "Shit, you're... *unh*... so... damn... *good*."

Ellis growled and thrust himself as deep as he could. He wrapped an arm around Randall's waist, and another under his armpit and up over his shoulder.

A pressure built deep within him. As he drove himself into Randall's welcoming heat, he felt that pressure well up and expand, and if he didn't let it out it was going to drown him.

His knees burned against the carpet, and he didn't care. The only thing that mattered now was the warm body in his arms, the tightness of the muscle around his cock, the cries of pleasure Randall made.

Randall bucked and fell out of rhythm. He howled. His insides gripped like a vice, and the air became sharp with the scent of his cum.

It was too much to bear. The pressure deep within Ellis surged, and then he was falling. His cock twitched, his juices slicked Randall's insides and filled him.

The dam burst with release, and Ellis collapsed over Randall's back. He lay, boneless and complete, and basked in the warmth of his lover's body.

They hadn't even made it as far as the living room.

THEY SHOWERED AND DRESSED. Randall was adorably tactile, touching Ellis as much as he could, stealing kisses and brushing against his chest every other minute.

Ellis would be lying if he'd claimed he didn't enjoy it.

"We'll have to go east," Randall said as he made himself toast for breakfast. "Hughes says once they realise you're out they'll hunt for you. If we can get you to Tower Hamlets my pack can protect you."

Ellis wore his spare glasses. They usually hid in his bedside table, and they felt heavier than his normal pair. "They going to be areet with that?"

"I'll have to ask."

Ellis scratched his stubble slowly. He didn't like the idea of passing through unknown territories, but to stay in one seemed a whole lot worse.

"Oh." Randall hesitated, then the toaster popped. Ellis listened as a knife scraped over two slices, and then the knife slid into the sink. "I, uh. I should have mentioned something else, too."

Ellis frowned. "This doesn't sound at all ominous," he murmured. "What is it?"

Randall padded through to the living room in socked feet and settled lightly on the sofa by Ellis' side. "Jay came to look for you last night," he began cautiously, "because Han's situation…"

Ellis turned toward him urgently. "What?"

Randall swallowed, then took a quick breath. "Han… had a heart attack last night. He's alive," he added quickly. "He's in intensive care—"

Ellis' jaw worked as he tried to find the words. How could Randall have left this out earlier? Did he not think it was important? Did he just not *care*?

"Where's Jay?" he breathed.

"With Han. Once Hughes came up with the plan there wasn't any need for Jay to stick around, so he went back to the hospital." Randall sounded meek, at least. Contrite.

The door buzzer sounded. Ellis ignored it.

"My priority was to get you out safely," Randall added. "Jay said he'd be in touch to let us know what he needed."

"What if he tries my phone?" Ellis stood quickly.

"El, it's okay. He knows my number. He'll be in touch. He promised."

The buzzer sounded again.

"Shall I get that?" Randall added. He sounded eager to have his attention dragged elsewhere.

Ellis grit his teeth, then nodded. "It might be Jay."

Randall's footsteps padded softly toward the door. Ellis heard him chew and swallow toast as he went, then there was a click.

"Hello?" Randall said.

"Where's Ellis?" barked a familiar voice. Ellis heard it in stereo: once from the doorstep downstairs, and an echo of it through the tinny intercom speaker. "Ellis? I know you're in there, you little shitweasel! You don't get out of bed until noon!"

Ellis felt like he'd been doused in ice water. "You have got to be joking," he whispered.

"Open this damn door," Edison snapped, "or I'll press every bloody buzzer until *someone* lets me in!"

TWENTY-THREE

ELLIS SHOOK his head frantically at Randall.

"Ellis isn't here," he heard Randall say. "He's at work—"

"No he bloody isn't, I just came from the gallery! Do you want me to piss off all the neighbours? Ellis, open the damn door!"

"Hang on." The button clicked as Randall lifted his finger from it. "Shall I go let him in?"

Ellis paced and shook his head. "Shitting hell, we don't have time for this!"

"Is there an emergency exit?"

"The window?"

Randall snorted. "I think it might be a bit suspect if we both survive a three storey drop onto the pavement."

Ellis could hear Edison's fist against the front door, then the buzz of another apartment's intercom. "He isn't going to give up," he groaned. "He'll be on the doorstep all day if he has to."

"Want me to call the police?" Randall offered.

It was tempting. Sorely tempting. But Ellis didn't like

having to involve himself with the police if he didn't need to. It was one thing to run through a park jacked up on werewolf blood in the middle of December, but what if something ended up needing him to spend days on end in court during the height of summer? No, it was better to just stay under the police radar as much as he could.

"Better let him in," Ellis sighed.

He felt Randall's touch, and then the warmth of his soft lips against Ellis' own, but they were gone too quickly. Randall's boots patted their way down the six flights of stairs.

"Edison O'Neill?" Ellis heard him ask.

"Aye. Get out of the way."

Ellis grimaced. Edison had always been the bolshy one. The oldest of three brothers and the only one who could remember what their mother looked like, Edison had wanted to follow in dad's footsteps for as long as Ellis had lived. Ellis was pretty sure his eldest brother's first words were things like *subpoena* and *habeas corpus*.

Two sets of sounds hurried up the stairs. Randall made it to the door first and clattered through it with a jangle of keys.

Ellis grabbed the back of his armchair and gripped it with both hands. He felt the need for some sort of physical barrier, and had a moment's silent debate with himself on whether it may have been better to still be stuck in a cell.

"You're a slippery get, Ellis," was Edison's idea of a greeting.

"Good to see you too. How was the journey?" Ellis didn't even attempt to keep the sarcasm from his voice.

"Shite. Train was delayed for over an hour. Hotel's passable. Nice flat you've got here." His last sentence bore a sneer.

Edison had retained much more of his Yorkshire accent than Ellis. While Ellis only slid into it when he stopped concentrating on fitting in with the Londoners, Edison still lived up North and still had the strong accent which Ellis obviously hadn't noticed while he still lived there, but suddenly in his flat ten years after he'd moved to London was like a blast from the past.

"Dad's sent papers," Edison said. Buckles unfastened and soft leather whispered through them.

"Oh that's great. What am I supposed to do with them?"

"In braille, smart-arse." The sound of a heavy envelope thudded against the coffee table.

Ellis' retort was cut off before he could even begin. Randall's phone rang, the jangling ringtone loud enough for the werewolf to hear it on busy London streets.

"Sorry," Randall mumbled. "Oh. I gotta take this. Hey, Jay!"

"Who the hell's this bloke anyroad?" Edison muttered as he came closer to Ellis. "Turned out to be a poofter, did you? Is this yer boyfriend?"

"Randall! Did you get Ellis? Is he okay?" Jay's voice was easily audible from Randall's phone, but Ellis had to concentrate to pick it out over Edison's insults.

"Yeah, he's here," Randall said softly. "In and out, just like Hughes said."

"Hey. I'm talking to you." Edison was right beside him now, and Ellis cursed himself for letting his brother sneak up on him.

"Not really," Ellis muttered. "You're talking *at* me. Yes, I'm gay. Yes, he's my lover."

Edison snorted. "Da' won't be pleased."

"When is he ever?"

"—need him like yesterday. How long will it take you to get here?"

"Are you at Guy's?" Randall murmured.

"No. Han discharged himself. I couldn't stop him. We're in his office."

"I don't know—" Randall began.

"I know where it is," Ellis interrupted. "Tell him we'll be right there."

Everyone spoke at once, then. Jay had begun to recite the address. Edison wanted to know where that non-sequitur had come from. Randall was trying to repeat what Ellis had asked him to.

Ellis' grip on the back of the armchair tightened.

He didn't have time for any of this. The Council would discover him gone, and there didn't seem to be any plan to make that problem go away. Was he supposed to hide out with werewolves for two or three months until Barb got her revolution underway? That didn't seem feasible. Christy couldn't possibly run the gallery herself. She wasn't remotely able to make purchasing decisions, let alone put in the hours it would require to run it as a one-woman show.

He didn't have a million pounds loitering around, either. Thank heavens dad had at least said he could have it interest-free, because ten years of interest on that kind of sum didn't bear thinking about. He couldn't be angry that his father had got sick of waiting for it, either. That had to be one hell of a chunk of change even for a man as wealthy as he was.

Ellis frowned and forced himself to release the armchair. He faced toward Edison and lifted his chin. His brother was an inch or so taller than Ellis himself, and while Ellis couldn't see him, he had an extremely vivid picture in his mind, though he realised with a pang that even that picture had to be out of date by several years now. He'd last seen Edison at the man's wedding, and that had been seven years back.

"Why doesn't dad just knock it out of the inheritance?" Ellis suggested.

"Maybe he'd like to spend his own money while he's still alive? Maybe once he finds out you're a woofter he'll not want to leave you a penny anyway? Who knows?" Edison sniffed. "Not my problem, is it? I'm just down here to get you to sign a repayment agreement."

"He looks really bad," Jay whispered, as though afraid Han might overhear him. *"Hurry. He shouldn't even be here, but he isn't listening to me."*

"We'll be right there," Randall promised.

"I have to go," Ellis said.

"No, we're going to sit down and go over this paperwork, and if you need changes made I'll get them made, but I have to get your signature before I head home." Edison was firm. The man was a practising solicitor, for crying out loud.

Taking a stand and arguing well ran in the family. Negotiation, reading a situation, understanding the flow of influence in a room and taking advantage of it were all skills Ellis had learned at home, whether he liked it or not. Edison and Elijah had both followed in dad's footsteps, but Ellis hadn't missed out on the education. He'd just applied it differently.

"Ellis," Randall said calmly. "Jay needs you."

"Aye." Ellis nodded. "Let's go."

Fingers closed around his arm. "You can do that later, Ellis. First we sit down and go over the terms and conditions. The quicker you sign this stuff the faster I can be out of your hair. And that's a lot of hair. Do they not have barbers down here?"

Ellis bared his teeth. "Let go of me." He spoke slowly, his voice soft.

Edison hesitated, then his grip withdrew. "Come on. Sit down and we can get through the paperwork in well under an hour, then I'll be gone."

Randall cleared his throat.

Ellis turned toward the werewolf and lifted his eyebrows.

"I don't think," Randall said gently, "Jay can wait."

"I'm inclined to agree." Ellis stepped back from the chair, then moved past Edison and toward his desk. It was set up against the wall furthest from the window, and he trailed a hand against the wall once he'd counted the right amount of steps to reach it. Three more and he felt for the desk, then found the middle drawer and felt inside for his cane.

He didn't often use the cane. Now he had Tiberius there was no need for it, so it lived in his drawer and remained largely forgotten, but he preferred to take it with him in case they went straight from Han's onward to Randall's pack. Stumbling around the east end without it had been downright miserable. His fingers slid across the smooth aluminium tubing and he withdrew it, then unfolded it. Each segment slotted neatly into the next and held fast by strong elastic cord, and he nudged the drawer closed once it was done.

"Right," he decided. He faced Randall. "We go to Jay and do what we have to. Then you drop me off and come back here for Tiberius. If Jay can look after him for a while that'd be great. We'll work that out when we get there."

Edison took a deep breath, then released it slowly.

"Okay." Randall came towards him and drew his fingers softly over Ellis' palm before he turned his own hand away.

Ellis' touch fell to the back of Randall's hand, and he slid it up the werewolf's arm until he could nestle fingers comfortably in the crook of Randall's elbow. "Let's go."

"Ellis!" Edison bellowed.

Ellis winced. That sort of shouting might work well in a courtroom, but it was horribly invasive in his own home. "No, Edison. I'm too busy, and I do *not* have time to sit around reading paperwork. A friend of mine is dying. Do you understand? He has a heart disease and he is *dying*, and I am not going to haggle over repayment terms and whatever other gobshite is in those documents while Han has another damned heart attack. So if you really damn well want to you can shut the hell up and come with me, or you can take dad's stupid documents back to your hotel and wait for me to contact you, but I will *not* be delayed any more. Is that clear?" He gestured toward the door with his cane and nodded to Randall. "Let's go."

Randall began to move. He led Ellis toward the door and paused to open it.

Edison's footfalls hurried to the coffee table. The folder scraped softly over the wooden surface, and then Ellis heard it return to the satchel Edison had removed it from and the buckles fasten. Then Edison chased them to the door. "I'm coming with you," he stated.

Randall took in a sharp little breath. "Are you sure about this?" he asked quietly.

"No," Ellis muttered. "But I'm not in the mood to let him waste any more of our time."

The door closed, and they began their way down the stairs.

"How long is this likely to take?" Edison demanded.

"I don't know," Ellis barked. "I don't care. And don't blame me if, as of about now, your life turns to ratshit. I gave you the option to go back to your hotel and wait this out. Just remember that, Edison. And if you start screaming, I'll ask Randall to punch you until you stop."

"Why the hell would I scream?"

Ellis shook his head. "God I'm going to enjoy saying 'I told you so'."

TWENTY-FOUR

HAN'S OFFICE WAS, thankfully, north of the river. The address was close to Blackfriars train station, in a building Ellis remembered as a fairly squat three-storey thing with one-way glass. Most of the offices nearby were in converted old houses, but some had been purpose-built, and Han's was of the latter variety.

The trouble with one-way glass was that it was nice and reflective to the outside world regardless of whether it was mirrored or simply darkened. Randall had the taxi drop them right at the front door, but it was something Han would have to take into account if he chose to go through with Ellis' offer.

Edison had tried to get Ellis to read during the taxi ride, but Ellis had steadfastly ignored him. He'd sat in silence instead, fingers sometimes drifting to his wrist only to remember that his watch was gone. Christ, he hoped Hughes knew where everything was, because that would be a pain in the backside to replace.

The taxi stopped, and Ellis heard the handbrake. When he also heard the Velcro of Randall's wallet, Ellis slipped quietly out of the cab and used his cane to guide him a foot away, silently hoping that he wasn't too obvious. The pavements around here weren't all that broad, so he had very little space to hide in.

Edison was next out. "It's like a bloody maze," he grunted. "I don't know how as you find your way around these parts."

Ellis shrugged. "I don't know what you're complaining about. You can see where you're going."

"You're on Disability, aren't you? And I suppose your boy toy gets a carer's allowance."

"No, he doesn't. Don't be ridiculous. He runs his own business."

"Oh, then maybe *he* can repay—"

"Will you shut up," Ellis snarled, "for five fucking minutes?"

Edison clicked his tongue. "I'll let you have that one," he finally groused. "But only 'cause your mate's in a bad way."

"Christ on a bike," Ellis muttered. "Hurry up, Randall, before I have to kill him."

"You bloody wish."

Randall's boots landed against the pavement and the cab door slammed shut. "You know what? If you don't kill him, I damn well will."

Edison spluttered.

"I have never loved you more," Ellis said as he took Randall's arm.

JAY CAME DOWNSTAIRS to meet them and get them past security. Ellis heard the disdain once he told Jay that the stranger with him was Edison, and Jay kindly offered Edison the opportunity to remain in the foyer. Naturally Edison refused, as though afraid that once Ellis was out of his sight he'd be unable to find him again.

It was a reasonable fear. If Ellis had the opportunity to give Edison the slip he had no doubt he'd take it, just to be rid of the obnoxious bastard.

They took the lift up to the third floor and Jay hurried them through a bustling office. Ellis wouldn't strictly use the word *busy* to describe it, as he easily made out the sound of three different videos (one of which was most certainly the adorable squeaking of kittens), two non-work conversations (last night's television and weekend plans), and one phone call to a landlord (the rent will be there next week, honest). Jade Enterprises obviously slowed down before Christmas. Still, Ellis supposed that a lot of offices did.

His attention focused the moment he picked up one pulse that didn't fit in, and he quickened his pace.

It was a stumbling thing, this heartbeat. It limped along, one weak beat chasing on the heels of every strong one. Half that heart wasn't pulling its weight, and the sound felt wrong to Ellis on an entirely instinctive level, as though some part of him — some awful, predatory part that he wished he could ignore — had marked the owner of that heart as easy prey.

He wondered whether this was what it was like to be a lion on the Serengeti. Did they feel this laser focus the moment they picked a weak antelope from the herd? The young, the injured, the easily-felled...

"Ellis?" Han said. "Who's your friend?"

Ellis stopped abruptly and tightened his grip on his cane. God damn it he'd been away with the fairies again. "Is the door closed?"

"Yeah," Randall murmured.

"I'm Edison O'Neill," Edison announced. He breezed past Ellis and toward Han.

"Uh huh. Ellis, what's he doing here?" Han's question came in a terse breath. A difficult breath.

"He wouldn't damn well leave me alone. What are *you* doing here? You're supposed to be in the hospital, Han."

"Oh do *not* get me started!" Jay said wearily.

Randall moved. Ellis hoped he had reason to, and retained hold of his arm. When his cane bumped against something metal he nodded faintly and thanked Randall, then released him and moved his hand to find the back of the chair he'd been led to instead.

"I had to—" Han paused for breath "—get Jay set up. In the system. And test his access."

"All right," Ellis said quietly. "I assume I'm here because you want to go ahead with this?" He faced the last location Han's voice had come from.

"I don't have a choice."

Ellis shook his head. "You're the only one here who does, Han. It's all down to you. But there's a problem."

Han sighed. "Of course. What is it?"

"As of about eight this morning I'm a fugitive." He ignored Edison's sharp breath. "If you get caught they'll destroy you without any hesitation whatsoever."

Han snorted. "I thought they would anyway."

"Aye." Ellis paused and listened to Han's erratic pulse.

That wasn't a heart which had much left to give. Ellis wasn't a doctor, but he was surer of this knowledge than he was of anything else right now. Han was dying, and it was no longer some abstract fact or talk of an unknown future. It was something which was in progress right now, as they talked. Ellis didn't know how long it might take, but he was certain Han wouldn't make it to the end of the week like this.

"You're a hundred percent?" he finally added.

"Can you do it now," Han answered, "or do we have to wait until tonight?"

"Now is fine."

"What the hell are you two even talking about?" Edison muttered.

"Jay," Ellis said. "Can you lock the door? And if there are blinds, close them. Otherwise do whatever you have to to stop anyone out there getting a look in here."

"I'm on it." Jay hurried to the door.

"Randall, petal?"

"Yeah?"

"If Edison so much as squeaks, start punching him until he shuts the hell up."

"I'd love to," Randall growled.

"Edison?"

"What?"

Ellis shook his head. "Keep quiet. I mean it. I'm not asking. Not a damn sound out of you until I'm done. Han?"

"I'm here," Han murmured.

"Areet." Ellis stepped away from the chair with care and used can and hand to feel his way toward Han's desk. Once he had it, he was able to use the edge to guide himself around to Han's side of it.

His thigh stopped against Han's and he folded his cane, then set it on the desk. "Have you got room on your desk to lie down?"

"Not really," Han said. "There's stuff all over it."

"Right. On the floor with you, then."

"Can we not just do it here?"

Ellis shrugged. "Here's the thing. When someone dies, all their muscles relax. Either you fall out of your chair, or we start off with you on the floor and save me the effort of trying to get you there without banging you up."

Han laughed weakly. "I'll be dead, right? Will it really matter? Okay. Fine. God, this is weird. Hang on."

Ellis listened as Han's chair rocked on its castors and his body eased to the carpet.

"What the hell is going on?" Edison whispered.

Ellis turned faintly toward his brother. It was enough to indicate that he'd heard, and Randall cleared his throat.

"Fine," Edison muttered. "Not a bloody word."

"Jay?" Ellis asked.

"Coast is clear," Jay murmured. "Nobody's getting in, nobody can see in."

Ellis slipped his glasses off so that they wouldn't dig in to Han's face. He didn't want the man he was about to kill to be any more uncomfortable than necessary.

He eased down to his knees and used the back of his hand to find Han's arm, then worked up to his shoulder. "You're shaved? Happy with your hair? Your nails are okay? Nothing ingrown you want to take care of first?"

Jay laughed weakly. "We stopped at the barber on the way here." He hurried closer and sank down the other side of Han's body. "This is such a weird day." Skin slid against skin. "Are you okay, sweetie?"

"I'm lying on the floor of my own office waiting for my best friend to kill me," Han wheezed.

"Areet." Ellis leaned in slightly. "This is going to be horrible. I don't want to sugar-coat it. It'll feel amazing, and then your brain will realise that you're dying and there won't be a damn thing you can do about it. You can't move. You can't make a sound. You'll be paralysed for the duration, and you'll have another heart attack. You've done that once already and woken up after, aye? You are going to be all right. But when your brain knows you're dying, its only goal is to try and get you to save yourself and you can't."

Han let out a slow breath. "Yeah. Okay. Do your worst. I'm ready."

Ellis placed his hand on Han's chest. There was the soft silk of a tie, so he found the knot and loosened it. He unbuttoned Han's shirt collar. It felt intimate, and that wasn't a word he liked to apply to anyone other than Randall — especially not with Han's husband watching.

Once he was sure Han wouldn't get blood on his shirt, Ellis leaned in. The thrum of Han's pulse below his skin was like a beacon. He didn't need to find this with his hands, his own body knew exactly where to go. He gently nosed Han's jaw aside to make room.

Han's breathing was already ragged. Not aroused — not yet — but it couldn't be comfortable to be in this situation, surrounded by people, one of whom was a total stranger. The quicker Ellis did this the better for all present it would be.

His lips found Han's skin. It was smooth from his earlier shave, with the acrid taste of aftershave. He had to push past that, to ignore that his mouth was on the wrong man.

Ellis fangs descended and pierced Han's skin. The body beneath him gave a faint whimper which softly transmuted into a sigh as Ellis began to suck at the wound.

Nothing else mattered now. The office all but ceased to exist for him. There was just darkness and blood and a man beneath him who Ellis fervently hoped would get through the next few hours with his sanity intact.

TWENTY-FIVE

RANDALL STARED IN MOUNTING HORROR. Jay was a wreck, clinging to Han's hand while Ellis bowed over him to drain him dry. Hell, even Edison had been stunned into shutting up at last.

This was what Jonas had done to Ellis, wasn't it? Except without any of the care, none of the attention to detail or fuss over his victim's comfort and wellbeing. He'd bitten into Ellis' neck and sucked and swallowed and *god how long does this take?*

The room was eerily quiet, punctuated only by Jay's sniffles and Ellis' swallows. Both were regular, though Ellis was faster.

Gulp. Gulp. Gulp. One every two seconds, by Randall's count.

How much blood would be in a man Han's size? He was fit and healthy, a couple of inches taller than Randall, not quite thirty yet... All in all Randall reckoned there should be about five litres of blood. Did Ellis have to take every last bit? Surely Han's heart would give out after losing about three litres, so how would Ellis get to the last two if the heart wasn't pumping anymore? Was this some weird magic vampire stuff?

Vampires seemed to ignore all laws of biology when it came to blood. Blood went into them, but no waste seemed to come out, yet they always needed more and didn't get any larger. Randall thought maybe their innards were essentially constructed out of blood, since Ellis always needed more when he was injured. But they didn't bleed if you cut into them, so the stuff wasn't circulating, and Ellis certainly didn't have a heartbeat. The amount of times Randall woke up next to what seemed unnervingly like a corpse had confirmed that the man had no pulse. He didn't even want to try to fathom how the hell Ellis could get an erection.

It was all stuff Randall found easy to blot out of his thoughts when Ellis held him in his arms, kissed him, even when the vampire bit into him and took just a little to survive. It was *Ellis*. He wasn't some terrifying undead horror. He was just a guy with a particular condition and very specific dietary requirements.

Now, though, Randall watched as the man he loved was unable to hide the truth of what he was.

Ellis was killing a living, breathing human being. Every ounce that he took from Han seemed to bring a small flush to his cheeks, and the way his body undulated with each swallow was obscene.

And Han... Randall ground his teeth. He could see Han's erection from here. That was what it was like to be fed on. The bite brought such pleasure intermingled with the pain that Randall had grown almost addicted to it. He would cry out during sex, begging Ellis to bite him, and the intense sensation always pushed him over the edge. He loved the helplessness, he loved being trapped between Ellis' mouth and his cock, unable to do anything but come explosively until he was left a quivering wreck.

He didn't love seeing it in someone else. His wolf all but bristled at the sight of Ellis bestowing that feeling on another, while his human half was increasingly repulsed by it.

Han's body jerked slightly, and then his skin became a sickly, ashen shade. It was horrible how quickly it turned from wan to unmistakably dead as though at the flick of a switch.

Ellis broke away and exhaled over Han's skin, then he bit into his own wrist. He sucked on it, and when he lifted his mouth away Randall couldn't tell whether that was Han's blood or his own across his skin.

Ellis felt for Han's mouth and prised his jaw further apart. He pressed his wrist to Han's lips and twisted, leaving a smear of vivid red across the greyed-out mouth. The juxtaposition of blood and death was carnal in a way Randall found grotesquely disturbing.

Finally Ellis ran his tongue over his wrist to clean himself up and he sat back on the carpet, looking flush with life. Randall couldn't help but glance to his crotch, but Ellis folded his arms in his lap and Randall couldn't see whether it had had the sort of effect on Ellis that it had on Han.

Jay clung desperately to Han's hand. Tears trickled down his cheeks. He looked between Han and Ellis, then whispered, "It didn't work."

"It takes time," Ellis said quietly.

"How *much* time?"

"I honestly don't know." Ellis slowly licked his lips, then pushed his hair back from his face. "The only time I've been through it I was too dead to pay any attention to the passage of time."

Edison took a shaky step back, and Randall was grateful for

the distraction. He turned to watch Ellis' brother and almost hoped he'd start screaming so that Randall had somewhere to direct all the weird energy coalescing within himself.

The older O'Neill didn't have too close a resemblance to Ellis. He didn't have the fine features or the slender form. He was a broad-shouldered man with dark, neat hair which had a smattering of silvery strands at each temple. His eyes were a deep blue, and maybe that was what Ellis' had once looked like, but that was where their similarities ended. Edison's jaw was square and his lips thin. Feather lines crept around his eyes. He was clean-shaven. He kept himself active, and beneath the lines of his suit was the unmistakable shape of a gym-fit body. Maybe Edison took after one parent and Ellis the other, because if Randall had seen them side-by-side without knowing that they were brothers he wouldn't have guessed it. Their only shared feature now was the accent, but even there Edison's was far stronger than Ellis'.

"What the fuck," Edison said slowly, "is going on here?" At least he kept his voice down.

"Shut up," Jay whimpered. "Just shut up. God. You're an arsehole on the phone and you're an arsehole in person." He turned toward Ellis. "Why is he even here?"

Ellis waved a hand vaguely in Edison's direction. "Apparently dad got tired of waiting and sent him down to get me to repay the loan. He caught us at home and wouldn't leave us alone and I didn't have time to argue with him."

"Is he dead?" Edison insisted.

"It won't last." Ellis slowly eased to his feet and felt for Jay's shoulder, which he squeezed.

"It's horrible," Jay whispered. "You're *sure* this will work?" He didn't look away from Han, and his free hand began to comb through Han's hair.

"It'll work," Ellis murmured. "Give it time, Jay. It'll work."

Jay nodded weakly. He drew Han into his lap and coiled his arms around the body, and Randall had to look away. This wasn't something to watch. It wasn't television, it wasn't staged.

A man had died, and they all stood there like lemons.

"You're a vampire," Edison said.

Ellis felt for his cane and began to assemble it. "Randall?"

Randall pulled his shoulders up. "Yeah?"

"Are you okay?"

No. No I am not okay! How can anyone be okay with this?

Randall swallowed and shoved his hands into the pockets of his jeans where they could form fists without anyone noticing them. He couldn't lie to Ellis. The man's hearing was like a bat's. He could pick out the heartbeats of everyone in this building, let alone this one room, and he could pinpoint them to within inches. The vampire knew that Randall's was running like a thoroughbred, and a lie would ring like an alarm bell to his senses.

"I'll do better when Han's back on his feet," he said quietly.

Ellis inclined his head, then moved with care around the desk and approached Edison. The tip of his cane made delicate taps against the carpet to be sure his path was clear, and he raised his chin once he was a couple of feet from his brother.

Randall glanced up at Edison and felt a twinge of sympathy for the man. His skin was pale and his expression was one of barely-contained shock. The man probably hadn't even seen Ellis since he'd been turned.

Randall took a couple of steps to fetch the wheeled chair he'd shown Ellis to earlier, and led it over toward Edison. "Here," he said gently. "We'll explain everything. I promise. But you might want a bit of a sit down, yeah?"

Edison's glare turned on him, but Randall held his ground.

He didn't fear a man like this. There was nothing that Edison could do to him, but more than that Edison was in pain. It was evident in the tightness around his eyes and the hunch of his shoulders, and despite Ellis' usual compassion he didn't seem to have picked up on it.

Of course he didn't. They were visual clues, and Edison's voice was steady as a rock.

Randall looked up at Edison and gestured toward the chair. "Go on," he prompted. "It's all right."

Edison's glower began to ebb, and then he sighed and sat down. He set his satchel across his lap as a comforting barrier against the rest of the office and his gaze drifted back toward Jay and Han.

Ellis' brows tugged together in confusion, so Randall ran a hand down his back briefly, then went to fetch another chair. He wheeled it over and settled on it in front of Edison to help distract him from the body behind the desk.

"Ellis is a vampire," Randall said softly. He dipped his head to make eye contact without it becoming threatening. "He doesn't have a reflection, and it affects technology too. He can't use the phone, or an intercom. He can't pick up Skype calls. Cameras don't see him, microphones don't detect him. He hasn't been ignoring your calls, Edison. He just can't answer them. That's why you get Jay, or Christy, or myself. None of us can tell you when Ellis will be able to speak to you, because he can't. He'd transfer the money back electronically if he could, but he hasn't got a million lying around. He can't travel across town because vampires have really tight restrictions on that kind of thing, so he has to live right by the gallery, and that eats almost all of his wages, which he thankfully doesn't have to spend on food or heating so there's that. Now I've moved in that frees up a little bit of cash, but it's hardly hundreds of thousands of pounds. Everything he's earned he had to reinvest to get the gallery where it is today."

Ellis' hand came to rest against Randall's shoulder, but Randall didn't look away from Edison.

Edison regarded Randall like the werewolf was talking out of his backside. But he didn't argue. He sat and digested the information and looked as though he was working hard to apply some sort of logic or intelligence to it.

"The fact remains," Edison finally said, "that there's a significant sum outstanding, and dad's got no intention of forgetting it." He pointed toward Han. "Who's this guy? He runs his own business. Is he loaded?"

"Edison!" Ellis snarled.

"No." Edison sounded calm. He looked calm. "If you can't solve a problem, you pool your resources. You're too artsy, Ellis. You don't think analytically. Never have done. If you've just turned him into a vampire because he's dying, then he owes you his existence. Assuming he gets back up again. He *is* going to get back up again, reet?"

"Aye. He is."

"Then see what he can do for you. You won't be negotiating from a position of strength, but—"

"No." Ellis' fingers tightened on Randall's shoulder.

"Ellis."

"No!" Ellis flashed teeth, and Randall was struck by how wolflike the gesture was. "Han is my *friend*, Edison. That isn't how you treat friends. Not that you'd know—"

"Ellis!" Jay sounded tired.

Randall turned in time to see Han's eyes flit open. The man still looked horribly grey, his skin sallow. Dead.

"Holy shit," Edison breathed.

Ellis turned. "Jay, be careful. He's practically empty. His only instinct will be to feed."

Jay nodded weakly and ran his hands across Han's chest. "It's okay, sweetie. I'm right here. Do whatever you have to, okay?"

Han turned toward him, and Randall caught a glimpse of teeth before Han buried himself against Jay's throat.

TWENTY-SIX

ELLIS LISTENED. He heard the minuscule tear as fangs penetrated flesh. He heard the ravenous swallows. Jay's heart hammered ten to the dozen and his lungs laboured in that unique mix of fear and arousal that typified the reaction most people had to being fed from.

"Shit," Edison snapped. Ellis heard him spring to his feet. "Someone stop him!"

"Shh." Ellis held a finger to his lips. "I need to listen."

"To what?"

"I need to make sure Han doesn't do any lasting harm. He doesn't know what he's doing, he might pull too hard, collapse blood vessels, cause a heart attack. So please, Edison. Please let me listen."

To his relief, Edison sat again and said nothing.

Ellis moved as quietly as he could toward Han and Jay. Small slurps suggested that Han hadn't perfected the art of the vacuum in any way, which was a relief. It meant that he couldn't possibly draw so fast as to do any damage, but it might also mean that Jay was losing more blood than what went into Han's mouth.

He sniffed a little. There was blood in the air, but not much. Han had probably missed any major vessels.

Jay's heart was going strong. It didn't falter. He wasn't losing anywhere near enough for it to be dangerous, but that wouldn't last if Han suddenly figured out all the wrong things at once.

Ellis counted another ten seconds. That ought to be enough for Han to at least have some wits about him now.

"Han," he said. "That's enough."

Jay whimpered weakly, a faint little sound in the back of his throat.

Han didn't stop.

"Han!" Ellis poked him with the tip of his cane. "Pack it in!"

That had about as much effect as his previous effort.

"Randall," Ellis said urgently. "Stop him."

"You're on." Randall hurried past and there was a thud.

Bloody hell. Had Randall rugby-tackled Han? There were certainly sounds of a struggle.

"Han!" Ellis snapped. "Get off him, before you fucking kill him, you bloody idiot!"

Jay's breathing changed, and he groaned.

The wrestling sounds came to an end.

Ellis pushed his hair back slowly and said, "Han, listen to me. You have to breathe in. You've got to do it deliberately, then you breathe out over the bite mark, okay? That'll stop Jay bleeding and help him heal up fast. Areet? You do that, then we can talk."

There was an odd breath. A false breath. Jay's own paused, then picked up again in relief.

Han croaked faintly.

"You have to breathe to talk, too. Just like you used to, but now you have to think about it. It doesn't come automatically anymore." Ellis pressed his lips together.

Christ, not being able to see what was happening here was a real pain in the arse.

"Right," Han whispered. He cleared his throat, then said "Right!" far more loudly.

Ellis winced. "Yeah. Volume takes practice, too. You're not firing on all cylinders yet. You'll need another feed. But it's something like lunchtime, and I don't know if you can go out in the daylight. I certainly wouldn't recommend it when you're half empty. I'm going to have to teach you to feed so that you don't hurt your donor, too."

"He can have me," Jay insisted. He sounded faint.

"No. You need to drink water, and rest for a day or two. Let your body make more to replace what you've lost."

"He can take what he needs from me," Edison said quietly.

Ellis turned sharply. *That* was unexpected.

Edison couldn't possibly know what would happen to him. He had a wife, for god's sake. The last thing Ellis wanted to be responsible for was any confusion over his sexuality that might arise from Han's bite. Suppose Edison got it into his head that his reaction meant that he was attracted to men?

Worse, what if Han got it wrong second time around and did Edison some serious harm? Ellis didn't exactly have a great deal of love in his heart for either of his brothers, but that didn't mean he wished them any harm.

He wasn't about to tell Edison that, though. Instead he said "If Han kills you we'll have a bugger of a time explaining how you died in his office."

"I won't kill him," Han croaked, barely above a whisper. "Shit, this is weird. I can hear *everything*."

Han would be able to see everything too. Ellis pressed his

lips together and rubbed his nose before he could pass comment, though. He was weary, true, but there was no need to be bitter.

His friend seemed to have all his marbles. That was what mattered. Han was conscious, lucid, and seemed to be sane.

So had Marcus, though. In Ellis' vision of him the young man was capable of maintaining a conversation. He was upset, desperate, and he'd done terrible things, but he wasn't outwardly crazy just to look at him. If Han had been driven over the edge it might not show for some time.

If it did come, and if Jay was harmed because of it, Ellis wasn't sure that he could ever forgive himself. He'd given Han the choice, Han had been the one to agree, but Ellis knew the risks and he'd gone through with it anyway.

Any harm that Han caused would be on Ellis' conscience.

Surely, then, it was better to give him a quick grounding in how to feed *before* Ellis had to run off and hide with a pack of werewolves?

"Areet," he relented. "Fine. Ellis O'Neill's quick start guide to feeding from human beings." He leaned against Han's desk and folded his cane while he organised his thoughts. "Your fangs will puncture without much pressure. They are sharp. You already found that when you prodded mine."

"Yeah." Han sighed.

"They taper to a point, so you go in to make a hole, then withdraw a little to give you space to draw from. Don't withdraw all the way or they'll start screaming. Close your lips over the skin like you're giving 'em a love bite, then suck *gently*. If you pull on 'em hard you might do serious damage."

Han wheezed. It could be an attempt at a laugh, but it didn't sound much like one. "How serious can it be?"

"Depends. If you've stuck yourself into an artery then you suck like a vacuum cleaner you could collapse the blood vessel. They'll black out because you've cut air supply to their brain. Then they die because they're oxygen-starved."

Randall swore faintly. "That's pretty serious," he said softly.

"Aye. And I'm not having that. You're safer going in at the neck than the wrist. Skin at the neck is thicker than the inner wrist. Means you're less likely to have an accident. Don't go for the groin unless you're a doctor, got it?"

"Got it," Han said. He spoke carefully, and while his voice was oddly modulated, he was almost at a reasonable volume at last.

"Don't get funny ideas about aiming for the jugular, either. The crook of the neck, the shoulder, they're both absolutely fine." Ellis slipped his index finger into his own collar and tugged it aside, then drew his fingertip to the side of his neck. "Around here is pretty safe. If you hit anything vital, breathe on it immediately and wait for it to heal. It only takes a couple of seconds. If you leave an artery open your donor *will* die. That shit does not fix itself."

"Loud and clear," Han replied.

Ellis nodded and tipped his head toward Edison. "Are you sure? This will paralyse you until he's done. You can't—"

"Move, can't talk. Aye, I heard it all earlier," Edison stated.

Ellis pursed his lips. "It's, uh. It's a very... different experience."

"It's amazing," Jay breathed. "It's super sexy. I always took the mickey out of Ellis for it, but actually it's seriously hot—"

"You're probably not helping," Randall muttered.

Ellis dipped his chin. Was there something in Randall's voice there? He sounded distant, but Ellis couldn't quite identify the undercurrent to his words.

"Come on," Edison grunted. "Get on with it."

Footsteps. The *shht* of another bite.

Ellis walked away from the desk and toward Randall's heartbeat, a mounting guilt scrabbling to be heard somewhere deep inside him. No amount of telling it that Edison had volunteered would get it to shut up.

His cane tapped against Randall's foot, and Ellis raised his chin, but Randall said nothing.

This could all have been too much for the werewolf. He'd been through so much recently: lost his pack; lost the closest he had to a sister; become an Alpha. The poor man was struggling to find himself, and among all that Ellis had turned his own best friend, then let that man feed on his own brother.

From the outside, this couldn't look good. Hell, from the inside it didn't exactly seem much better.

And now Randall wasn't even talking to him.

Ellis turned away and ran his thumb slowly over the handle of his cane. He tried to think of something to say, but the sound of Han feeding distracted him. It added a backdrop to the growing voice within him.

You're a monster, Ellis.

"That's enough," he whispered, voice thick with self-loathing.

Edison released a shaky breath, but whatever he said was lost in the racket from Randall's phone.

"Sorry," Randall mumbled. "I, um. I better take this." He walked toward the door, then affected false cheer. "Hi mum! What's up?"

"Randall! Thank god! Is everything all right?" The woman Ellis could hear sounded concerned. Her accent had a twinge of Jamaican to it.

Three months into a relationship and he still hadn't met Randall's mum. He rubbed his jaw and tossed that revelation onto the pile of things to hate himself for.

"Bloody hell!" Han sounded startled. "I can hear the other end of that phone call!"

Ellis nodded grimly, but couldn't find the words to answer him. That or he was too invested in eavesdropping. Yet another thing decent human beings didn't do to their lovers.

"Yeah, uh. I'm with a client right now, mum." Randall spoke quickly. "Can I call you back later?"

"Are you in trouble? The police just came by and asked for your whereabouts. I think they're looking to arrest you for something. I said 'have you got him confused for his brother?' but they insisted it was you they wanted."

"No, I'm not in trouble, mum." Randall sounded confused.

"They said they've been to your place and it's a mess and the landlord says he hasn't seen you in weeks!"

"Uh—"

"You aren't mixing with bad people? You're too bright for that nonsense!"

"No, mum, I'm not—"

"I told them! I said 'my boy Randall's a good boy! Whatever you think he did, he didn't do it!'"

"Mum," Randall said, strained. "I have to go. I'm fine, I swear. I'll call you later, okay?"

"You better!"

"Bye, mum!"

The room was quiet. All eyes were likely on Randall. Even Ellis turned that way.

Han broke the silence. "What're the police after you for?"

"The police?" Jay squeaked. "Oh, god! Nobody saw you break into the church, did they?"

"Church?" Edison paused. "Wait. Ellis, you said you're a fugitive now, aye?"

Ellis nodded faintly. "Aye, but not from the police."

"Unless someone made a call." Edison snorted.

"Anonymous, or connected, either way it sounds like whoever's after you is utilising their resources better than you do."

"You reckon the Council has the Met in their pocket?" Randall's pulse raced. He sounded aghast, as well he had every right to be. "They can't, can they?"

Ellis had the horrible feeling that he knew the answer.

"They don't have to," he said quietly. "There's one man in this city who can have whoever he *wants* under his thumb."

TWENTY-SEVEN

RANDALL SHIFTED his weight from one foot to the other, but that wasn't any more comfortable. "Hang on. This bloke with the mind control?"

Ellis' head bobbed. "Aye."

Randall glanced to his phone. "It's two in the afternoon. He can't have phoned the police, he can't have gone to them…"

"Which means he has people who do all that for him." Ellis tapped his cane against the carpet while his expression drifted into some thought or other. "We have to go get Tiberius."

Edison strode toward Ellis. "Give me your keys."

"What?" Ellis pulled his shoulders up. "I don't have them. They took everything I had on me when they dragged me off and threw me into a cell."

Randall winced at the anger on Edison's features. The big fella might be an arsehole, but he seemed righteously indignant that his brother had been treated so poorly.

"You." Edison looked to Randall now. "You got keys?"

"Yeah." Randall fumbled them out of his pocket and tossed them over. "Key card for the ground floor, keys for the flat."

"I'll be in an out, then I'll take your dog to my hotel. Your vampire fella won't recognise me, I can pass meself off as another tenant if I have to."

"Edison—" Ellis broke off awkwardly and tightened the grip on his cane. "Thank you."

"Don't get soft on me." Edison dropped the keys into his satchel and shouldered it. He adjusted his collar and tie, and made for the door.

Randall stepped aside for him. "Good luck," he said softly.

Edison gave him a nod and twisted the door's lock, then slipped out and closed the door after him.

Randall locked the door. He stood with his back to it and regarded the room.

Han's office was spotless. Shelves and walls were dotted with awards and certificates. His desk was covered phones and tablets, a laptop, and a small collection of plastic Daleks.

Han himself looked almost human again. He hadn't mastered the art of breathing, but otherwise he could pass for a man who just needed a good night's sleep.

Jay... Poor Jay. He looked like hell. His eyes were reddened, his skin pale. He looked about at the end of his tether, and Randall couldn't blame him. He'd watched his husband *die*.

"Edison's right." Han said it quietly, but he seemed like he'd meant to do so. "You've got to use your resources better."

"People aren't resources." Ellis turned away and found the chair that Randall had brought for his brother. He sat down with care to stop the wheeled chair escaping before he was done.

"Yes. They are." Han grabbed Jay's hand. "They're not *only* resources, but every one of us can bring something to the table and if you ignore what people have to give, you will sink."

Randall rubbed his arm uncomfortably. "It's all biometrics around here, right? Jay had to come down to let us in?"

Han nodded to him. "Yeah."

"Okay. So you've got somewhere no vampires can get into, so you should be safe while we figure this out."

Ellis cast a small smile. "Aye," he agreed. "I need to speak with Barb. And Hughes, if she's really managed to convince him over."

"How do I go about turning into a flock of bats?" Han smirked.

"If you figure that one out, let me know." Ellis stood again and came toward the door. "Jay?"

"Yes, sweetie?"

"Eat something, and get some sleep."

Randall unlocked the door, let Ellis out, then with a nod to the married couple, he followed.

RANDALL LET Ellis take his arm as they hurried out onto the street. He steered aimlessly and stuck to the shade of the tallest buildings he could find.

"Where are we going?"

"I have no idea," Ellis sighed. "Hughes won't be able to get north of the Thames until after sunset, which won't be for another couple of hours yet. I don't know if I can stay outside that long."

"The amount of blood you've got inside you, I would've thought you could stay out for hours."

Randall winced the moment the words came out. God, he sounded like a total bitch! Where had *that* come from?

Ellis' head drooped. His cane tapped quietly over the pavement.

"Shit, I'm sorry." Randall turned to face him. "I'm sorry. You've been to hell and back and I'm not helping. I didn't mean it—"

"It's all right." Ellis took his hand from Randall's elbow and laid it on his chest. "I'm not Briar, petal. You don't have to apologise for every little thing around me. I love you. I know everything's fucked up and I'm sorry, but I *do* love you."

"I know." Randall held himself still. If he fidgeted, Ellis would know. He'd want to know what was wrong. He'd want to *talk*, and Randall didn't know if he felt up to a conversation.

Ellis leaned in to kiss Randall's cheek. "What's wrong?" he whispered.

"Jesus." Randall glanced around quickly. Anything to look away, even though Ellis couldn't see him.

The streets hereabouts were hardly busy. This was office land, and the few who came and went were in suits, on their phones or with earbuds in as they hurried from one place to the next. It didn't leave anywhere convenient for them to duck out of sight for a private conversation. The best they could probably do around here was find a café and tuck themselves into the back.

Randall didn't want that. He didn't *want* to talk. There were things he absolutely did not want to say, and the person he didn't want to say them to stood so close to him that nobody could mistake them for anything but lovers.

"Do I disgust you?" Ellis breathed.

Randall jolted like he'd been exposed to a current. He stared up at Ellis and tried to find an answer that wouldn't make him sound guilty or come off like a gigantic arsehole, and the longer he took the worse it got.

Ellis dropped his hand. "I see."

"No," Randall choked. "It's not like that."

What *was* it like? Desperation and panic vied with revulsion and fear. Neither won. The memory of Ellis sucking on Han's neck like a remora came to him in all its repugnant, vivid glory, and Briar's words came with it.

He's a vampire. A leech. A flea.

Had Briar been right? That would be galling. No, it would be worse than that. It would be unbearable. The man was smarter than he pretended to be most of the time. Had he had some idea of what Ellis could be beneath the veneer of humanity?

It had to be more than a veneer. It *had* to be. Randall *loved* him. He couldn't be an Alpha unless he loved someone, and he'd got his pack through two full moons so far. There was no way Randall's feelings could be in doubt.

Could Ellis'?

"Are you leaving?" Ellis said quietly.

"I can't." Randall's voice constricted around his words. "I love you."

"And I love you, petal. I love you more than I ever thought possible. You're everything I never knew I needed and if I didn't have you I don't think I could go on another night." Ellis spoke softly. He didn't raise his voice, he didn't beg or implore, he simply let the truth come out of him like a man who had already lost the will to fight. "You gave me everything you had. Your secrets, your kindness, your heart. What've I given you in return?" Those delicate lips clamped together a moment. "Pain. Fear. Disgust. I've taken your beauty and I've given you nothing in return."

"That's not true," Randall argued. "It isn't! I'm sorry. I just —" He hesitated, then crossed his arms. "Fine. It was horrible, okay? That's what you want me to say? You fed off Han and it was unbearable."

Ellis dipped his hand into his trouser pocket. His head fell forward again. "I can imagine."

"I don't know what to think." Randall looked away. His gaze fell to a pigeon which waddled across the road, so he stared at it. It was something normal in a staggeringly abnormal day. "It was proper gross, okay? And it upset me, and I know Jonas did it to you and *that* upset me, and Han was obviously turned on by it, and it sounded horrible, and then he *died*, and... and..." He came to a trembling halt and rubbed at his eyes when they began to sting.

"My poor, sweet Randall," Ellis whispered. He came in closer and slipped his hand to Randall's hip. "Is that it?"

"Is what it?" Randall mumbled.

"Are you jealous?"

Randall opened his mouth. He shut it again.

"You like it when I bite you, don't you?" Ellis whispered. "You ask me to. You *beg* me to do it." His lips twitched gently. "Come here, my little flower." His arm eased around Randall's waist and tugged him closer.

"It's not that," Randall mumbled. He looped his arms around Ellis, though, and clung to him tightly.

"It's maybe a *little* bit that, aye?" Ellis breathed against his cheek.

Randall gripped the back of Ellis' jacket and buried his face into the vampire's shoulder.

"Oh, Randall." Ellis rubbed the small of his back. "I love you so much. I'm sorry. If there were any other way to save Han I would have leaped at it."

"Yeah." Randall inhaled deeply, but Ellis' only scent was the faint lingering touch of shampoo from the morning's shower. "I know. I'm not jealous. I swear, I'm..." He sighed and leaned into Ellis' hug. "Maybe a bit jealous," he relented.

"It's areet." Ellis pressed his lips against Randall's hair. "I don't feed from anyone else, petal, I swear. I couldn't. After I met you, I just couldn't do it. God, it isn't even... It's not..." Ellis laughed weakly. "I don't know. It's such a sexual thing, isn't it? There's no way to feed from anywhere else. People can't just bleed into a cup, it doesn't work like that. So I couldn't do it. Not once I found you." He snorted. "How messed up is that? I'm standing here telling you this like I'm trying to convince you I haven't cheated on you. It's all... bunched together in my head. Love. Sex. Feeding. It's all tangled up and I can't... I can't separate it. I couldn't then, and I can't now. I can't feed from anyone but you because it *would* be cheating. And I feel like I've betrayed you. To save Han's life, I've done this... horrible thing, and I can't... I don't know what to say or do to make it better."

Randall felt dizzy. He clung to Ellis and squeezed his eyes shut, but the sick sensation wouldn't stop. "You had to save Han," he stated, voice muffled against Ellis' clothes. "There wasn't any other way. When we got there he looked sick as a dog, El. I honestly thought he was going to drop dead on the bloody spot. He needed to be in hospital, but that wouldn't have saved him, would it? It just would've prolonged the misery. You've given him a chance. It isn't your fault that what you are does this... *thing* to us. It's designed to protect you, isn't it? It's so that your—" he cut himself off before he could say *victims* "—donors don't know they've been fed from. It feels nice, you take a little, you move on, and everybody lives. It's like a—" he grappled for a metaphor, fast. "A mosquito." He winced. *Nice choice!* "They're in and out, and they inject an anticoagulant, but you never notice them until well after they're gone..." He tailed off.

"Keep digging," Ellis murmured wryly.

Randall huffed and lifted his head, only to find Ellis waiting to kiss him. His lips parted slowly, but the contact soothed him in a way no other touch could, and he began to breathe more calmly.

"We'll work it out, petal," Ellis said. His smile faded. "Please tell me you aren't going to leave."

The thought of losing Ellis hurt more than he could find a way to express. "I'm not leaving you, El. I'm never leaving you. Just… Gimme a bit of time to work it all out, yeah?"

Ellis nodded. "Of course. Whatever you need, it's yours."

Randall gazed up at him and winced at how pained Ellis looked. Added to that, the vampire's pale skin had begun to grow pink across the forehead and the tip of his nose.

"Let's get you inside," he said softly. "You're burning already."

Randall waited for Ellis to take his arm, then hurried for the first Starbucks he could find.

TWENTY-EIGHT

THEY WHILED AWAY a couple of hours tucked away near the loo. It wasn't Ellis' favourite place to be — filled with smells and sounds nobody should have to put up with — but it beat being outside in the sunlight.

Randall had gone through three cups of tea and a brownie in that time. They'd talked about safe subjects and pretended that Randall hadn't just confessed to how utterly disgusting he found Ellis.

Or was Ellis being too harsh? Not on Randall, but himself. Randall had told him the truth, and Ellis would be absolutely childish to hold that against him. What would he prefer? Lies?

No. No, Randall's honesty was something Ellis loved about him, and truth often had a price. Today the price was Ellis' pride, and he would have to suck it up, because Randall's love was worth more than a bit of a knock to Ellis' self-esteem.

And at the end of the day, Randall was right. People were repulsed by anything that drank blood: fleas, mosquitoes, leeches. They all caused a visceral disgust within people. There was something about parasites which deeply disturbed the human psyche, and if Ellis weren't one himself he'd be sickened too.

Unless that was why he'd taken Randall's honesty so hard. Did he have some sort of internalised revulsion over his own existence? He hadn't been a vampire for long and he certainly wasn't born one. It could well be that Randall's words had torn at a raw nerve; that Ellis despised what he was and it was his own self-loathing which hurt more than Randall's honesty.

It was a strange idea to wrestle with. He wished he hadn't thought of it.

Ellis hadn't really had any trouble accepting his sexuality. That was a privilege of his upbringing, he supposed. He'd attended good schools, and university was considered the natural progression, not a rare thing he was fortunate to be able to do. The main arguments at home had been over Ellis' interests in art and his refusal to study law, not who he might be interested in having sex with. He went from school to university to London in very short order, and while York was cosmopolitan, London was the very definition of the word — especially in the circles Ellis moved in.

He'd never mentioned his preference at home, but even if it had led to an argument he had no fear that he might be cast out onto the streets or beaten senseless. His father was confident, even arrogant at times, but he wasn't a thug.

The very idea that Ellis had managed to build up such a wellspring of self-hatred, then, was an alien concept to him. Like a loose tooth, the more he probed at it, the more painful yet irresistible it became to do so. Worst was his realisation that, only a few months ago, he trudged through his existence in a mechanical fashion while he loathed every second of it. He'd yearned for it to end. Even as he fought to survive Jasiński's attack, part of him had hoped the artist would finish him off and end his miserable unlife.

"It's dark out," Randall said.

"Mm?" Ellis dragged himself out of his thoughts. "God, already? What time is it, petal?"

"Quarter past four."

Ellis nodded to himself. Sunset in December was usually just before four in the afternoon, but Randall could have been delayed by streetlights and their burial at the far rear of the Starbucks they'd hidden in. Quarter past was well and truly into what any other vampire would consider safe territory, so he felt for the folded cane on the cushioned seat to the side of his hip and stood once he had it in hand. "Shall we?"

"Yeah." Randall's chair scraped over the carpet, and he waited until Ellis took his arm. "Taxi?"

"Aye." Ellis offered him the best smile he could muster. "Thanks, petal."

THE TAXI DEPOSITED them outside the chocolatier's shop, but this time it was open, and the bustle of people buying or ordering chocolates in preparation for Christmas was little less than a hectic din which made Ellis glad that his own customers came in small, hushed groups and the most crowded his gallery ever became was during a launch party. People didn't push and shove in art galleries, and they certainly didn't have screaming children with them.

"Blimey," Randall muttered after he'd paid for the taxi and joined Ellis on the street. "It's like a free-for-all in there. I've seen more orderly behaviour in a scrum."

Ellis grinned at him. "Tell me you play rugby," he challenged. "Actually, don't tell me. I can imagine your bum in tight shorts without facts getting in the way."

Randall snorted in amusement, which gave Ellis some

measure of relief. The werewolf's sense of humour hadn't dissipated entirely, then. "Fine," he chuckled. "I'm telling you nothing. Want me to go see if I can fish her out of there?"

"Please."

He waited as Randall dove into the shop. Someone's child jostled him while he waited, but a woman quickly apologised, and Ellis simply showed a polite smile and a tip of his head.

Several minutes passed before Randall emerged again.

"Nice," Barb said. "Coming 'round here, scaring my customers." She sounded amused. "C'mon, this way."

"At least you have customers," Ellis replied dryly.

"Yeah, that's 'cause I don't charge fifty grand for a chocolate, duh."

ELLIS SETTLED on Barb's slightly dog-eared old sofa. Randall sat by his side, and even rested a hand on his thigh.

Things were looking up.

"Nice one, Randall," Barb said once she'd shut the door. "You managed to get him out. Any problems?"

"Nothing to do with the rescue. Hughes' information was solid," Randall said. "I thought he was gonna be here by now, though."

Ellis' eyebrows lifted. "Hughes was supposed to be here?"

"Yeah," Barb muttered. "Said he'd come over as soon as he could to make sure you got out okay."

"You don't sound all that happy," he said, turning to face her.

"It's weird having a Constable drop over. I dunno. I kinda worry he might be playing the whole double-agent line."

Ellis gave a grim nod. "I can understand that," he admitted. "But even if he is, he might not be once he gets here."

"Yeah?" She flopped into the armchair. "Why'd you say that?"

"Because I've got some information for him."

Barb sucked at her teeth, then said, "Okay. I won't ask what it is. No point making you repeat yourself."

"I appreciate that." Ellis idly traced his fingertips over the back of Randall's hand, and was rewarded by a soft squeeze of his thigh in return.

"So who goes on top, anyway?" Barb said cheerfully.

Randall coughed so hard that Ellis felt a strong urge to pat him on the back.

"Oh, it's like that, eh?" she cooed. "I thought it'd be the other way around!"

"I'm not sure how it's your business," Ellis said lightly.

"Oh, it ain't." She snorted. "I'm just nosey. Anyway, I—" She broke off.

Ellis heard it too. A soft voice out on the street, separate from the hubbub of the busy shopping stretch.

"I'm here," was all Hughes had said.

"Hang on," Barb said. She hurried out of the little flat and clattered down the stairs.

"Hughes?" Randall asked softly.

"Aye."

She returned soon enough, another set of footsteps behind her.

"Christ, O'Neill, you're a sight for sore eyes," Hughes said. "Sorry I'm late. Place has gone to shit since you killed Dickens."

"Who?" Randall sounded startled.

"Holy shit, you killed a Councillor?" Barb's tone was more one of awe. "How'd that happen?"

"It didn't," Ellis groaned.

"Well you need to lay low," Hughes muttered, "'cause

Dickens went into your cell and didn't come out, and there's two witnesses say you killed him."

"Charles and Victor," Ellis said.

"Hole in one." Hughes paced slowly. "What happened?"

"Charles killed him." Ellis rubbed his forehead while he tried to form a passable timeline of events which left out incriminating information. "I was dumped in the cell and left there for a while. I thought I might find something useful down there if I felt my way around, tried to find out whether there were any visions to be had, and I found something." He hesitated. "I saw Charles with Marcus."

Randall tensed at his side. He'd heard the name, then. Was this how Barb had talked Hughes onto her side, by going over the past?

"You were in Marcus' cell?" Hughes's seat creaked. "What'd you see?"

"Charles turned Marcus. Marcus had done something, killed some people after he was turned. Charles went to see him in his cell and used his power. He forced Marcus to say that you—" he nodded to Hughes "—had turned him. He made Marcus forget that Charles went to visit him. Marcus begged, but Charles ordered him to tell the council that you'd turned him without their permission, that you were lovers."

Hughes hissed in anger. "I fucking *knew* it! That utter bastard!"

Ellis tipped his head forward and gave Randall's hand a firm squeeze. "I'm sorry."

"It's okay." Hughes' teeth ground together. "Go on."

"Devitt and Dickens came in to question me. They wanted to know whether it was worth hauling me up in front of the Council. I managed to tell Dickens that Devitt had been the one to turn Marcus." Ellis shook his head. "Devitt killed him. Murdered him in cold blood. And if I go in front of the

Council I'll tell them I did it." He pushed his hands into his hair and gripped tightly. "I know I will. He's ordered me to."

"Shit." Aaron sat back. "Devitt's baying for your blood. He wants you hunted down and executed for the murder of Mark Dickens, and he's rousing the entire Constabulary against you. He's got you pegged as public enemy number one. Had me picking over your entire territory last night trying to find you, and I wouldn't be surprised if he's pulled some strings to get people after Randall an' all."

Randall growled at that. "The police called on my mum looking for me earlier."

"Devitt's got people in the police. He uses 'em to bury any evidence of vampires if someone messes up, then holds that over their heads. One way or another he pulls most of the strings in this city, whether you're livin' or dead."

"I didn't realise he was *that* fecking dangerous!" Barb let out a low whistle. "He's never going to let us change the way things are done 'round here, is he?"

"Not likely," Ellis said. "After he'd killed Mark he made some comment about there being a spare seat on the Council at last."

"He's wanted that seat back for donkey's years." Hughes paused as a phone vibrated. "S'cuse me," he added.

The phone vibrated again.

And *again*.

"Holy shit," Hughes muttered.

"What is it?" Ellis raised his head.

"Apparently you've killed Councillor Clarke now," Hughes muttered. "Oh, Jesus. He's making it look like you're on a fucking rampage!"

"He's killing off the whole Council." Horror crept through Ellis' gut and settled like a coiled snake around his spine.

He was *eating* the whole Council. Except he couldn't tell

Hughes that, could he? Not without admitting everything. Not without revealing what he'd done to Jonas, or that he now had Jonas' power as well as his own. He'd have to tell Hughes and Barb what it meant to consume another vampire, and that Devitt would be accumulating more than political power; he was gaining whatever abilities each Councillor had possessed.

"That's gonna be one mean-arse power vacuum if he wipes 'em all out," Barb mused. "What's his endgame? Install himself as dictator?"

"I wouldn't be surprised." Ellis grimaced at the thought. "Nobody to answer to, nobody to strip him of his control. Nobody to stand up to him if they don't like his rule." He shook his head. "We've got to stop him."

Hughes tapped away at his phone. The soft tap of a rubber-tipped stylus patted over glass with remarkable speed. "I'll try to put the Constabulary on protecting the last three," he said as he worked, "but they're out scouring town for you, and the Council themselves might argue that they're best protected if you're caught. I'll go to Asquith and see if I can't get a guard on Hillier and Stanley."

"And if Devitt turns up? What happens to you?" Randall leaned forward.

"I'm okay. He can't get me. If he opens his damn mouth near me I'll shove a stake in him so fast he won't get a word out. I can't be in three places at once, though."

"He has to speak to use his power?" Randall asked.

"Yeah. If you can't hear him, he can't use you. I'll do everything I can, but he's gotta go home sooner or later, and you, me ole china, are a werewolf."

Ellis pursed his lips. "You're suggesting Randall lies in wait?"

"It's the best we got," Hughes said. "You gotta make sure you can't hear him, okay? Take an iPod or something. Crank it up full volume. Don't muck about, don't give him a chance. Put a stake in him and I can come arrest him."

"I've got an iPod," said Barb. "Hang on."

Ellis heard her search around. Papers and other things were shunted aside, then plastic *tinked* lightly against metal and her boots crossed to Randall.

"Here," she said. "If that don't drown out the evil old bastard, nothing will."

"Cheers."

"Where do we get a stake?" Ellis began to stand.

"You don't have any?" Barb sounded gobsmacked. "What if someone comes into your turf to kick off?"

"Er." *I usually eat them* probably wouldn't go down well.

"Christ, how the heck do you survive so long, eh?" She tromped away, and was back far more quickly this time. "Here. I've got spares. Keep it."

"Oh," Hughes added. "I managed to pull your stuff from the Church, too." He stood and came closer, then began to tuck items into Ellis' pockets. He moved at a normal pace, but everything went back into the pockets he'd originally taken them from. "Text me once you've got Devitt in the bag, yeah?"

"Sounds like a plan." Ellis nodded.

He hated plans.

TWENTY-NINE

RANDALL FLAGGED a taxi to get them to the address Hughes provided. While it was only a couple of miles, the fastest route cut through Ellis' own territory, which had to be crawling with vampires hunting him right now. He even messed the driver around a bit, originally asking to go to Charing Cross before he faked a text and change of plan once the cab sailed past Nelson's Column.

The taxi trundled down Whitehall and Randall gazed out of the window. What began as pubs and fast food places quickly turned into white-walled government buildings built in the 1800's and lacking any sort of identifying marks other than their street numbers. The centre of the wide road was dotted with memorials and statues. And up ahead, the Palace of Westminster. The road was so wide and straight that Randall could see the clock of Big Ben several minutes before they passed the seat of Parliament.

Was all this how Devitt exercised his control? God, that was a terrible thought. The whole country was run from offices within Devitt's territory. Did his reach extend beyond the city?

The hard wood of the short stake Barb gave him nestled against his thigh. The tip dug into his skin slightly, having found itself a slight hole in the pocket of Randall's jeans. He'd been assured that it wouldn't kill Devitt, only paralyse him, but maybe it would be for the best if Devitt were dealt with more permanently. What would stop him talking his way out of a cell and right back to seizing control of the city?

Randall wasn't an executioner. He sure as hell wasn't a judge, either. Hughes knew what he was doing. All Randall had to do was stick to the plan.

They passed the Houses of Parliament and on into Pimlico's rows of obscenely expensive properties. They looked as old as the government buildings on Whitehall, if not older, and each and every one was pristine and white.

"Bloody hell," he grunted. "Devitt has to be rolling in it."

"When you can tell people to sign everything they own over to you," Ellis said quietly, "why live in poverty?"

Randall grimaced. He'd grown up in what Ellis would probably call poverty: a tiny two-bed Council flat in Spitalfields. He shared one bedroom with his brother Kieran and his mum had the other. The heating often conked out in winter, and there was no air conditioning in summer. Sometimes the radiators banged loudly when you turned them on. Almost every pipe and cable was exposed, painted to match the walls. The walls were so thin you could hear the neighbours unplugging the kettle after every cup of tea.

Yeah, they could maybe have done with a bit more space. But they had a roof overhead. Electricity. Running water that usually came with a hot option. He'd had a great time as a kid playing with the other children on the estate out in the playground shared by three tower blocks. He couldn't imagine

AMELIA FAULKNER

children playing in the neatly-manicured park which faced the row of townhouses they got dropped at.

"Yeah," he finally breathed as he steered Ellis toward a massive house at the end of the row. "Well. Bloody thing's like six storeys high." He peered over a tidy iron railing and added "And it's got a proper basement."

"How do we get in?" Ellis asked as Randall gently guided him up four wide marble steps to the black lacquered door. "You can't exactly tear the door off, petal."

Randall grinned and crossed the porch to the door. "If he's that minted, he'll have staff, won't he?"

Ellis' head turned, and he tipped one ear toward the door, face a mask of concentration. "Three people," he murmured, a slow grin creeping across his features. "You're a genius."

"Oh, you know." Randall banged his fist against the door three times. "I do my best."

Ellis' smile warmed, but instead of an answer he gestured toward the door seconds before it opened.

Randall turned just in time to punch the butler in the face.

THEY WERE INSIDE WITHIN MOMENTS. Randall didn't have time to hold back, and when his second punch hit the older man in the throat he pushed inside and heard Ellis close the door behind him.

The man wasn't a fighter, and it didn't take long for Randall to wrestle him deeper inside the house.

"I'm really sorry," he gasped as he propelled the other man through into a small kitchen which had a view over a secluded back garden.

Who the hell could afford a *garden* in London?

The man in his arms struggled, so Randall headbutted him.

While the butler reeled and bounced into the wall Randall managed to get the man's tie off and loop it around one of his wrists. He used the hold to drag his arms behind him and soon had him trussed up like a chicken.

"Randall!" Ellis called from the hallway.

"Shit. Stay right there!" Randall burst out of the kitchen in time to hear feet clamouring down the stairs.

These men weren't domestic staff. Or if they were, Devitt had a thing for late-night cleaners who dressed like bodyguards.

They fought like them, too.

Randall took a fist to the stomach and another to his temple. He lashed out while his body quickly recovered, but they were good. They were *trained*. Randall's usual style revolved around defending himself while other people took down a bully or an attacker. He was strong, fit, but he never wanted to hurt anyone, and punching the butler in the face moments ago was as close as he'd come to doing intentional harm.

He landed a blow somewhere in the chaos and heard a grunt of pain, but they were hitting him far more often than he hit them.

He had two ways to win this, as far as he could see. One was to shift and become twice his size. That seemed harsh, especially against humans who might only be here as employees. The other was to win through attrition and hope that ultimately they would wear themselves out trying to beat him.

Randall chose the latter. He gave as good as he could and did his best to avoid being pinned in a corner, but the fact was that they couldn't possibly match his stamina, and every injury they did him was healed in a matter of seconds.

His attackers panted hard. They were flagging. Fit, strong,

trained, but the prolonged fight and the adrenaline crash were taking their toll. It made it easier for Randall to hit them, easier for him to land blows which were effective.

By the time one finally fell, the other only had a couple more punches in him. Randall elbowed him in the face and heard the satisfying crunch of a nose breaking.

"Randall?" Ellis asked. He sounded uncertain.

"I'm okay," he panted as he looked down the hall to where Ellis stood, his back to the wall.

"Oh, thank god." Ellis's shoulders slowly relaxed, and he turned toward Randall. He took cautious steps, one hand against the wall to guide him. "Best to get them as high as you can. You said it was six storeys?"

Randall groaned at the thought of hefting three people up so many flights of stairs, but he nodded. It made sense. The more distant they were, the less chance Devitt would immediately hear something was wrong. "Stay here," he panted. "I'll do it."

Ellis gave a small nod, and Randall began the long, hard slog of dragging three men, one at a time, up to the top floor and finding something to tie and gag them all with.

———

THEY BEGAN a search of the ground floor once Randall had finished that job. There was the kitchen and a small utilities room, a cramped sitting room which lacked either television or radio, and a larger room which occupied most of the level.

There was something strangely familiar about the last room. It held a broad desk polished to within an inch of its life, and was lined with shelves that were sparsely decorated with all sorts of odds and sods: books, mostly, but also the occasional ornament. Randall had the strangest feeling that he'd been here before, but it could have been any number of rooms in half a dozen stately homes that were used as sets on television programmes. He must have seen one like it in an advert, but he couldn't place where.

Ellis gently felt the desk, and his hands paused while he drew a vision from it. His beautiful features contorted in concentration, and then he sighed a little and felt for something else to touch.

"What I don't get," Randall mused as he slowly turned a globe on its axis, "is why Devitt killed Dickens. If he can just order people to forget stuff, why not make Dickens forget what you said about Marcus?"

The globe was large, and the paper faded with age. The world it showed was from another time, before Germany had lost land and Russia had broken up into smaller countries. It niggled at him. He couldn't have seen this exact globe on an advert, could he? The thing looked like an antique, maybe even one of a kind.

"Aye," Ellis muttered. His hands were on the back of a broad oxblood leather chair. "You've no idea how glad I am Hughes didn't ask that question. Devitt made me tell him about Jonas."

Randall gasped and turned to face Ellis. "Shit."

Ellis' nose crinkled. "I told him everything. God, it was horrible. I just couldn't stop. Devitt knows I stole Jonas' power, so he turned on Dickens and bloody ate him. Whatever power Dickens had, Devitt now has it. And Clarke as well."

Randall hurried to Ellis' side. "Do you know what Clarke's power was?"

"No idea." Ellis shook his head, and his chestnut hair cascaded over his shoulders with the movement. "That's the thing about the Council. They all want to know everything about you but you don't get to know a bloody thing about them. All we can do is hope that even if either of their powers were remotely useful to Devitt, he hasn't worked out how to control them yet."

"Oh, you are kidding me." Randall ran a hand over his head and rubbed slowly at his scalp. "What are you looking for?"

"Anything. Anything we can use against him. There has to be something he's done here, something he wouldn't want known, a weakness, or evidence we can collect." Ellis trapped his lower lip between his teeth and worried at it slowly.

Randall nodded. He pulled away and hurried around the room while Ellis fell silent with his hands on the chair.

His gaze was drawn to an ornately shaped picture frame. It was silver, with an incredibly complex pattern of vines and leaves around the outer edges, and it housed an old sepia photograph of a handsome young man with fair hair, and a beautiful woman at his side with long hair elegantly piled atop her head. The man wore an old-fashioned dark suit, and the woman was dressed in a white, flowing dress.

"Ellis," he murmured. "I think I've got something."

Ellis turned toward him, one hand on the chair still. "What is it?"

"It's a wedding photo. Looks old. It's in a silver frame. A vampire wouldn't want silver in the house, would he?"

"I wouldn't," Ellis agreed. He felt his way around the desk and moved cautiously toward Randall.

"You're clear," Randall said once Ellis had an obstacle-free path.

"Thanks, petal." The vampire strode over and raised a hand. "Where is it?"

"Here." Randall gently steered Ellis' fingers to the glass over the photograph, careful not to touch the silver himself.

Ellis dipped his chin and focused. His eyebrows pulled

together. A smile flickered briefly across his lips, then faded again. "Elizabeth," he whispered.

"That's the only one," Randall said after a quick look around. "I don't see any other pictures of her."

"Something must have happened," Ellis said softly. "No pictures of children anywhere?"

"No."

Ellis grimaced. "Okay. Keep an ear out, petal. I'm going to keep looking."

Randall dropped a hand into his pocket and tugged the iPod earbuds out. "Gotcha."

He slipped the earbuds in and left his thumb lingering over the iPod, ready to hit play the moment anyone came in through that door.

THIRTY

ELLIS HAD PIECED TOGETHER SNATCHES of stolen glimpses of this room, yet they seemed to match the layout of it he found in the present day. Devitt wasn't one for redecorating.

Was this how his wife had left it, or did Devitt simply not care to modernise his surroundings?

His thigh brushed against something hard, and he reached for it. It was the arm of a chair, but this chair wasn't like the one behind the desk. That chair had been a thing made for comfort, designed to be worked in for hours on end. This chair was solid wood, heavy and unpadded. There was some carving along the back, but it was rather austere so far as he could tell.

It didn't fit with the aesthetic of the room very well. Not to Ellis' idea of it, anyway. Devitt seemed to favour ornate things, yet this chair was a blunt object in an otherwise fine room.

He settled his hands across the back of it and tipped his head forward to concentrate.

"Stay seated, Mr. Carter."

Ellis stared at the man behind the desk. His suit was impeccable; his golden hair groomed to perfection. His eyes were bright, gleaming amber.

Charles Devitt.

He looked down at the chair. The man squirming in it was dark skinned, breathtakingly beautiful, his warm skin and even warmer eyes contorted in anger as he fought against the plastic zip-ties which cut into his wrists.

Randall.

Oh, god, he really was stunning. Handsome, muscular, wholly masculine, with that delectable woodsy scent and soft, full lips.

Lips which curved in impotent fury.

Ellis tore his attention from the sight of Randall. His first real opportunity to get a good look at the man he loved, and it was in Devitt's home.

When the hell had Randall been here?

Ellis searched the room desperately while Charles gave permission to speak and robbed Randall of the ability to shapeshift. His gaze fell on the Tupperware container on Devitt's desk.

Mrs. Uddin's samosas.

God damn it. Devitt had begun to move against Ellis before Ellis was even aware the man was a serious threat.

Ellis turned his attention back to Randall. It hurt. God, it hurt to see this, to see the man that he loved with such fear in his eyes. Randall fought against his bindings, but Devitt had forbidden shapeshifting, and Randall was stuck like a fly in honey.

Anger roiled within him. He wanted to destroy Charles, wanted to bring him suffering for what he was doing to Randall. God, the vision was nothing but pain. How could he stand by and watch Devitt do this?

"Tell me: are you aware that Mr. O'Neill is a vampire?"

"Yes." Randall twisted in the chair and pulled at the zip ties so hard that the scent of blood broke free from his skin.

"Relax, Mr. Carter. Don't bleed on the rug. I understand it to be quite the bother to wash out." Devitt circled the desk like a panther and dragged a finger through the bright red specks. He sniffed at the blood, and Ellis' rage escalated, but all Devitt did was wipe the blood off onto a handkerchief. "Well, now I see your appeal, Mr. Carter. I've never thought to actually feed from one of your sort. All that hair and muscle is quite off-putting. But that still doesn't explain what you see in O'Neill." Devitt perched against the edge of his desk, calm and confident. The bastard knew full well that he was in control here. "Where shall we begin?"

"I don't know," Randall whimpered.

Ellis snarled. He wanted to tell Randall that he'd be safe, that it would be all right, that they'd kill Charles any moment now. Sod Hughes' plan. Once that stake went in, Ellis was going to grab that silver picture frame and hack the bastard to pieces with it.

"Then let us begin where O'Neill would not wish us to. The man has secrets, Mr. Carter. If you know what he is, then I'm certain you know what other secrets he holds. Let those be our guide. Tell me something about him that he would not want me to know."

Ellis' insides ran cold.

Randall's lips parted, but nothing came out.

Ellis felt a brief flicker of hope. Had Randall somehow found a way to disregard Devitt's orders? Was he about to break free any moment now?

No, if he'd done that, he would have told Ellis he'd met Devitt. But perhaps if there were at least some hope that Randall could resist Devitt's power, and Ellis could divine how that worked, they might have an ace up their sleeve in case things went wrong when Devitt came home.

Devitt leaned forward. He stared into Randall's eyes.

"It seems," Devitt murmured as he straightened up again, "that Mr. O'Neill has far too many secrets under that ridiculous hair of his. Very well. We shall go through them one at a time." Charles grinned. "Tell me how he killed Tomasz Jasiński. You may know him as Peter Barnes."

"Barnes had a silver knife. He cut Ellis' shoulder and Ellis' arm

turned to dust. He started cutting Ellis' chest, so I bit his arm and dragged him clear. Then Ellis found the knife and stabbed him with it."
Randall looked mortified as his mouth betrayed them both.

"You bit him..." Devitt's eyebrows lifted, then he added "Ah! You were a wolf at the time?"

"Yes."

"I see. Where is the knife?"

"I don't know. Ellis got rid of it."

Devitt nodded to himself. "See? Isn't this pleasant. We're getting somewhere. Now, Mr. Carter. Do you know how Mr. O'Neill killed the vampire who created him? His name was Jonas."

"Yes," Randall spat. Specks of blood coated his lips. He'd resisted so hard that he'd tried to bite his own tongue.

"Wonderful. Tell me."

"Jonas came to kill Ellis," Randall groaned. Tears were in his eyes. "He went to the gallery and called Ellis out. He threatened to kill Jay and Tiberius. Ellis went to confront him but Jonas attacked him."

Ellis snarled. He reached for Randall's shoulder, but it wasn't really there. His other hand remained locked in place around the seat back as though he were being electrocuted. He couldn't break free.

"Ellis couldn't defend himself," Randall continued, his voice seething with hatred. If it was possible to kill a man with a look, Randall's gaze should have turned Devitt to ash by now. "He bit Jonas and it worked. Jonas was paralysed, but Ellis figured that Jonas would go back to killing him the moment he let Jonas go, so he fed from him."

Devitt stood, his gaze sharp as glass now. He really would be good looking, Ellis realised, if he wasn't such a bastard. "O'Neill cannibalised Jonas?"

"Yes." Randall's admission was a plea, a desperate cry for this to end.

Devitt ignored it. "How delightful. I assume he would also very much like for me not to know that you are a werewolf. We can move past that. What's next, Mr. Carter? What else are you hanging on to?"

Randall let out a whine from the back of his throat. "Ellis has Jonas' power."

Devitt blinked. "The languages?"

"Yes," Randall groaned.

"As well as the visions? Or instead of?"

"As well as." Tears began to roll down Randall's cheeks.

Ellis snarled. Devitt knew. He damn well knew before he even set foot in Ellis' cell that Ellis had Jonas' power. He'd acted like it was a surprise, like Ellis had revealed new information to him, but the fucker had already known!

Oh, god.

Devitt had always intended to kill Dickens. That's why he'd taken the man to Ellis' cell in the first place. One way or another he was going to force Ellis to admit to taking Jonas' power, then kill Dickens for his. He'd made Ellis think it was Ellis' fault Dickens had been killed.

God damn it! The rat bastard! Ellis had been so sure Devitt killed Dickens in a spur of the moment decision, but the whole thing was a set-up, a construct to put Ellis behind bars and pin Dickens' murder on him.

Had he relied on Randall breaking him out, too? Was this all Devitt's plan? Had he known that Randall would find Ellis sooner or later, and laid in wait for him to do just that so he could then cherry-pick the best of the city's powers and blame it all on Ellis?

Devitt had been on the council. He had fingers in every pie. He probably knew who every single vampire in the city was, and what their power was.

He'd be unstoppable.

"Miss Ryan says that O'Neill has begun to attend the gallery in the afternoon," Devitt said. "How is that possible?"

Ellis reeled.

Christy?

Had the bastard dragged Christy in here, too? Who else? Jay? Han? Was there anyone Devitt hadn't interrogated?

"It's my blood," Randall snarled. "We think it lets him heal faster."

One of Devitt's eyebrows lifted delicately. "He feeds from you," he surmised. Then he leaned in to examine Randall's wrists. "You werewolves do heal remarkably quickly, don't you?" he noted. "Where is the rest of your pack?"

"East End," Randall whispered. He blinked and tears glittered among his eyelashes.

"How many of them?"

"Twenty-one."

Devitt let out a low whistle and sat back against his desk. "Who is the Alpha?"

"I am."

Devitt narrowed his eyes and looked Randall over slowly. His lips pursed before he appeared to reach a decision. "Once you leave this house," he said calmly, "you are going to forget that you were here. You will forget that you saw me, that you met me, that we had this conversation. You will not involve your pack in my business. My staff will take you somewhere and drop you off, and once they do you will forget them, too. You will not speak a word of this to anyone."

"I'll kill you," Randall snarled. His fingers dug into the arm rests of the chair. "Somehow, I'll find a way, and I will fucking end you."

Devitt feigned a wince. "Such fire," he snorted, full of disdain. "You silly little creature. You have no idea what I'm capable of." He leaned forward and pressed a palm to Randall's forehead, pinning the shifter's head to the back of the chair. His fangs descended briefly, and his gaze hardened. "So let me show you," he whispered as he forced his fangs to retreat. "Look at me, Mr. Carter. The next time you see me, you will forget who you are."

Randall's gaze burned with loathing. "Not bloody likely."

"Oh, you will, Mr. Carter. I won't have something so dangerous as you in my presence without precautions, and you follow O'Neill like a puppy. He relies on you for protection. Well, he won't have it. You, Mr. Carter, are my new favourite toy."

Randall spat a mixture of blood and saliva into Devitt's face.

"Victor," Devitt said as he stepped back. "Come in here and clean Mr. Carter up, would you? We can't have a speck of blood on him when he returns to O'Neill."

Ellis snarled and tried to break his hold on the chair. Randall's emotions were too strong, and he felt pinned by them, trapped in a vision he had to escape.

He wrenched one hand free and tore at the other, frantic.

This was a trap. The whole damn thing was a trap.

Ellis kicked against the chair and tore free with a frustrated scream.

His world sank into darkness as he fell to the floor. Was it over? Was the vision done?

"Randall?" he croaked.

THIRTY-ONE

HE HEARD QUEEN. Tinny, muffled, but that was unmistakably Freddie Mercury. The man's voice was legendary and utterly irreplaceable. Don't Stop Me Now, though? Seriously?

Ellis grabbed at the chair and pulled himself to his feet. "Randall!"

There were footsteps in the house.

Oh god.

Ellis ran toward the sound of the iPod. He had to grab Randall, tell him to get the hell out of here.

"Well now," came Devitt's voice. "Isn't this a delight?"

Ellis reached for Randall and caught a fistful of his jacket, so he pulled on it and tried to drag Randall around. "Randall!"

The music grew louder. Less muted.

"Uh," Randall said hesitantly. "Sorry, I, um. I don't... Sorry. Where am I?"

Ellis' heart sank.

He was too late.

"Randall," he breathed.

"Is that..." Randall hesitated. "Oh god. I don't... I don't remember anything..." Panic touched the edges of his words.

Ellis tightened his hold on Randall's jacket and snarled at Devitt. "Undo this. Give him back!"

Devitt laughed. "Go find the others," he said absently. "They're upstairs."

Footsteps left the room and hurried down the hall.

"And you, young man," Devitt added. "Your confusion is amusing, but do keep quiet and wait."

Randall fell silent. Ellis shook him, but he didn't say a word.

Of course he didn't. He *couldn't*.

Charles crossed to the desk and the soft leather of his chair creaked discreetly as he sat. "I must say I hadn't thought to look for you here, O'Neill," he chuckled. "You really are full of surprises, aren't you?"

Ellis couldn't bear to let go of Randall. He clung to the werewolf's jacket as though his touch could return Randall's memories, his very identity to him, but he turned to follow the sound of Devitt's movements.

"Let Randall go," Ellis breathed. "Please. Let him go back to his pack. Give him back who he is and make him forget all about you, or me, or any of this, and let him live."

Charles clicked his tongue. "Possibly. I haven't yet decided. After all, his blood is remarkable, isn't it? It allows you out in the sun. You have youth on your side there, but even the young cannot survive as you do."

Ellis grit his teeth and tried not to allow Charles' words to worm their way under his skin. "If you let him go," he said, his voice soft, "you can have me."

The sound of manicured fingernails tapping against wood rattled for a few moments. "The value of that offer rests solely on whether the ability to steal the power of another includes those *that* vampire has already stolen," he decided. "I have no interest in your silly little visions, O'Neill. But Jonas' gift? That would be valuable enough to me to do as you ask."

Ellis loosened his hold and shook his head. "Why?"

"You can't be *this* stupid." Charles tutted. "This city used to have only a handful of languages. Now it has *hundreds*."

It all fell into place. "Oh god," Ellis whispered. "You can't control anyone who doesn't understand you."

"Correct." Charles's seat creaked faintly and he gave a faint sigh. "Still, you are a tremendous problem. I sent Jonas to kill you, and the idiot couldn't manage it. I found Jasiński and crafted him into the perfect tool to destroy you with, and *he* couldn't manage it."

"Why?" Ellis finally released Randall and stepped toward the desk. "Why go to all this trouble? I never even knew you existed! I was *never* a threat to you!"

"You were on *my territory!*" Devitt roared as his fist hit the desk's surface. "That cretinous weasel Jonas was so blinded by what was in your bloody trousers that he didn't stop to think about where you lived! I'm a damn laughing stock, O'Neill! I used to *own* this city, and now I have *squatters!*"

Ellis shook his head numbly.

Devitt had every right to destroy Ellis if what he'd said was true. The laws allowed for territory disputes to lead to fatalities — the very technicality on which Ellis had initially got away with killing Jonas.

"Why didn't you just take care of it yourself?" Ellis reached for the back of the wooden chair and his fingers gripped it tightly to steady himself with. "If it's just territory why did you go to all that trouble?"

"A gentleman does not sully himself with these things. I detest having to involve myself at this sort of level. You should have died and never even known my name." Charles sighed.

"But you are too much of a problem to leave lying around. Too resourceful, too clever, and too dangerous. Time and again I have underestimated you, and I keep making the mistake of allowing you to survive. No more, O'Neill."

"Devitt, wait!"

"You," Charles snapped. "Kill him."

Ellis turned quickly. Nobody had entered the room, had they? He heard no pulse other than Randall's, and no footsteps bar those of the werewolf who was sprinting toward him.

Cold, hard realisation hit him a split second before Randall's fist did the same.

It was Jonas all over again. This time without all the blood, all the screaming and the threats, but otherwise it was uncannily familiar. Randall's fists slammed into him in a flurry of punches, and while Randall had little training, he had more strength than Jonas ever mustered.

Randall was a powerhouse, and he could see.

Ellis tried to put the chair between them, but Randall grabbed him by the hair and tore him away from it, then a boot connected with his thigh and something snapped.

"Randall!" Ellis grabbed at him and managed to snag his t-shirt. Fat lot of good that would do him. "Stop!"

A fist collided with his gut, then the other snapped two of his ribs.

His leg repaired itself. His ribs realigned and re-knit.

A hold on Randall's t-shirt wasn't going to cut the mustard.

"Charles!" he screamed. "Stop this!"

The other vampire chuckled. "The only way I will stop

this," he said as casually as a man discussing the weather, "is by telling him what he truly is."

Ellis pushed back from Randall in horror. Randall used his fists because he'd forgotten who *and what* he was. He didn't know he had claws, or that he could double his mass and power with a thought. He could tear Ellis limb from limb with nothing more than a word from Devitt to give him that knowledge.

Once Randall knew that, it really would be over.

Randall grabbed his wrist and used his hold to throw Ellis against a wall. God knows how many of his bones cracked there. It all happened too fast to count them.

He was disoriented. Before he'd fully healed Randall landed three more blows against his lower back: good, solid punches that would have permanently wrecked a human's kidneys.

Ellis dropped like a stone and heard Randall's fist impact against the solid brick wall a hair's breadth above his head. This time it was Randall's body which made a faint *snap*, and Randall yelped in pain.

"I'm sorry," Ellis whispered. He scrambled out and away from Randall's heaving breaths, but within seconds collided with something at shoulder height. A shelf, perhaps? He didn't remember any other obstacles at that kind of height within the room.

The force of his impact cut his legs out from beneath him and he grabbed wildly. One hand bashed against the shelf and another grabbed something with soft leather sides that came free-

Elizabeth clutched the leatherbound book to her chest and sobbed softly. She sat on the edge of a beautiful four-poster bed and wore only an ankle-length nightgown.

Ellis stumbled and fell. Not now. Oh, Christ, not now!

"Darling?" Charles hurried into the bedroom. He was only in his

233

shirtsleeves, and smelled strongly of cigars and whisky. His hair was in slight disarray, and his skin flush with life. "My sweetheart! What's wrong?"

Elizabeth rubbed quickly at her cheeks. "It's nothing," she whispered. "Oh, Charles, I didn't mean for you to worry."

He sat beside her and reached for her hands. It took a moment, but he managed to prise one from the book. "You are my wife," he said softly. "It's my proud duty to worry when you cry." He leaned in to kiss her cheek. "What is wrong?"

Something sharp gouged through Ellis' stomach. He kicked blindly, all the while trying to let go of the goddamned book.

"Will we ever have children?" Elizabeth whispered. "What if I am barren? Oh, Charles, I couldn't bear it!"

"Shh. Shh, my sweet. It hasn't been more than half a year." Charles squeezed her fingers. "You mustn't worry. We have all the time in the world."

This time the stab punctured his diaphragm.

Ellis's fingers jerked and the book fell from his hand. The darkness closed in around him. Randall's weight was on him, and whatever was in Ellis' gut withdrew as Randall pulled it out.

The stake. Oh, Christ, Randall had found the stake.

Ellis' gums itched as his body repaired itself from yet another round of damage. He writhed to try and push Randall off him. The stake dragged across his arm this time and snagged in his jacket's sleeve. It failed to break through the material.

Ellis bucked and twisted until he could wriggle free, but Randall grabbed the back of his jacket and dragged Ellis toward him, so Ellis thrashed and fought until he managed to escape his own jacket.

He was hungry. Christ, he'd already burned through all the blood he'd taken from Han?

The stake clattered dully against the rug. Ellis didn't wait for Randall to pick it up again. He launched to his feet and tried to run.

This time it was Charles' desk which stopped him, and he sprawled across it. It offered little traction, and soon Randall's hands had him around one thigh and dragged him back across the polished surface. A fist pummelled against his spine.

Ellis's tolerance for pain was ebbing away. What had been mere warnings about damage were now alarms clamouring in his head. Randall's strength, his persistence, his lack of restraint had all taken their toll on Ellis' body, and the next hit made him cry out weakly.

This couldn't go on. Not for much longer. Ellis' body was at its limit. Any more hits and he'd tip over from hungry to ravenous, and then-

Then he'd be the one to kill Randall.

Ellis snarled. He clawed at the desk to try and pull away. And all the while, Queen blasted out from those bloody earbuds.

No, I am not having a good time! I'm not having a fucking ball!

Randall grabbed him by the hair and slammed his face into the desk, and Ellis screamed.

THIRTY-TWO

HIS GLASSES JOLTED FREE, but not before the rigid plastic had broken his nose again.

Ellis flopped and kicked out. His foot collided with something, and Randall grunted. The hand in his hair released him and Ellis slid from the desk and landed heavily on the floor.

There wasn't enough light in here to make out anything more than the vaguest shapes. One of those shapes loomed out of the darkness at him, and Ellis launched himself at it.

Randall's familiar body was hard and unyielding. He grabbed Ellis and flexed for another headbutt.

Ellis surged forward and sank his fangs into Randall's shoulder.

Everything stopped. Randall's balance was precarious, and with Ellis wrapped around him gravity won. They fell together until the breath was knocked from Randall's lungs.

Ellis didn't dare release him. He took a little blood to prevent himself from losing control, and Randall whimpered with need.

I'm sorry. Oh, god, I'm so sorry.

He heard footsteps from far above. Charles' men were free at last.

Ellis was out of time.

A slow clap sounded from the direction of the desk. Charles chuckled. "Absolutely wonderful," he crowed. "What will you do, Mr. O'Neill? Kill him?"

Ellis screwed his eyes shut. He couldn't release Randall and both vampires knew it.

"Whichever way this goes, I win." Charles clicked his tongue. "If you kill the werewolf, Victor will kill you. If the werewolf kills you, I get to keep him. Which way would *you* like it to go?"

Randall's cock swelled against Ellis' groin, and Ellis groaned weakly. He couldn't help but swallow the blood which slowly trickled over his tongue.

"Would you like to know what Dickens' power was?" Charles almost sounded bored. "Quite staggering. The man was completely immune to silver. Oh, it isn't outwardly impressive, but nor does it require any effort to learn. It merely *is*."

Devitt's men were coming down the stairs.

"Clarke's will take some experimentation," Devitt continued. "It's some sort of limited telepathy, from what I understand. He could see auras. It may take a little while to figure it out, but I imagine it will be rather useful."

There was no reasoning with Charles. None. Whatever kind of man he may once have been, he wasn't anymore. Ellis fumbled along Randall's body and snagged the iPod, then stuffed it into the pocket of his own trousers. One hand quickly located the earbuds.

His other hand lightly touched Randall's cheek before he

withdrew his fangs and jumped back from the werewolf's body.

"You're a coward, Mr. O'Neill. You must realise that if you are to survive in this existence you must be prepared to lose everything."

Ellis snarled and turned toward the desk. He heard Randall groan and move sluggishly, hopefully just a little distracted by the bulge in his jeans.

"All this is because you were firing blanks, isn't it?" Ellis sneered. He fell forward and landed a hand against the desk's surface, and tried to make out the hazy figure the far side of it. "It wasn't Elizabeth who was sterile, was it? It was you. *You* failed her!" Randall clambered to his feet and Ellis had to ignore him. "You couldn't give her the one thing she wanted the most. You couldn't make her *happy*, and now this entire city suffers because you can't find anything worth living for because she is *dead* and you *failed her!*"

Charles's hands slapped lightly against the desk and his blurred shape grew larger. No, not larger. Taller. "You wretched rat," he hissed as he leaned toward Ellis. "What would you know about life or love, you filthy little molly!"

"That was probably an insult a century or two ago," Ellis snarled.

Randall's fist planted into his back, and he cried out with the force of it.

"Mr. Carter," Charles sneered. "I think it's high time you remembered that you are a werewolf. Why are you lightly poking Mr. O'Neill to death? Get on with it. Do it properly."

Ellis heard the terrible sounds of tearing flesh. He had three or four seconds at most before Randall dug claws into him and turned him to dust.

He jammed the earbuds into his own ears and launched himself up onto the desk.

Christ, it was deafening! They were at full volume, and his hearing was too sensitive for comfort.

Ellis planted a foot against the desk and threw himself at Charles. The blur of Devitt's body withdrew, but Ellis grabbed for it, and they both fell against Charles' plush leather seat.

Something pulled against the cable of the earbuds. If Charles got them free it was all over.

Ellis was out of time.

He extended his fangs and lunged forward, praying that he'd penetrate skin.

The earbuds fell away.

Charles' body was still.

Ellis froze.

Footsteps and heartbeats drew nearer.

Claws raked across his back.

Ellis screamed and almost pulled away from Charles in agony. Those claws would most definitely turn him to ash if he took another couple of blows like that one. If he released Charles he would die. If he didn't stop Randall he would die.

Pretty much every option he could think of led to his death. Except the one which might give him what he needed to stop all of this.

He gripped Charles' hair and began to feed.

EACH MOUTHFUL WAS A SHORT-LIVED VICTORY, spent almost immediately to heal every wound Randall inflicted on him. Randall's claws dug in again and again. They tore chunks from him which struggled to heal before the next wounds were inflicted.

Ellis sucked as hard as he dared. It didn't matter whether he damaged any blood vessels; his victim was already a damn corpse. The faster he fed the quicker he healed, but he couldn't possibly hope to finish in under two minutes. Not to drain an entire body.

The pain was unbelievable. It boiled in his flesh and seared through his brain as horrendously as the silver blade had when it took his arm. He heard scattered dust fall like rain against the floor.

Ellis no longer cared whether he survived this, but he was buggered if Charles was going to see another night.

He endured. He *had* to. He tried to blot out the agony, and pulled mouthful after mouthful of Charles' blood. He swallowed as fast as he could.

He felt as though he might go insane. How much pain could one man take? How long before he simply gave in and begged for it to end?

Tears rolled down his cheeks. He couldn't go any further. His mind was filled with fire and agony and regrets he wouldn't ever put to rest.

I love you. He couldn't say it. He daren't pull his mouth from Charles long enough to say goodbye. *I forgive you. This isn't your fault, Randall. Please, please don't blame yourself for this.*

You didn't have a choice. And neither did I.

The body beneath him turned to dust.

Ellis fell awkwardly against the chair and immediately rolled to the floor. He pushed himself towards darkness and fervently hoped that it was the underside of Devitt's desk.

It was.

He wedged himself beneath it and sobbed while his body continued to knit itself back together.

THIRTY-THREE

RANDALL'S CLAWS sliced through the body over and over. It refused to die.

What kind of thing was he fighting? No wonder the blond man wanted it dead. It looked like a man, but it didn't bleed, and its flesh constantly regenerated itself.

He sank them in again and tore out what had to be half the creature's insides, but even that didn't stop it.

Then it was too late. The man with the blond hair evaporated. One second he was there, and the next he was gone.

No, not gone.

He fell apart like a sandcastle blown by the wind, and the creature that had killed him darted under the desk, a cockroach hiding from the light.

Randall leaped off the desk and threw the little chair aside. If he couldn't save the blond man, the least he could do was take revenge for his murder.

He crouched down and peered under the desk. Huddled

beneath it, crying like a child, was the creature, its clothes mostly destroyed, and its exposed flesh white as porcelain.

The creature.

Ellis.

Randall's thoughts flooded with images strung together so fast that they barely made sense. Ellis, who had come here with him to trap Charles. Ellis who had helped him end the fight between two packs with unparalleled bravery in the face of monsters who outnumbered him and would easily overpower him. Ellis, who Randall had almost destroyed.

Ellis, who he loved with all his heart.

Randall howled in anguish and shifted into his human shape. "Ellis," he whimpered. He offered a hand under the desk toward him, only to realise Ellis couldn't see it. Instead, he touched it to Ellis' ankle.

Ellis shook his head in numb terror. "I'm sorry," he whimpered, flinching at the touch. "I had to. I *had* to!"

"It's okay." Randall blinked away wetness that blurred his vision. "Ellis it's me. It's Randall. I remember it. I know who I am. Oh, god, he... He made me forget everything!"

He felt sick. Devitt had forced him to betray Ellis' trust, and then wiped the whole thing away. Christ, no wonder he was confused as hell on the way back from Mrs. Uddin's party. He'd been here, in this damn room, and given Devitt every single secret he had.

Randall bristled and glanced toward the chair, but the clothes which had been strewn across it had since fallen to the floor. Piles of dust were scattered. It looked like someone had upended a vacuum cleaner and kicked the mess around then left it there.

"Randall?" Ellis whispered.

Randall turned back to him and nodded. "Yeah, I'm here.

I'm sorry. I love you. Please, come out. Let me take you home. I won't hurt you, El, I swear. I won't ever hurt you."

Jesus, he felt sick. How the hell could Ellis ever believe him?

Ellis wiped his cheeks with the back of his hand and slowly crawled toward Randall. "It wasn't you," he breathed. "It wasn't you, petal. It was Charles, not you. Don't blame yourself. Please, don't."

You don't understand! If I'd fought him, if I'd killed him, if I hadn't let him take me off the street...

Ellis crept into his arms and nuzzled weakly against him, and Randall held him tight against his chest.

"It's worn off." Ellis spoke cautiously, and his hand pressed against Randall's bare chest. "You remember."

"Yeah." Randall buried his face against Ellis' soft, silken hair.

"Oh, Christ."

Randall pulled back and frowned. How was that a *bad* thing?

A shadow fell across him and he looked up to the figures which surrounded them.

"Oh, Christ," he agreed.

RANDALL EASED ELLIS UP ONTO CHARLES' discarded chair, one eye on the figures looming over them.

Devitt's men had them surrounded, but they hadn't started a fight yet. The nearest, the only one Randall suspected might be a vampire himself, looked unsettled. Two cradled broken noses. One held his arm to his chest and eyed Randall with open fear.

Oh god. Had any of them seen what he was?

Randall swallowed and drew himself up to his full height. Under normal circumstances nobody would be impressed by that, but these men all shuffled or outright stepped back.

Yeah. They'd seen.

"Devitt's gone." He squared his shoulders. "I don't know what he's done to any of you, but if you've suddenly got memories you didn't have earlier—"

Victor's lip curled. "His tricks have ended with him, it seems."

"Yeah." Randall glanced between them. "I'm sorry. I don't know what kind of situation that's left you in, but we won't just toss you out on your ear. If you want a little time to work through some stuff, that's totally understandable."

"They—" Victor thumbed toward the others, "—can't leave here."

Randall blinked up at him. "Why not?"

"Because they know," Ellis answered. "If what Devitt did to them is all gone now, they know."

"I won't tell anyone," supplied the butler. His white gloves were stained with the blood from his own nose.

The others chorused in, all shaking their heads. They seemed as terrified of Randall as they were Victor.

"Go home," Ellis said, his voice soft. "Come back tomorrow night, ten at night. We'll work it out then. Tell nobody what has happened here until then."

Every last one of them turned on their heel and marched to the door.

Randall opened his mouth, but he couldn't find anything to say. He stood in silence as they took themselves off out of the house. When he hurried to the window and nudged the curtain aside, he caught sight of them marching toward Pimlico station.

"Bollocks," he breathed.

Ellis drew his feet up onto the chair and coiled his arms around his knees.

"You've taken it, haven't you?" Randall closed the curtain and crossed to Ellis' side.

Ellis nodded. His gaze was blank, and he tightened his hold around his legs. "I didn't have a choice," he whispered.

"I know, baby." Randall laid his hand over Ellis' shoulder, and when the vampire didn't flinch away from him he gave it a gentle squeeze. "I think we're gonna have to work out how to control this one before you accidentally order people around and they get suspicious." He swallowed tightly and sank into a crouch. "I'll tell Hughes that Devitt is dead and his power's worn off everyone who was affected. That might keep the Constabulary busy for a while. Who knows what the fallout of that kind of thing's gonna be? Especially if he's ever revealed what he is to more than his own people."

Ellis groaned. "Christy. He's had Christy here. I don't know what he's told her, or what she's told him. If he's had her here, what if he's brought Jay in too?"

"At least Jay already knows." Randall brushed his fingers over the back of Ellis' hand. "We'll work it out, but you're exhausted. Let me take you home and we can sort this shit out tomorrow, yeah?"

Ellis unfolded himself as though afraid everything were about to come crashing down around him. He placed a hand against the desk when he stood, and leaned against it as his other drifted hesitantly down himself. "We can't go out like this," he said. "I know it's London, but that's stretching it."

Randall blinked, then laughed briefly and glanced down at his own ruined shreds of clothing. All that was left on him were, absurdly, half his t-shirt still attached to the stretched collar of it, and flaps of denim which hung from his belt.

He laughed harder.

Ellis tilted his head toward him, and his ice-blue eyes narrowed as he tried to see Randall. "What is it?"

"Oh god." Randall ditched the belt, then tugged the scraps of his t-shirt off over his head. "We're pretty much butt naked, the pair of us."

Ellis blinked slowly, then pressed his lips together. "Oh."

"Yeah. They must've gotten a good eyeful…"

Ellis rubbed his stubble. "Reckon they liked what they saw?"

"Ellis!"

"'Cause I've seen you now, you know. Properly." Ellis placed a hand on his hip. "And I were right all along, it turns out."

"Right?" Randall rubbed his forearm. "What about?"

"How beautiful you are." Ellis smiled slowly and offered his hand.

Randall's cheeks warmed, and he drew Ellis into his arms. "I reckon a place this size must have somewhere we can spend a day," he whispered as he nuzzled against Ellis' jaw.

"A day?" Ellis countered. "Sod that for a game of soldiers. He spent a year trying to kill me. I'm having his bloody house, and anyone who's got a problem with that can kiss my arse."

THIRTY-FOUR

ELLIS HAD an unsettled night filled with Devitt's cold laughter and memories of his flesh being torn from his bones. When he woke, it was to an unfamiliar place where the heartbeats of the nearest neighbours sounded as though they may as well be in Hertfordshire. There were no electrical sounds, no beeps or hums. Traffic was a distant rumble.

He could get used to this. Well, not the nightmares. God, please, not the nightmares. But the house? Yes, he could absolutely get used to it.

Randall was curled up against his side, and Ellis lay there a while as he listened to his lover's gentle breaths and strong heart. The werewolf deserved better.

And while they lay together in peace and quiet, Ellis hatched a plan to give it to him.

CHRISTY ARRIVED a little after ten o'clock. Ellis had texted her the address and asked her to meet him there, and transferred a couple of hundred pounds to her number so that she could pick up some clothes along the way. That she actually did gave him some measure of hope.

He borrowed a silk robe Randall found hanging in the bedroom in order to answer the door to her, and sat her in the cozy little study rather than Devitt's office. She showed little recognition of the house, and he didn't want her to leg it before he could get dressed.

Ellis sat with her while Randall bustled around making tea in the kitchen.

"You've been here before," he said gently.

"I have?" She sounded uncertain.

"Aye." He rubbed his jaw and tried to work out how best to proceed.

Randall came into the room. Ellis heard a little *tink* of fine china, and Christy thanked him.

The werewolf sat by Ellis' side and slid an arm around his waist. Ellis rested a hand on Randall's thigh and took strength from his presence.

"You've been here," Ellis began, "and answered questions about me. You've spoken with—"

"Oh my god!" she cut in. The china rattled. "The blond guy. With his heavies! Oh, shit, why didn't I remember any of that?"

"It's all right. He isn't here." Ellis briefly wished he'd asked her to grab a pair of glasses, if only to fiddle with while he spoke, but it was better for her to see his eyes. It would help her. "He's dead."

Christy gasped. "What's going on? Are you guys spies or something?"

Ellis smirked at the idea, then wiped the expression from his face. "Ah, no. No. It's worse than that."

"Worse than spies," she echoed.

"Considerably worse." He pursed his lips. "I'm a vampire. So was he."

"Vampires." She snorted. "I suppose you are too?"

"No," Randall answered. "I'm not a vampire. I'm a werewolf."

"Oh, a hundred percent of all the crazy in this room is *totally* over your side," she said. "Okay. Vampire and werewolf. Prove it."

Ellis sighed.

Here we go again.

EDISON DIDN'T SHOW until noon, but he brought Tiberius with him, who was ecstatic to be reunited with Ellis. By that point the study didn't have enough room for them all, so Ellis relocated them to Devitt's office instead.

Edison let out a low whistle. "Areet. What're we here for?"

Ellis felt his way around the vast desk which had been a battleground only hours earlier. He found the leather chair and sat in it.

Yes, he could absolutely get used to this.

"Devitt lived here for over a hundred years," he began. "Which means that he must have owned this property or it would have changed hands by now."

"'Cause if he was a tenant the landlord could have sold it from under him?" Christy asked.

"Aye. And even if he used his powers on the new landlord ultimately it makes more sense for him to own it outright. Why mess around renting if you have the power to buy?" Ellis slid one hand against the polished desk and found a deep groove along the top. His fingers hesitated, then withdrew from the scar. "And if he's had the house that long, then he must also have the deeds for it somewhere."

Edison let out an *Oh* of comprehension. "And since he's been sole owner for all that time he likely didn't register, therefore is still the legal owner of the property. We need to find the deeds, notify the Land Registry, and put you down as the executor of Devitt's estate."

"That all sounded like you know what it means, so, yes." Ellis grinned. "That."

"We're searching this place for paperwork?" Christy clarified.

"Aye."

"Great." Edison sounded far too cheerful. "Then we flog the place, you repay dad, pay me my fees for the assist, and everyone parts ways happy."

"No." Ellis shook his head. "I'm not selling."

"Ellis—"

"I'm *not* selling. The place is probably stuffed to the gills with valuables and I've got no use for those. If we find particulars of Devitt's financials you can add those to the pile, too. But the house stays."

Edison huffed. "Fine. This bastard was reet loaded, you reckon?"

"He doesn't strike me as a man willing to live in poverty," Ellis said dryly. "Think of it as a treasure hunt."

"There'd better bloody be treasure," Edison groused.

DEVITT'S NEATNESS extended to his personal effects. Once Randall found the drawer in which the elder vampire had stored all his paperwork, Edison took it away to his hotel room to sift through. Ellis had no choice but to trust him with it, and since Edison's fees relied on the value he could find in Devitt's affairs he had reason to believe Edison would be honest.

Christy returned to the gallery after that to make sure it would be open to customers throughout the evening. She promised she wouldn't give away any secrets, but she also demanded that Ellis sit down with her in the new year and give her more details about all this vampire stuff. That seemed reasonable, and he agreed.

By the time Hughes arrived, Randall had done his best to tidy the place up, and they'd gone for a short stroll to give Tiberius a little exercise.

"It's weird," Hughes said as he wandered around the office. "Spent all that time hoping I'd never be in this room ever again. Didn't occur to me that it'd be okay as long as that arsehole was gone."

"Are you all right?" Randall asked, his soft voice filled with compassion.

"Yeah. Yeah, I will be. You takin' up residence, then, Ellis?"

Ellis nodded a little. "That's the plan."

"Yer well within the laws doin' so," Hughes mused. "God, I'm glad the fucker's dead."

"I won't be the sword of Damocles," Ellis promised quietly. "Your lover is your business, Aaron. You have my word."

"He was gonna turn Jude, you know," Aaron mused as he sat in the heavy wooden chair. "Right here in this seat. He was gonna turn him and make him tell the Council I did it. Marcus all over again. I got here just in time to stop him."

"Why didn't you kill him then?" Ellis blinked.

"He agreed to pull some strings in the Met. Got them to

bury some stuff I'd done in Battersea Park. I'd killed some guy to protect Jude but there was CCTV."

Ellis winced.

"Yeah. We called it even."

"Well, it's done now." Ellis leaned back. He heard Randall step up against the side of his chair, and he reached out and idly ran a hand down the back of the werewolf's leg. It was like steel, a pillar of muscle even in his human form. "But it seems that with Devitt's death, anyone he's ever used his power on now remembers everything."

"Oh you have *got* to be kidding me," Hughes hissed. He leaped from his chair and began to pace. "The only reason he was ever allowed to keep his Thralls was because they were forbidden from passing on what they knew. Are you telling me he's got a bunch of people out there — most of whom we don't have any idea who they are — who can remember him fucking with their heads?"

"Yeah." Ellis gripped the back of Randall's thigh.

"What about Victor? Where's he gone?"

"He said he'd come back later," Ellis lied.

"Be careful of him. He's been loyal since the Sixties. He used to be Charles' Vassal when Charles was still on the Council."

"Vassal?" Randall murmured.

"His representative," Ellis supplied. "Like a secretary, but with the power to go wherever he needs to and speak with his Councillor's authority."

Randall let out a puff of air. "What if he'd been coerced, though?"

"That's what I'm hoping to find out when he gets here." Ellis nodded.

"Right." Hughes sat again. "You do that. I'll get what's left of the Council together, tell them what went down with

Devitt, get your name cleared. Then we can work on making them agree to give you and Barb the spare seats."

"What? No!" Ellis let go of Randall and sat bolt upright.

"Oi. Shut it. It's perfect. We'll get you installed and then you two have got the perfect opportunity to make changes. You won't have a majority, but it's a start, and we'll be in a better position when it comes to changing the way shit is done 'round here."

"Aaron, I'm not a politician! I'm not a leader!"

"Yeah. I reckon that makes you more qualified than the current lot, dunnit?"

Ellis winced at that. "I dunno about that. There is… *one* other thing."

"I get the feeling I ain't gonna like the sound of this."

"You're probably not. I've turned someone without the Council's permission."

Hughes groaned. "You are gonna overcomplicate my life, ain't you? I can tell."

ELLIS MANAGED to do away with Hughes before Victor and Devitt's Thralls returned. He also managed to convince them all to forget Devitt and move on with life before he shooed them all out of the house. It would have to do for now until he worked out a longer-term plan.

"Areet," he said, and rubbed at his nose. "Please tell me we can relax at last."

Randall laughed and eased into his lap. "Jay says Han's doing fine. I reckon we should pop 'round there tomorrow and make sure, but for now… Yeah. We can relax."

Ellis gripped Randall's t-shirt and drew him in for a slow, lingering kiss. The shifter's lips were every bit as soft and warm as they always had been, and he gained reassurance from that. Something in his life was still trustworthy, still reliable.

"Do you reckon the police are still after me?" Randall murmured as he pulled back.

"I don't know." Ellis pressed his palms to Randall's chest and let his touch roam across barely-concealed muscle. "If they are, I can stop them."

Randall sucked his teeth faintly. "I don't know if that's something you want to start doing," he said, his tone cautious.

"Me either. But if nothing else I have got to learn to control it so I don't do it accidentally." He dipped his lips to Randall's shoulder and ran his teeth lightly along it.

Randall shuddered and his pulse quickened.

"Will you be all right?" Ellis asked. "With what I am? What I've done?"

"You had to." Randall ran his knuckles along Ellis' collarbone. "He didn't give you any choice. Will *you* be okay?"

Ellis closed his eyes. The desk bore permanent wounds from Randall's attack, and while Randall had been as helpless as Ellis, the thought of those claws sinking into him, of the man he loved brutally tearing pieces off him, had left him unable to sleep without the memory floating to the surface like a dead fish.

"I'll be fine, petal," he said. "I'll need a little time, but I'll be okay."

"Good. How about you take me upstairs and do nasty things to me, then tomorrow we can get our Christmas shopping sorted, yeah?"

Ellis nibbled softly at Randall's shoulder as he grinned. "You know how to make a fella feel special."

Randall laughed. "Not just any fella. You, El. You're the only man that matters to me."

"Better get up, or we aren't going to make it as far as the stairs."

"And that's a problem because?"

Ellis chuckled, and began to push Randall's t-shirt up his body. "Areet. Have it your way!"

THIRTY-FIVE

A WEEK LATER, Randall guided Ellis through the bustle of Spitalfields. Despite the heavy rain, the area was overflowing with last-minute shoppers.

It was Christmas Eve, and people still hadn't bought all their presents.

Ellis held Randall's elbow with his right hand and an umbrella in his left. The combination of rain and brolly meant that he was virtually unharmed by what little sunlight could occasionally make it past the clouds, but he disliked leaving Tiberius at home. He still debated whether he should have left the umbrella and brought Tiberius instead.

"Is it much further?" He grimaced as a market stall-holder bellowed inches from his ear.

"'Bout half a mile, if that," Randall said. "You okay?"

"Just a bit hectic is all, petal." Ellis chuckled. "This is why I do my shopping online."

"Uh huh." Randall sounded amused.

They both knew Ellis did his shopping online to avoid

CCTV and mirrors. Ellis had to admit that it did mean he'd forgotten what the press of Londoners on a deadline was like, though.

"You wanna be grateful we don't actually have to enter the market to get there," Randall added.

Ellis' eyebrows lifted. "But—"

"Nah, this is just the outer edge of it!"

Ellis tightened his grip on Randall's elbow. "Bloody hell."

"It'll be fine. I'm right here." Randall's tone softened. His words were ones of reassurance, not of dismissal.

Ellis nodded and fell quiet until they'd left all the crush and noise and odours behind.

"You're sure you wanna do this?"

Ellis chuckled at that. "It has to be done sooner or later, petal. Besides, It'll be fine. I'm lovable! Nobody can hate me." Well apart from all the people who had tried to kill him. They didn't count.

"You are lovable." Randall stopped. His arm twisted in Ellis' grip and he leaned in to press a soft, slow kiss to the vampire's lips.

Ellis tilted his head as he dipped forward to return it. The rain pattered overhead as it hit fabric, and that sound helped drown out the distant market chatter. Randall's warmth nestled against him and for a moment the rest of the world ceased to exist.

He withdrew a little. His mind's eye supplied Randall's likeness for him, although Ellis had to paint in a few details for himself: a little pinkness to his lips after a kiss, perhaps, or a flush to his cheeks.

The vision of Randall was far more detailed than the image he'd assembled after close study of Randall's face with his hands and eyes. It was so clear, so vivid, from the curve of his neck to the depths of his eyes. Jay had been right: Randall *was* gorgeous. He'd known where Ellis' tastes lay, both in art and men, and Ellis should have trusted that from the moment Randall stepped into his office three months ago.

Maybe it was better this way around. The loss of his sight had forced him to get to know Randall. They'd spent night after night in close proximity while Randall tried to help with Tiberius' behaviour, and the werewolf's kindness and compassion won Ellis over far more thoroughly than a one night stand over pretty lips and cheekbones would have.

God, a proper relationship. It had only been weeks but it felt as though they'd known one-another all their lives. Was this the difference between love and attraction? All those years of the staid old "you'll know love when you feel it", but he'd been convinced before, yet those times were *nothing* like what he felt now.

He'd die to protect Randall. He knew it, deep within his heart. There wasn't a damn thing he wouldn't do for this man.

"Everything all right?" Randall brushed his lips over Ellis' as he asked.

"Mm." Ellis smiled slowly. "Aye. I think it is." He kissed Randall's cheek.

"Good."

Randall got moving again, and Ellis relaxed his grip. "Are your pack not doing Christmas things?"

"Not together, no," Randall said. "Most of them are Muslims, so mostly they just hang out with family 'cause everything's shut." He chuckled. "I think Ameera's mum's got another party going on later."

"Won't she be disappointed that you aren't there?" Ellis paused as Randall stopped.

Randall took the umbrella and steered Ellis through a door.

He shook the umbrella and closed it as he followed, then gave Ellis his arm again. "Nah. She's good. Besides, she thinks this is a great idea."

"Mrs. Uddin sounds like a troublemaker," Ellis muttered.

Randall chuckled and led Ellis forward. "The lift usually smells of pee," he said. "Mind if we take the stairs?"

Ellis reached for the umbrella and nodded once he had it. "Let's go meet our doom."

He used the umbrella as an impromptu cane for the first few stairs until he was sure that they were even and reliable. Randall led him up ten flights, each of which were thirteen steps with a switchback after a small landing.

"Fifth floor?"

"Yeah."

Ellis nodded to himself and they emerged out of the stairwell into a corridor. He could hear laughter and televisions, all behind closed doors.

They stopped. Randall knocked on a door which sounded thin and plasticky.

Footsteps. A good, solid pulse. The door opened, and the smells which wafted out over them made Ellis wish he wouldn't have to evict whatever he ate later.

"Randall!" Mrs. Carter almost shouted with delight. "And you must be Ellis! I have heard so much about you!"

The next thing he knew, Ellis was engulfed in a large woman's arms. She was short, warm, and smelled of flour and salt.

"Mum!" Randall sounded horribly embarrassed.

"Skinny little thing, aren't you?" She squeezed Ellis' waist the let out a genuine and raucous laugh. "Well, don't just stand out here! Come in! Come in! We've got a lot of work to do if we're going to put some meat on those bones!"

Ellis laughed, and it felt like the weight of the world sloughed from his shoulders.

Christmas with family. New family, family he didn't know yet, but after ten years alone it felt like things were finally looking up.

TOOTH & CLAW

Blind Man's Wolf

Blood Moon Rising

Balance of Power

Monsters Within

Mirror Flower, Water Moon

———

Visit https://ravenswordpress.com to discover more about the characters and world of Tooth & Claw, and to sign up to the newsletter.

Join the Discord server at https://ravenswordpress.com/discord.

INHERITANCE

Laurence Riley has too many problems, and his uncontrolled psychic powers are just the tip of the iceberg. But when he accidentally summons a god, his only hope for survival might be another wild talent: the enigmatic and aloof British earl, Quentin d'Arcy.

Lose yourself in a world like no other in this award-winning series.

RAVENSWORDPRESS.COM

ACKNOWLEDGMENTS

Thank you for reading this far! Balance of Power was, looking back on it from the heady heights of 2024, the end of a three-book arc (duh, I hear you say) which I immensely enjoyed writing.

Onwards!

If you'd like to get sneak peeks of upcoming releases, why not join my Discord server? You can find it here:

ravenswordpress.com/discord

Love,

Amelia Faulkner, London UK, July 2024.

ABOUT THE AUTHOR

Raised on a steady diet of Star Trek and Doctor Who, Amelia Faulkner stood no chance in not becoming a grade-A geek. They have sat on the board of the British Fantasy Society, contributed fiction and fluff to various published roleplaying games, and written non-fiction for SciFiNow and SFX Magazines. For every positive there is an equal and opposite negative, and Amelia is forced to admit that they love Wild Wild West.

In their spare time they enjoy travel, photography, walking their Corgi, and trying to convince their friends to replay the Pathfinder Adventure Card Game with all the Goblins decks.

RAVENSWORDPRESS.COM